ROOFTOPS

A *Just Cause Universe* Novel

IAN THOMAS HEALY

Local Hero Press Edition

Rooftops
Published by Local Hero Press, LLC
http://localheropress.com

1st Printing
Local Hero Press: trade paperback, October 1, 2019
Printed in the United States of America

ISBN-13: 9781971445168

Cover art by Scott A. Story
Book design by Local Hero Press, LLC

Books by Local Hero Press

The *Just Cause Universe*

Just Cause
The Archmage
Day of the Destroyer
Deep Six
Jackrabbit
Champion
Castles
The Lion and the Five Deadly Serpents
Tusks
The Neighborhood Watch
Jackrabbit: Big In Japan
Arena
Hero Academy
The Path
Cinco de Mayo
Search and Rescue
Rooftops
Plague
Soldiers of Fortune
Just Cause Universe Compendium
Destroyer of Earth
Flint and Steel
The Club
Jackrabbit: Rinse and Repeat
Posse
Extinction Event
Rain Must Fall

Pariah of Verigo

Pariah's Moon
Pariah's War

Three Flavors of Tacos

The Guitarist
Making the Cut
The Scene Stealers

Collections

Airship Lies
High Contrast
The Good Fight
The Good Fight 3: Sidekicks
The Good Fight 4: Homefront
The Good Fight 5: The Golden Age
Muddy Creek Tales
Caped

Other Novels

Assassin
Blood on the Ice
Funeral Games
Hope and Undead Elvis
Horde
The Murder Squad (2026)
Roast Wyvern (and Other Recipes)
*Starf*cker*
Strings
The Oilman's Daughter
Troubleshooters

Nonfiction

Action! Writing Better Action Using Cinematic Techniques

Author Notes

Some stories come together as easily as Superman leaping a tall building or moving faster than a speeding bullet. Others are brought into the world kicking and screaming and fighting every inch of the way. *Rooftops* is one of the latter ones. The first draft was written in November of 2010 for National Novel Writing Month. At the time, I was looking to cash in on the vampire/werewolf craze (and I still am, obviously), but wanted to combine it with my love for superhero fiction. The *Just Cause Universe* was ticking along, but I didn't want to "pollute" it with supernatural influences, so I set the book in a fictional locale called Mesa City—a tip of the hat to all the fictional cities in the DC Comics universe. Rooftops eventually made it out as an ebook, but I was never happy with it. I couldn't get a cover I liked. I couldn't get any traction with it. Eventually I took it off sale and trunked it, as I have done with other projects.

Fast forward to 2019, when the Just Cause Universe is zooming along, and I'm branching out stories into different character arcs, sometimes with long-reaching plot lines. If you've been reading along since the beginning, you'll know, for example, that things I set up in *Just Cause* paid off eleven books later in *Arena*. This is all by design. Earlier this year, I started planning ahead for a huge crossover story that would involve characters from multiple story arcs coming together in a massive tale called *Extinction Event*. Before I can write that one, I have to write multiple books to set the stage for it—moving pieces around the board of the Just Cause Universe. In some cases, I have to write books to set up the set-up stories. Suddenly, I realized that *Rooftops* could be, with some tweaking, one of those set-up books.

A lot has changed from the original story. Now it's set in a real location, like the rest of the JCU tales: Reno, Nevada. Characters have changed gender and sexual preference more than once in the course of revisions. Plot points have been switched around, dispensed of, or changed entirely from the original book. What does this mean for you? Hopefully a better experience as a reader, and the knowledge that werewolves and vampires *do* exist within the Just Cause Universe.

They just keep it a secret.

* * *

As always, I have a list of people without whom this book would never have come to pass. I have my original editor Allison to thank, and my more recent beta reading team of Ira, Adrienne, and newcomer Andrew—who is working on a JCU project himself. Between them, they have helped bring this project together. I want to thank my original cover artist Cat, who never quite found her footing with the first cover, and my current artist Scott, who bucked conventional comic book-style art to produce the fantastic bold cover gracing this volume. My family, as always, has been incredibly supportive of this ridiculous *eccentric writer lifestyle*, as Jackie's Jenn called it. And finally, thank you to all my fans who buy books, write reviews, and spread the word. I love you the mostest!

-Ian Thomas Healy
September, 2019

Chapter One

November 2012
Reno, Nevada

Jackie was a nighttime costumed vigilante, and that wasn't even the most interesting thing about her.

The waning Moon hid behind a mask of clouds, dropping a chill rain on the rooftops of Reno. Jackie was glad of the fur over her head and shoulders. The cold-weather version of her matte-black bodysuit kept her warm and dry, but rainwater still seeped in through the eye holes of the cowl and ran down her face to soak her undershirt collar. Maybe Dominica could fashion artificial tear ducts to route water down the sides of the mask's snout instead.

The sound of rapid splashing footsteps pulled her attention from the discomfort of the damp collar and reminded her that out here, she wasn't some spoiled writer, she was the masked vigilante known as White Fang. She padded to the edge of the rooftop and peered into the alley below. *Someone didn't have the sense to get out of the rain.* The irony of the observation was not lost upon her.

A slender man ran up the alley. He turned to look behind him, tripped over a trash bin, and splashed face-first into a puddle. A large, leather-bound portfolio spun from his grasp. Two more figures entered the alley, moving with swift, silent purpose. The man scrambled to his feet, slipped on some trash, and fell again. He didn't cry out for help, perhaps too frightened of what appeared to be an attempted mugging.

Jackie would even the odds. Nothing warmed one on a chilly night like administering a good old-fashioned beating. She reached into her belt and triggered Dominica's bollix device. The short-range signal blocker interfered with cell phones, radios, and CCTV cameras. The best way to maintain the urban legend of White Fang was to make it difficult for anyone to obtain tangible proof of her existence. The beast within her breast yammered, screaming to be let loose, shrieking for *blood*. She bit her own lip until it bled. The sharp pain and coppery taste helped her focus without becoming the monster.

She went over the side.

Her superhuman muscles absorbed the impact of dropping a few stories with no more effort than if she'd jumped off a curb. She landed in a crouch behind the two aggressors. One of them withdrew a spray can from inside his jacket and blasted it in the face of their intended victim as he tried to regain his footing. The young man collapsed without another sound.

The cloying spray was sweet, a mixture of flowers and incense and opiates, strong enough to make Jackie's head spin. Despite the heavy scent, Jackie's tainted blood kept her alert. Tungsten steel claws at the toes of her boots sparked against the wet cement. She spread her hands wide to display similar claws at the fingertips of her gauntlets, lowered her head to emphasize the wolf's-head cowl. "*Let him go.*" The growling voice sounded rough and masculine thanks to the modulator Dominica built into the cowl because Jackie's own voice wasn't threatening enough.

The men didn't even turn to look.

They bent down to pick up their unconscious victim. Nonplussed, Jackie stepped forward, grabbed one by the shoulder, and spun him around. "I said, let him go."

A rotting stench of death and chemicals washed over Jackie, thick and powerful even in the rain. Greening tumors grew on the cheeks of the man's dead-white face. Jackie froze with the horror of the man's appearance.

The man swept his arm back and flung Jackie across the alley. She smashed against the concrete wall. Pain shot through her as ribs cracked at the collision, too much for even her kevlar-weave bodysuit to absorb. Her unnatural healing knitted the bones back together in an instant, but the impact still jarred her. Stunned more than hurt, she shook herself and jumped back to her feet. The man who'd struck her wore what might have once been a nice suit, but it hung in tattered rags. *Why does he smell like a dead man? And what the hell is he, a super-strong parahuman?*

Her lip curled into a snarl. Two could play at that game.

She growled like her namesake, blood boiling. Her face tingled as the beast within her struggled to free itself and her bones and muscles tried to reshape themselves into something much less human. She forced it back and tempered the rage as she dug her tungsten claws into the man's shoulder and threw him against the concrete. The wall cracked when he hit it, but even then, he uttered no sound as he collapsed to the pavement.

Jackie whirled to confront the other aggressor, whose face was even more decayed. She saw yellowed teeth through an actual hole in the side of his face. The reek of death and decay made her head spin. She had no doubt the man before her was *very* dead, yet moving with an offensive semblance of life.

Zombie!

Even in a world where people could fly unaided, shoot lightning bolts from their hands, or shatter buildings with a single blow, Jackie had never heard of such a thing.

Moving with surprising speed, the zombie hooked its fingers into claws and swung awkward but fast strikes at her. Jackie deflected them with the tungsten-plated gauntlets, backing away as the monster advanced. Her breath steamed in the chilly rain, but no breath came from the animated corpse.

She forgot the other zombie and nearly paid for it with her head. As hard as she'd thrown him against the wall, he should have been unconscious and broken, but instead he swung a section of pipe at her from the side. She ducked one blow and deflected another with her forearm, cracking both bones. In the moment when she couldn't use her arm, the other zombie grabbed her from behind and squeezed, trapping her elbows against her ribs. The zombie with the pipe raised it and shoved the rusty end at Jackie's face. She bent forward at the waist to pull the zombie behind her into the blow.

The pipe hit the zombie's face with a juicy splatter. The creature released Jackie and staggered back a few steps. Jackie braced her hands on the ground and kicked hard with both feet, driving the zombie back farther, the length of pipe still embedded in his face. He fell onto his back, hands flailing at the pipe sticking straight up from his head.

Hole-in-the-face zombie, once again unarmed, went for Jackie. with decaying fingers hooked into claws. Even with his unschooled lunges and swipes, she was hard-pressed to avoid his grasp. He was far and away the strongest, fastest foe she'd ever battled—a far cry from the drug dealers and petty lowlifes she normally fought.

He caught her with a glancing blow off her shoulder and his other hand hooked onto her cowl. Before he could tear it off, Jackie slashed with her tungsten claws and ripped the zombie's face off his skull.

Except instead of a skull, another face lurked beneath the gruesome, decayed ribbons of flesh, as if it had been wearing the dead human as a costume. It had no features save for a mouth three times as wide as it should have been, with at least a hundred gleaming teeth. The remaining shreds of the zombie's face tore away. The apparition hissed at her like a pressure valve releasing on a boiler, its breath as foul as an open sewer.

Jackie, desperate to destroy this new horror, grabbed the pipe stuck through the other zombie's skull and yanked, tearing the head loose. Rancid green smoke poured from its stump of neck. She whirled and lunged at the mouth-creature, impaling it right through its gaping maw with the broken pipe. The horrible face vanished, leaving only a dead body with a pipe shoved through its face. Jackie twisted and wrenched the pipe to one side and, with a meaty rip, separated the zombie's head from its body. Common lore said decapitation was effective against the undead. She didn't know if that was true in reality but it seemed safer than any other immediate alternative.

Blood thundered in Jackie's ears as she balanced on the balls of her feet, waiting to see if the zombies would rise again. Smoke ceased pouring from their neck stumps after a few seconds. A minute later, when neither creature had moved, she decided she'd won. Her heartbeat slowed from its combat rate and her body ached as it worked to heal the damage she'd sustained.

"Man," she said aloud. "I need to give myself a raise." Then she smiled beneath her cowl; that wasn't a White Fang statement so much as a Jacquelyn Langdon phrase—something a character from one of her *Silverback* books would say.

The stench of decay and unfamiliar chemicals made her wonder if they'd been borne from tubs of some evil concoction. *How does one make a zombie, anyway?*

She removed one of her gauntlets and knelt to check on their victim, who lay unmoving in a puddle. His pulse beat strong and his breathing was slow but regular. The zombies had intended to capture this young man alive instead of kill him and eat his brains— if that was what real-life zombies did. What good was he to them? Or were the zombies following orders?

Jackie loved a good mystery, and White Fang was just the vigilante to solve it.

She touched a hidden button on her belt to recall her self-driving truck. Two miles away, the large black pickup with the sloped camper shell engaged its engine so the onboard computer could guide it to her.

While the truck approached, Jackie considered the best way to dispose of the bodies. She didn't consider herself having killed them, as they had clearly already been dead when they'd attacked. The police wouldn't see it that way, and she was already wanted in connection with dozens of assaults. They took murder investigations much more seriously, and if they decided she was a parahuman, she might wind up having to contend with Just Cause coming after her. If she was in custody at the wrong time of the month, her secret would be out and she'd never see the outside of a cage ever again. They'd send her to Deep Six—or worse, a black site science lab. She'd spend the rest of her life as a lab animal, being poked and prodded by scientists and doctors trying to understand what she was.

The grocery store's large trash compactor would be the best bet, pulping the bodies into unrecognizable jelly. She popped open an access hatch atop the huge steel bin and was rewarded with the stench of rotting produce and piles of boxes not yet crushed. With tenements right behind the store, the manager probably had established rules about when the compactor could be used. Jackie wondered if anyone had heard the noises of the battle, but after replaying it in her mind, she realized that as far as fights went, it had been strangely quiet.

Jackie lifted the two zombie bodies up to the hatch and shoved them inside the bin one at a time, using the broken pipe to push them deep enough into the garbage that they wouldn't pop out with compaction. Their heads went in next, along with what gore she could wipe away from her costume. Dominica was going to be furious about the stains, but upon reflection, they were better than stains from Jackie's blood.

She sealed the access hatch just as her truck rolled into the alley. It sickened her how calm she'd been about the killing and disposal of the bodies, but she and death had been close companions her entire life. She had vivid memories of tearing open the throats of animals and feasting upon their steaming innards. A human had never died in her jaws, but she lived in constant fear that it wasn't a question of *if* she would kill, but *when*. She risked it every night she went out as White Fang. One bad injury or loss of control, and the beast would escape, even on a moonless night.

Instead of suffering in silence, fighting criminals had given her an outlet for her aggression. *Therapeutic violence*, her doctor friend called it. Like some alcoholics had to maintain a certain blood alcohol percentage just to function, Jackie needed a certain level of violence to keep her beastly alter ego satisfied without letting it subsume her. She turned that violence toward the predatory elements of the city. Criminals feared pain, loss of respect, and embarrassment, and Jackie fought them by using those fears against them. She'd built up a decently fearful reputation among the denizens of the criminal underworld, and she grinned whenever she overheard whispers of "The Wolf" who hunted them.

The *Gazette-Journal* had also gotten wind of her, and they were quietly offering a reward for a picture of White Fang. Dominica's bollix made that nearly impossible, but Jackie knew sooner or later someone would snap a picture with a camera using actual film, and that would take some of the mystery away. Just Cause was a distant concern, but so far, she'd kept a low enough profile that the Parahuman Resources Administration hadn't sent anyone to investigate her. At least, she didn't think they had. The smartest thing would have been for her to hang up her cowl and never go on the hunt again, but crime wouldn't stop just because she did, and she would still need a way to keep her brutal side under control.

She followed her nose to the zombies' discarded spray canister and sealed it into a plastic container for further investigation.

Last, she lifted the man into the passenger seat of the truck. He was slender, with dark hair and eyes showing Asian heritage. His face was composed and serene in unconsciousness. Jackie strapped him into the seat and debated whether to bind his hands, just in case. She opted not to; she didn't want to treat him as an opponent if she didn't have to. He was a victim, and Jackie had a duty to see he would be all right. She retrieved his portfolio and slipped it behind the seat.

Jackie slipped behind the wheel and shifted the truck into gear. As she guided the large black vehicle from the alley, she thumbed the button on the wheel to call her doctor, Alix.

"Yes, Jackie, what is it?"

"I've got a victim here that I want you to take a look at. He was attacked by . . . well, by zombies."

A normal doctor might have argued there was no such thing, but six months as part of White Fang's team had opened Alix's mind to many possibilities.

"Sounds intriguing. You want a dissection and autopsy, then?"

Jackie glanced at the young man in the seat beside her. "No, he's still alive. I'm hoping you can keep him that way."

"Is he cute?"

"Alix, he's a victim."

"You never let me have any fun."

"You've got lots of nifty toys in that lab. How is that not fun?"

"Good point. Bring him in, then. I'll do my best, but I warn you. I'm having a bad day at the office."

"Your bad days are still better than most doctors' best days."

"Flattery will get you everywhere, Jackie. See you soon."

She broke the connection and left Jackie to drive south in silence, heading for the mountains and her secret den.

Chapter Two

November 2012
San Francisco, California

Charlotte Pastor strode across the expensive granite floor. She was dark-skinned with tight black curls cropped close to her skull and the child of Jamaican slaves. To anyone not in the know, the San Francisco office building was just another faceless corporation, but to her and others like her, it was the North American home of the Midnight Collective, a centuries-old organization dedicated to the survival and anonymity of vampirekind. She flashed her badge to the human guards waiting at the metal detector and they waved her through.

The guards were a precaution only against unwelcome human visitors. The chief of security, an old-school vampire who'd been turned around the time of the American Revolution, believed humans were the best deterrents against their own kind. Charlotte would have preferred a couple of trained dogs and naked assault rifles like they used in Israel, but she wasn't in charge of Collective security. Her calling lay on other, bloodier paths.

She gave her bag to a waiting thrall and asked to have it taken to her room. The young woman gave a polite bow and left to comply

Her boot heels clacked on the floor as she traversed the main hall, heading for the elevators. Hunting werewolves was hungry, tiresome work, and some days not even fresh blood could cure Charlotte's exhaustion at the never-ending chore. Werewolves delighted in killing humans, and vampires couldn't survive without human blood. If too many humans died, they might discover the existence of the undead, and then a culling would begin. It had many times throughout history. Charlotte worked to prevent that, defending humans who never knew about the desperate, bloody war being fought in the alleys and sub-basements of their world.

It was a noble, honorable job among her kind, and she was one of the best in the world.

The elevator door slid open and a tall native American man emerged, hair plaited neatly into two braids over his shoulders and turquoise conchas decorating the band of his cowboy hat. "Welcome home, Nightfall. I heard you were in Asia."

"Hunan Province." Charlotte stepped onto the elevator and pushed the button for descent. "Another colony."

"There's always another colony. Don't you ever get tired?"

"No," she lied. "Not until they're all dead."

"I wish I had your dedication." He tipped his hat to her. She didn't remember his name. It didn't matter.

"If more of you in the Collective did, we might not be needed any longer. Did you ever think about that?"

The doors shut before the other operative could formulate a response. In truth, Charlotte *was* tired. After several decades of hunting and slaughtering werewolves, it felt like she hadn't made the slightest bit of difference. It was like trying to redirect a river with a shovel. She leaned back against the wall of the elevator and practiced taking a deep breath. She reminded herself to breathe now and then just to retain the ability for when she spent time among humans. Even nearly a century since her embrace, she still found catharsis in a sigh.

Hunan had been a bad one. The colony was holed up in a cheap plaster-and-paper apartment building. With the local overpopulation, the werewolves had not only been well-fed, they'd taken to killing humans for fun. When she and a Chinese agent had assaulted the colony, they'd discovered bodies of children that had been torn apart without being eaten, women who'd been savaged in ways Charlotte didn't care to recall, and men kept in cages to be released and hunted daily.

All but the most deranged humans felt a mixture of revulsion, pity, and righteous anger when they happened upon mistreated dogs. Charlotte felt the same way about the humans she'd discovered in the werewolf colony.

She could still hear the human captives' terrified screams as she and Agent Huojin stormed the building with silver bullets and aconite spray—two dark avenging angels against a dozen of the dog-men. The vampires had been careless and overconfident, and a werewolf tore out Huojin's throat in the second while Charlotte reloaded her pistols.

Now, back in the States, all Charlotte wanted was a long, hot bath and to feel Anastasia's arms around her.

She found Anastasia in the *dojo*, giving a combat lesson to the latest batch of recruits. If it had been full of humans, the air would have been redolent with the stink of perspiration, but vampires didn't sweat. Charlotte leaned against the edge of the doorway to watch Anastasia conduct her class. Her *gi* hugged her hips and left her calves and slender ankles exposed. Anastasia shook out her reddish blonde curls and had a student approach her. She dispatched him swiftly using a combination of French savate kicks and finished with a Japanese jujitsu lock and throw. The victim crashed against a support pillar and before he could recover, Anastasia had a silver dagger resting point-first beneath his sternum. If he'd been a werewolf, he'd be dead.

"What you must understand," Anastasia said in her brusque peasant accent that she'd made no attempt to remove in forty years, "Is that as vampires, we stop growing, but we can still force change into our bodies with much practice and effort. Say you were big strong man before embrace and want to become bodybuilder afterward." She poked one of the recruits, a giant of a Pakistani man whose muscles strained to burst through his skin. "You must work much harder than human for much longer to condition and change vampire body. Great patience is needed. Same goes for learning fighting skills. Vampire muscle memory takes much time to instill. You will work hard to become skilled agents of Midnight Collective, *da*?"

The new recruits muttered agreement. Charlotte thought their enthusiasm left much to be desired, but Anastasia seemed satisfied. She looked up and caught Charlotte's eye, then returned her gaze to the recruits. Charlotte blinked in surprise. She hadn't seen the slightest bit of welcome in that brief eye contact.

"Comrades, we have a celebrity in our midst. Please welcome Agent Pastor, known as Nightfall. Perhaps she has wisdom to share for you."

Charlotte sighed again. She'd hoped for hot blood, peaceful quiet, and time alone with Anastasia. Instead, she was being recruited to teach. She put on her best smile, stepped out of her boots, and left them at the door to the *dojo*.

The recruits were a motley bunch, from the giant Pakistani to a skinny punk with a skateboarder's shaggy hairdo to a matronly housewife type. Charlotte couldn't see how a woman like that had even wound up embraced. Somewhere, a vampire had showed a serious lapse of judgment. It wasn't like in the movies, where one bite made a vampire. The process took time and dedication from both parties. It had been many generations since a human had been converted against his or her will.

"There isn't anything I can say that Anastasia can't explain to you better," Charlotte said. "She knows her stuff."

"You are too modest," Anastasia said. "Agent Pastor is a brilliant werewolf hunter who understands the nature of the beasts. When it comes to slaying them, she has no equal."

The Pakistani man stepped forward. Charlotte thought she could hear his muscles creak with every motion. He folded his massive arms across a barrel chest and looked down his nose at her. "Are they really that tough?"

Charlotte fixed him with a glare. "Short of a human with a hardwood stake and balls of steel, werewolves are the only creatures that can harm us. Their teeth and claws bypass the mystic energies that protect us and keep us alive. If a vampire loses a finger or hand to a werewolf, it won't grow back, and the shock to your system can be just as fatal as if you were human. They've got an incredible sense of smell and can pick you out of a crowded room. We are their most direct competition for human prey, and they won't hesitate to gut you given the chance."

The Pakistani put his hands on his hips and tilted his head to one side, cracking his neck. "You sound like you're afraid of them."

Charlotte didn't look away from his challenging gaze. "I am. I've lived for almost a hundred years in this body, and I kept it whole because I am careful around the most dangerous beasts in the world."

"Well, I'm not afraid." He grinned, showing his fangs in perverse aggression.

"Then you're a fool." She took pleasure in the way the muscles in his jaw bulged as he clenched his teeth at her retort. She'd seen his type before. Big ones were always convinced that their bodies were sufficient weapons to defeat werewolves. "Let me demonstrate for you." She pulled a device that resembled a thimble from one of her pouches and fixed it over one of her fingers. A yellow enamel tooth sat in silver solder built up on the end of the tip. "This is a werewolf's tooth. Want to bet I can scratch my initials in that pretty skin of yours?"

The Pakistani laughed. "And what's in it for me, Agent?"

Charlotte glanced at Anastasia. She looked pale and nervous. Charlotte wondered what Anastasia knew about the Pakistani that she didn't. She was tired, hungry, and annoyed by the big man's stupid attitude and self-centered superiority. Nevertheless, she wasn't one to back down from a challenge or to offer inadequate stakes. She would enjoy kicking his ass and maybe in the process he might learn a lesson about humility if nothing else. "Anything you want, big boy."

A leer of pure lust split his bearded face. "The name is Raheem," he said. "And this will be a true pleasure." He pulled off his t-shirt to show off an admirable physique, layered with slabs of hard muscle underneath his olive skin. Once upon a time, Charlotte would have lusted after his raw sexuality and longed to feel his cool skin against hers. She could appreciate the beauty, but no longer felt the attraction.

"Observe, class," Charlotte said. "The werewolf has a distinctive fighting style. Undisciplined. Animalistic."

Raheem charged at her, his hands raised in a skilled defensive posture. He'd been well-trained in a fighting method she didn't recognize. She'd have to channel all her knowledge of combat to get through this encounter unscathed.

She sprang at him, keeping low to attack his legs. She slashed the tooth at one muscular thigh, which he moved out of the way just in time. His elbow dropped to pummel her into the floor, but Charlotte rolled clear. Before he had a chance to turn, she jumped again. The tooth flashed in the glow of the overhead lights as she scratched a thin line down one of his shoulders. He hissed and struck her solar plexus with his open palm. The blow would have knocked a human down in writhing agony, but Charlotte shrugged it off and stepped back.

"Although the werewolf generally appears human," she said, "in moments of extreme stress, especially approaching the full Moon, he can take on aspects of his transformation, either intentionally or by accident. This makes him more powerful and unpredictable."

Raheem charged again, arms whirling like pinwheels. His fingers hooked into claws and Charlotte heard the whistle of displaced air as he approached. She shook her head. So much wasted effort in his showy actions. She dove toward his feet, underneath his hands. As he reached down to grapple with her, she kicked her feet up across his chest to hook her ankles behind his ears. He grabbed onto her ankles to toss her away and she used his hands as leverage to bend upward at the waist. As her body passed up and over his head, she added a curved loop to the scratch she'd left on his shoulder, making a recognizable *P*.

She hit the ground behind him and paused in shock. She'd caught a hint of Anastasia's scent as he moved—not her everyday smell, but one much more intimate. The brief stall nearly ended the bout, for Raheem closed a hand around her wrist and swung her into the ceiling. Plaster rained down as the masonry cracked where she struck. She twined her legs around his arm. He tried to fight her off and she moved like a snake around him, keeping herself tight against his body so he couldn't get enough leverage to punch at her again. They wrestled for a moment, he with the greater strength and she with the dexterity until she got the position she wanted and scratched a *C* next to the *P* already on his shoulder.

"Hold!" cried Anastasia. She'd gone white as a sheet, and Charlotte knew why.

She disengaged herself from Raheem, rolled back onto her feet, and bowed to him. Raheem bowed back, rubbing the welts on his shoulder. "If you ever find yourself unarmed and facing a werewolf under the light of the full Moon, my advice to you is to run away as fast as you can. A fully transformed werewolf is faster than the fastest of us, resistant to silver and aconite, and will slash you to shreds in the blink of an eye. And believe me, you'll feel every bit of pain as he . . . or she—" Charlotte fixed Anastasia square in her gaze. "Rips out your heart."

Anastasia wouldn't meet Charlotte's eyes. "Class dismissed," the Russian said. "We resume tomorrow to study vital points of werewolves."

Charlotte folded her arms and waited for the students to leave. Raheem was one of the last to go. He looked as if he wanted to say something to Anastasia but left after a meaningful glance from her.

At last, the two women were alone in the *dojo*. Anastasia put her hands on her hips and stood with one hip cocked aside in a pose Charlotte remembered from the first day they'd met. "All right. Let's hear it."

"Really, Ana? A student?" Charlotte struggled to keep her voice from breaking.

"How did you know? We are careful."

"I can smell you on him. Did you wait for me to leave for China before jumping into his arms or has this been going on even longer and I'm just too stupid to have seen it?"

Anastasia pointed at her. "Don't you put this on me. You are so intent on your war with the werewolves that it consumes you day and night. Especially at night. How can I be with someone who would rather be killing than fucking?"

"Is that all I am to you then? Your . . . your chew toy?" Charlotte felt her fangs poking at her lower lip.

"You are so self-righteous. I know you have had many men. Would you have me live forever without seeking new experiences? New sensations? You've never been one to forego those pleasures." Her jaw tightened, framed by those golden red curls Charlotte remembered twisting in her fingers.

"Don't you lecture at me like I'm some first-year student. I was doing this for a lifetime before you were even born. I've seen entire families wiped out by werewolf invasions. I've lost friends . . . mentors. Even—"

"Even lovers?" Anastasia's voice grew bitter. "Fucking me isn't going to bring them back. Your Spaniard is gone, Charlotte."

Charlotte gasped. The barb hurt like slavering teeth in her flesh. She still remembered Valdez like it was yesterday, even though the last time she'd seen him alive was 1953 in Peru, right before he was torn apart by a pack of werewolves. He'd taught her everything she knew about climbing. They'd hunted together in the jungles by the pale moonlight. He was the last man she'd ever loved.

"I won't live like this. Not with you being more focused on your war. It was fun while it lasted. Pleasant, even. But it's over. Go find yourself someone who doesn't mind sharing you with werewolves." Anastasia spun on her heel and left the *dojo*.

Charlotte shut her eyes. She remembered the play of her dusky skin against Anastasia's alabaster, the taste of her lips, the feel of their intertwined limbs as they dozed following their lovemaking. Anastasia had given her something she hadn't had in a long time: a reason to come home.

She punched a wall. Concrete cracked at the impact, but she felt no pain. She hadn't felt pain for decades and was terrified of losing the ability to feel anything at all. It took the thrill of the hunt, the terror of combat, or the tenderness of making love to broach that barrier. What if she lost those outlets entirely?

Her phone buzzed with a text from her superior, Blackstone. *Got a job for you if you're free. Come see me upstairs.*

Blackstone was the commander of the Midnight Collective. He wouldn't request her services for anything less than a whole pack of lycanthropes. A little unbridled violence would provide the kind of therapy Charlotte couldn't get anyplace else.

She texted back: *On my way.*

Chapter Three

November 2012
Reno, Nevada

The access road into White Fang's secret headquarters was just wide enough for the truck, with a vertical wall on the right and a sheer drop-off to the left. Jackie had driven it enough times that she didn't need to feather the brakes until right before she ran through the buttressed mine entrance. It was secured with a remotely operated gate, paid for not with a book advance, but with a bag of cash she'd confiscated from a drug dealer. Much of her equipment had been paid for over the past year by the drug trade. She figured by taking that money and investing it in her one-woman crusade against crime, she was giving back to the community in ways most charities hadn't considered. The drug trade was lucrative, and ran almost entirely on large amounts of untraceable cash. The more of it she took out of circulation, the worse it hurt their enterprises.

A century and a half ago, Mount Davidson was the center of a silver rush, transforming the sleepy trading post of Virginia City into a burgeoning boomtown rife with misadventure and opportunity. Diggings honeycombed the mountainside as miners scrabbled through rock and dirt in the hopes of finding nuggets of precious metal. In modern times, the nearby area of the VC Highlands was peppered with the large houses of the region's wealthiest citizens, and the mines had been filled in with concrete and sealed.

Except one.

With the help of her socially inept computer geek and engineer extraordinaire Dominica Altuna, Jackie removed all evidence of one particular silver mine from historical and online records. They hid the narrow access road behind a road sign and artificial rocks. A touch of the switch on the dashboard of her truck and the false barricade would slide aside. It took them months to prepare the area, both through a lot of backbreaking work with shovels, pickaxes, and rented heavy equipment. It was a rough, underdeveloped space because they'd only started using it three months ago. Still, having her own lair felt . . . *right.*

She parked the truck on the turntable, which hummed as it spun to rotate the truck around so it faced the entrance. Overhead lights bathed the headquarters in a warm yellow glow, comforting in its lack of resemblance to anything like moonlight. The utilitarian headquarters was functional in design but had a certain austere beauty Jackie appreciated. Her cage sat off to one side in the shadows, a constant reminder that no matter how she pretended otherwise, her life was governed by the lunar cycle. By the end of the week, she would be locked in that cage to claw and bite helplessly at the titanium bars and scream wordless fury at her friends.

Her staff awaited as she climbed from the truck. Dominica Altuna had her nose buried in her tablet, which was tied into the main computer center on a nearby platform. The diminutive Hispanic woman had a gift for designing and repairing machinery and had graduated at the top of her class from Cal Tech. Despite her academic success, Dominica had found difficulty seeking employment. Many industries spoke about needing women in STEM, but when one presented herself, she was passed over time and again for less-qualified male applicants.

Jackie knew she needed help for her crusade, and an engineer was the place to start. She made some discreet inquiries and did a lot of internet research—and if there was one thing writers were good at, it was research. She had her assistant Jenn put out some feelers and after Dominica's name had come up from a few different avenues of research, Jackie approached her as White Fang. Did Dominica want to design and maintain the equipment for vigilante operations? *Hell, yes she did!*

Doctor Alix Duchesne hovered by the passenger door of the truck. A heavyset, bespectacled redhead, she carried an air of authority and competency Jackie strove to emulate in the field. She already had a wheeled hospital bed and emergency kit at hand. Jackie lifted the young man onto the bed and Alix wheeled him to the medical lab. "Zombies, huh? You sure you're getting enough air inside that cowl?" the doctor asked over her shoulder.

One night, early in her career as the vigilante, Jackie ran afoul of a dogfighting ring and the perpetrators set their dogs upon her while making their escapes. The furious canines nearly tore her apart, driven mad by her unnatural scent only they could detect. Their assault nearly overwhelmed her healing ability, and she'd staggered into the street more dead than alive where Alix almost ran over her. The doctor carried Jackie into her nearby apartment and as she started treatment, she'd been astonished at the sight of Jackie's flesh knitting itself back together. At first, Jackie swore her to secrecy, and then offered her a job on the spot. Alix, tired of emergency room politics, was only too glad to accept.

"It's a good cowl," Dominica called as she plugged her laptop into the truck's data port to check its systems. "I've worn sleep masks that weren't as comfortable."

"Let me get out of my work clothes, Doc, and I'll be right over there."

A gentle clearing of a throat made Jackie cringe and she turned to regard an impatient blonde in a charcoal gray pencil skirt, a white Oxford shirt, and a strategically placed pencil holding up her hair in a bun. She glared at Jackie over the tops of her rectangular glasses. This was Jennifer Sproles, her personal assistant. "Jackie," she said in the tone that meant she was in trouble. "We need to talk."

When Jackie sold her first novel, it became a sensation. A film producer optioned the rights and the subsequent movie rocketed her to superstardom. Suddenly, Jackie was wealthy, and in demand at book signings, talk shows, and conferences around the country. She bought the house in the mountains and hired Jenn, who was young, fresh out of school with an M.B.A. and a sharp, quick mind. Three months after she'd started, on the day before the full moon was due to rise, Jackie had been pacing her house and snarling at the walls. Jenn understood something was wrong. She asked Jackie what it was, and Jackie overcame a lifetime of silence to explain.

That afternoon, with Jackie's blessing, Jenn locked her in the cage. She'd sat all night in front of it while the beast-that-was-Jackie screamed at her, howled its rage, and beat its head bloody against the iron bars. She didn't flinch once. In the morning, when Jackie's body wrenched itself back into human form, Jenn had unlocked the cage, helped her into bed, and dozed on the couch while Jackie slept off her monthly night of monstrosity.

Jackie pulled off her cowl and handed it to Jenn, exposing her short black hair and sharp features. "There were zombies out there tonight, Jenn. Real life zombies. Did I mention that?"

Jenn set the cowl upon the dressmaker's manikin in the ready area beside the truck. "You had an interview scheduled this evening."

"I did?" Jackie kicked her boots off in the general direction of the manikin.

"SKY News is doing a feature on the *Silverback* series and its famous author who chooses to stay here in Reno instead of jet-setting to the East Coast like other, more *professional* authors I could mention."

Jackie pulled off her gauntlets and inspected them. Underneath one of the tungsten steel claws she found a chunk of zombie flesh. She wrinkled her nose in distaste and dropped it into a plastic baggie from her utility belt. "Tell them I was jet-setting tonight. Can you reschedule it for me? Doc, there's a sample of zombie meat over here when you get a chance."

Jenn accepted Jackie's utility belt and hung it on the rack beside the gauntlets. "I already did. You're talking to them tomorrow evening if I have to bring them here into the mine and let them conduct it while you're working out on that contraption over there."

That contraption was the combination exercise machine and combat workout device Dominica had built in two weeks of feverish intensity. The mine had stunk of welding for days afterward, and the first time Jackie tried it, it had neatly snapped one of the bones in her left forearm.

"Hey, that's my masterpiece." Dominica looked up from her laptop to see if everything was still working since the last time she'd checked them a few hours earlier.

"It makes a medieval torture device look like a kids' bouncy castle," Jenn said.

"Kids, please," said Jackie. "We have a guest. Can we try to be on our best behavior?" She peeled out of her black bodysuit, quilted with layers of Kevlar. She wasn't self-conscious about her near nudity around the other women. Alix was busy examining their unconscious guest and Jenn—well, she'd seen the worst of Jackie without batting an eye. Showing her tautly muscled body certainly wasn't going to cause embarrassment for either of them. She wrapped a kimono-style bathrobe around herself and padded barefoot to the cave's kitchenette.

"And that's another thing." Jenn watched Jackie as she mixed a protein smoothie. "You think maybe we could talk about security for just a minute? I mean, you bring a civilian in here, of all places? Why didn't you take him to a hospital?"

"Zombies, remember?" Jackie dumped ingredients into the blender. "They did something to him. Knocked him out with gas. Oh, Dominica, I saved a sample for you. Canister in the passenger footwell."

"Sweet." Dominica opened the door and retrieved it.

"Careful with that. One good whiff put that dude down for the count. How is he, Doc?"

Alix wheeled the cart into the medical lab. "He seems to be in an induced coma. I'd need to do a brain scan to know for sure, and so far an MRI machine is still out of your budget."

"I'll write another *Silverback* novel after this one. Please the masses. Add a few more gizmos to the lab." The whine of the blender filled the air, echoing off the mine's walls.

"Maybe you should finish the one that's on deadline," Jenn said pointedly. The *Silverback* series featured a family of werewolves and their machinations in the world of men. It was popular with urban fantasy readers, and after five books the series' appeal was massive. There was even a television series in the works.

"Of course, I'll do the interview, Jenn. What would I do without you?" She looked around in futility for a cup, shrugged, and raised the blender pitcher to her lips.

"You'd lose everything," said Jenn. "Excuse me, I'm getting a call." She stepped away from the others and tapped the headset that seemed to be a permanent fixture on her right ear.

"So, what's the diagnosis, Doc?" Jackie ambled over to look down at her guest.

"Too soon to tell. I'll need twenty-four, maybe forty-eight hours before I can tell you more than that. Right now, all we can do is hook him up to monitoring machines and see if whatever the—"

"Zombies." Jackie took another sip of her smoothie. She thought about mentioning the face she'd seen beneath the zombie's face, but she still wasn't convinced it had been there.

"Yes, well, I'm not prepared to accept that on your word."

"I'm a werewolf, and you're having difficulty believing in zombies?"

Alix looked up from her monitor. "I'm a scientist, Jackie. I need a little more to go on than an eyewitness account. Especially when that eyewitness is unbalanced enough to dress up in a costume and pretend she's a superhero."

"I brought you home a piece of zombie face because I love you."

"Bullshit." Alix ran wires to electrodes she'd placed on the young man's head. "Put it in the fridge for me so I can look at it tomorrow." She looked back over her shoulder. "Try not to eat it."

"I do have standards, Doc."

"I've seen you eat a squirrel."

"It had attitude, and I can't be held responsible for my actions at peak lunar cycle."

"He's a pretty good artist, boss," said Dominica. Jackie looked over to see the mechanic thumbing through the man's portfolio. "Looks like lots of charcoal, colored pencils. Hey, check this out. Coincidence?" She held up a half-finished sketch of a wolf in a snowy forest.

"Good omen, maybe. Does he have any ID on him?" Jackie returned to the kitchenette and rinsed out her smoothie pitcher.

"Driver's license says his name is Mark Hu. He lives near Old Town." Dominica examined Mark's wallet. "Attends the School of the Arts. Looks like he's doing well with it from the quality of his work. He's got a bank card here, a bit of cash, and a cell phone. I disabled the GPS on it, by the way, even though the signal shouldn't reach into the mine without connecting to our wi-fi." She paused. "Wait a minute. I know this address from somewhere." She punched it into her tablet and crowed with triumph a minute later. "Ha! I knew it. He lives in the same building as the guy I bought the powder from for your smoke bombs. *Hu Makes Fireworks*. Must be his family. Small world, huh?"

"Indeed," Jackie said.

"So, what are you going to do with him?" Jenn rejoined them, finished with her call. "He's already late for wherever he was supposed to be. My guess would be home. You going to keep him here without notifying his family?"

"I kind of have to," Jackie said. "Doc needs to keep an eye on him. We're going to need a cover story to tell his family."

"We?" Jenn laughed. "You brought him into the mine, Jackie. This is on your head, dog-girl."

"Why do I pay you to insult me?"

"You pay me for other things." Jenn winked. "The insults are a free add-on service."

Jackie scratched at her chin. "How about this? Paranormal novelist Jackie Langdon was driving through Old Town tonight. She heard the sounds of a man in distress and found him in a bad way. Being that she has a private physician on hand, she took the young man back to her home where he is being cared for."

"The noble Samaritan," Jenn said. "That's so ridiculous everyone will probably believe it instead of thinking you just picked up some stranger in Old Town."

"Will you contact his family? Reassure them that he'll be fine. Invite them to the house. Ask them to please not mention it to the press because as a writer, I do like my privacy. Tell them I'm covering the costs of his treatment. That might alleviate their fears."

"Already on it." Jenn stepped away once more, tapping her earpiece.

"Doc, Dominica, let's get this kid moved upstairs."

They rolled the bed and supporting equipment out of the medical lab, past Dominica's workshop and the computer station to an old-fashioned cage elevator. They rode it up out of the mine where it arrived behind a bookcase in Jackie's library. The case swung aside with a gentle click and they wheeled the bed into one of the guest bedrooms.

"Don't forget to get dressed," Dominica said. "You're going to take the eccentric writer lifestyle thing a little too far."

"Don't you have a chemical compound to analyze?"

"Yes, ma'am, that I do. I'll be downstairs."

"Don't call me *ma'am*. It makes me feel old. And take the stairs," Jackie said. "You have no idea how loud that elevator is inside the house. You should have soundproofed it better."

Dominica smiled. "All it takes is more money, *señora Lobo*."

"It's like I'm the mother of teenagers," Jackie muttered to Alix.

The doctor chuckled. "Mom, can I borrow one of the cars tonight? Dominica said something about putting a mileage booster on mine and she's got it in pieces in one of the side bays. I'll need to replenish some supplies if we're going to have a patient here for a few days."

Jackie sighed. "Not the Jag. I've seen how you drive."

"The Mustang?"

Jackie shrugged. "Keys are by the garage door."

Alix left and a few minutes later the supercharged V8 roared as the dark blue Mustang with the chrome wheels raced down the drive to the main road.

Clouds still hung low and heavy over Reno, but the air was clearer up the side of the mountain, and the cold didn't bother Jackie the way it would a human. She stepped out onto the deck, closed her eyes, and sniffed deeply of the air with the tang of sumac, the sweetness of acacia, and the faint musk of a raccoon somewhere nearby. She could have hunted it down, slinking through the sparse mountainside woods with the grace of her namesake, torn it apart and eaten the bloody flesh while it was still warm. The temptation was always there, like the underlying hum of air conditioning in a downtown high-rise. Most times she could entomb it under the veneer of civilization.

But for those times she could not, that was why she had the cage.

Her transformation wasn't entirely at the mercy of the lunar cycle, and a few times growing up, her temper had started the transformation. The painful sensation of her spine rippling was usually enough to calm her. Even as a human, she had an acute sense of smell and taste, and found herself depending upon it nearly as much as she did her eyes and ears. Like so many parahumans in Just Cause and other superheroes or supervillains, she was much stronger and quicker than humans, and healed from injuries with unnatural speed.

Before Jenn came into her life, Jackie used a technique her parents had taught her when locking herself in the cage. She kept a hooked wand within reach to pull the key to her. Human hands could manipulate that wand, could fit the key into the lock and turn it. Wolf jaws would never manage such a complicated and precise task. It was how she kept herself from getting out, how she kept the rest of the world safe from her. Once Jenn had taken on monitoring her, the wand became an afterthought, until one day the year before, Jenn hadn't come to let her out.

She'd been carjacked. A thug yanked her door open at a stoplight, hauled her out of the car at gunpoint, hit her across the face with his pistol, and stole her car. He went on to use it while robbing a store then crashed it into a minivan, killing a young mother and her daughter. Jenn finally arrived at Jackie's house in a rented car with a cracked mandible and frazzled nerves, having forgone her own needs to help her employer. Jackie immediately took her to the hospital, appalled at what had happened.

That's when she realized she could do something about it.

"You planning to heat the entire mountainside?"

Jackie turned to see Jenn standing in the doorway of the deck. She was chewing on the end of a ballpoint pen in a coquettish fashion and had a blanket wrapped around her shoulders to ward off the chill.

"Sorry. Woolgathering."

She stepped a little closer. Jackie smelled her hair conditioner. It was the same brand her mother had used. It had been as much a factor as anything in hiring her. It reminded Jackie of happier times, when her parents still lived. "Does that make you a wolf in sheep's clothing?"

Jackie's somber mood lifted. "Perhaps."

"So, you're in a good mood then?" Jenn offered her a corner of the blanket. Jackie shook her head, not cold even though the chill rain threatened to turn to snow.

"Sure." Jackie narrowed her eyes. "Why?"

"Because after the Hus arrive to check on their son, I'll tell you all about the event you're going to be have to attend the day after tomorrow."

"An *event*?"

"Yep. In public. You'll have to dress up and everything."

Jackie sighed. So much for her eccentric writer lifestyle.

Chapter Four

November 2012
San Francisco, California

Charlotte rode the elevator to the top floor of the Midnight Collective building, trying to harden her heart against the pain of Anasasia's betrayal. Memories of the red-headed Russian's passion had been one of the few things to keep Charlotte able to focus on her werewolf-slaying duties. Anastasia had been her reward for a job well done, and now that reward had been yanked away from her. Her eyes wandered up to a flier taped on the inside of the elevator, warning of the H3N2 influenza outbreak and advising vampires not to feed on any sickened thralls. Vampires couldn't contract the flu—or any other disease—but sick thralls didn't provide much sustenance, and vampires could transmit viruses between thralls with their bites.

She should get back out in the field as quickly as possible, she thought. Find a werewolf den. Cleanse it. Psychosomatic itches plagued her fingers as she imagined herself tearing her way through vicious beast after vicious beast. No silver bullets, no aconite spray. Just her claws. The sound of their tainted blood splattering onto walls and floor, the feel of it on her skin. Charlotte didn't feel much of anything anymore, but she would feel that, and it would feel good. She could lose herself in that blood. It wouldn't heal the injury Anastasia had done to her soul, but it might cover it with crimson relief. Hopefully, Blackstone would have exactly the job she needed.

Blackstone was the oldest vampire Charlotte had ever met. He'd been converted sometime in the mid-1100s as a young man. Like her, he hadn't aged a day since his embrace, but he'd found ways to alter his body nonetheless. His dedication to that level of hard work had been inspirational for many vampires who'd followed him over the years as he formalized the creation of the Midnight Collective. She'd never learned his real name. As far as anyone knew, all he'd ever called himself was Blackstone. Upon the founding of the Midnight Collective, the other members chose to emulate him by adopting code names the way parahumans often did, and Charlotte had chosen *Nightfall* as hers.

When she entered his office, he was standing with his back to the door, staring out the polarized windows at the Bay. Without them, the sun would raise blisters upon his skin within minutes and if he couldn't escape, his skin, then flesh, and eventually his bones would burn to ash. His tailored suit jacket strained to contain his basketball-sized shoulders and accentuated his narrow waist and hips. Not only was he the oldest vampire Charlotte knew, he was also the strongest—capable of tearing through a wall or overturning a city bus. The only shortcoming in his physical perfection was his height. At only five and half feet tall, he'd have been a head taller than most men in the Tenth Century. His hands clasped behind his back and he didn't turn around.

"Sit down, Nightfall."

Charlotte sat in one of the leather-wrapped office chairs which had, like everything else in Blackstone's office, a distinctive Victorian style. She waited for him to speak. Blackstone never hurried anything.

"I read your report on Jishou City." He turned away from the windows and the bright sunshine beyond them. "Thorough and professional, as always."

"Thank you, sir."

A flicker of disappointment crossed his face. "So, it's *sir* now, is it?"

"Yes. This time." The tight black curls of his short beard and hair plus olive skin tone showed his Moorish ancestry. When Charlotte had first seen him, all those years ago, she'd thought he was a beautiful man. That hadn't changed, but her feelings had.

"I see." He sat behind his desk and clasped his hands in deliberate, precise motions. "I'm concerned that a foreign agent died."

Charlotte shrugged. "It was his mistake. If he'd timed his shots not to run out at the same time as me, he'd still be alive right now."

Blackstone raised an eyebrow. "Perhaps you haven't considered that you could have timed your shots not to run out at the same time as him."

Charlotte's mouth fell open. Was he going to pin this on her? "What are you getting at?"

"I've had you in the field for a long time. Before Jishou was Sapporo. Before that, Honolulu. Motor City. Urbanis. I've been running you ragged."

"I'm fine. Field work is what I enjoy . . . *sir*."

"And you're very good at it, *Charlotte*, but I'm worried you're overextending yourself."

Charlotte shrugged. "I'd rather be out there doing my job." She wasn't going to take his bait. Calling him anything besides *sir* would give him a chink in her armor, a place into which he could set a chisel and worm his way in.

"And I'm going to send you out again." Blackstone rested his elbows on his desk and touched his fingertips together. "But not in the type of job you're accustomed to. This one isn't search and destroy. It's an investigatory job."

"Sir, I'm fine, I swear!" She felt like he was about to punish her and wanted to forestall it.

Blackstone's voice grew so cold the temperature dropped. "You are what I say you are. Never forget that, Nightfall."

She'd left him because of that coldness. It still frightened her to have it directed at her. The last time she'd heard that tone directed at her, he'd been moments away from tearing into her after she broke off their relationship. If Blackstone was angry enough to speak to her in that tone, what else was he angry enough to do? Charlotte couldn't win a fight against him if he lashed out at her. He was too strong, too fast, too powerful. She needed to tread lightly. Stick to the plan. "What's the job?"

His tone softened a few degrees. "Have you ever been to Reno?"

"Nevada? No, sir. Is there a colony there?"

Blackstone's brows drew together. "Not exactly. There's something going on there, but I'm not sure what. Reno seems to have found itself a superhero. More specifically, a vigilante running around town in a wolf costume, breaking up organized crime and street-level thuggery. Descriptions vary but one thing they all seem to agree on is the wolf costume and that White Fang is very difficult to harm."

"So, he's a parahuman. They exist. Why couldn't there be one in Reno?"

"There could be," Blackstone said. "But it could also be something else."

"You think there's a werewolf underneath that costume? That seems unlikely. Werewolves live in colonies. They always have. It's their whole pack mentality. Could he be a vampire instead? Playing up the whole *look-at-me-I'm-a-scary-werewolf* thing?"

"That's a possibility. Local law enforcement hasn't admitted he exists yet. Most of my information is coming through underground sources. Apparently, he's extremely difficult to see on video. He causes localized signal interference."

"That sounds more like a parahuman ability if you ask me."

"Or technology. It exists, as you say." Blackstone pushed back from his desk and returned to the windows. There was a small spot where the glass wasn't polarized. He held his hand in the spot of sunlight for a moment until his skin started to smoke. He pulled it back and regarded the superficial damage to his skin for a moment. Then he brushed away the smudge of ash and clasped his hands behind him once more. "The bottom line is that I need to understand whatever is going on there in Reno. If this vigilante is a werewolf, or even a rogue vampire like you suggested, he's putting us all at risk with his foolhardy actions."

"Maybe he's just a parahuman. And a crazy one at that. Who'd put on a goofy costume and fight street crime outside the law when he could join the Champions or Just Cause and do it with a badge and a license? It's insane."

"Insane or not, we can't take the risk. The very survival of vampirekind is predicated on the humans not believing we are real. If this madman is a werewolf, and the humans discover the truth, how long will it be before they start seeking us as well?"

Charlotte shrugged. "Even so, there's nothing to tie him to us. Besides, it's a different world than it was five hundred years ago. Shit, it's a different world than it was fifty years ago. They accept parahumans now—even the really freaky ones. Why wouldn't they accept us?"

"Vampires and werewolves have preyed upon humans for millennia. We are the monsters of their nightmares, embedded into every culture on this planet. You think they'll just let that go? Humans leap to conclusions. Are you prepared to go to war against them? We would have found it difficult five hundred years ago. Today it might be the end of us forever."

"You're awfully judgmental of humans. Before our embraces, every one of us was a human being."

"Don't remind me. Humanity is sick. If we didn't need them for our own survival, I wonder if we wouldn't have wiped them out long ago."

Charlotte stood and put her hand on Blackstone's arm, gentle but insistent pressure to make him stop pacing. Many decades ago, she had soothed him the same way. And he responded in kind, becoming still and calm once more. "You don't mean that, Blackstone."

"No, I suppose I don't. Go to Reno. Find out who this man is. If he's a vampire, bring him in. I want to speak to him."

"What about a parahuman?"

"Use your judgment. If he's operating alone, that's unusual enough to let him live and see how things play out."

"And if he's a werewolf?"

"Put him down. They're vermin. Where there is one, there will inevitably be others."

"I'll take care of it. Hell, dealing with only one werewolf . . . It'll be like a vacation."

Blackstone smiled at her. "I heard about Anastasia. I'm sorry. Maybe a low-pressure job like this is just what you need."

Charlotte turned to leave.

"Agent Pastor . . . Charlotte . . ."

She turned to hear whatever Blackstone had to say.

"Be careful with this one. I've got a funny feeling something's not right."

"Do you have anything you're not telling me? Or is that just a hunch?"

Blackstone's desk phone beeped and his secretary spoke over the intercom. "Sir, I have a Mr. Gault holding for you."

He sat at his desk and picked up the receiver. "Just a hunch. Excuse me, Agent."

"I'll watch my back." Charlotte left to get her gear from her quarters.

When she arrived at her room, she paused before entering. The last time she'd been here, Anastasia had been staying with her. She wondered if the Russian vampire had left anything in her room or taken it all away long before Charlotte had returned home from China. She imagined Anastasia and Raheem making love in her room, on the very same bed she and Ana had shared. Her fangs elongated with her emotions and stabbed her lower gums. The hunger gnawed at her, amplifying her anger until she couldn't think straight. Had a human—*any* human—been anywhere nearby, she would have fed with savage glee.

She opened the door again and looked past the haphazard pile of gear she'd dropped just beyond the threshold. Otherwise, the room was neat and orderly— the bed made, the carpet vacuumed, even the polarized windows sparkling. It was so different from the tiny, cramped room she'd shared with Agent Huojin, where they rested upon dirty bamboo floors and fed on scrawny stray dogs because none of the local humans were healthy enough to be thralls. This room felt like a place someone only ever stayed instead of lived. Charlotte hadn't spent more than a few days at a time in this room. She wouldn't miss it.

She wouldn't dare.

She swallowed the burning knot of anger and called upon the only tangible thing she had left—her professionalism. She dumped her stained and soiled clothes out of her suitcase and repacked several days' worth of clean clothes ranging from a business suit to black cocktail dress, casual college attire to barfly floozy. Years of experience had taught her that the proper outfit could get her in almost anywhere. Since she didn't possess the mind control some members of her race had, she could only rely on her looks, brains, and ability to act in a convincing manner.

As she packed a selection of jewelry, she dropped an earring and it rolled under the bed. Grumbling, she stretched prone to look for it in the darkness amid the dust bunnies. Two sparkles beckoned to her. Curious, she retrieved them both. One was the earring she'd just dropped. The other was a bracelet Anastasia had lost months ago. Why they'd never looked under the bed for it, Charlotte would never know. She regarded the golden bangle in her palm. It was only a blend of semiprecious jaspers and carnelians, but Anastasia had loved it.

Charlotte hesitated, then raised the bracelet up to her nose and inhaled. Beneath the layers of dust and the dilution of time, she could still smell the gentle scent of jasmine Anastasia wore. She closed her eyes and remembered the last time she and Ana had really connected: an evening at the theater followed by a meal from willing thralls. As she'd crouched behind her kneeling thrall, lips locked over the open wound at the juncture of his neck and shoulder, she'd stared into Anastasia's eyes as her lover likewise fed, and she'd seen genuine tenderness and affection there. Still feeding, she'd reached out to clasp Anastasia's hand in hers. The simple touch had an intimacy Charlotte couldn't get anywhere else, no matter how many werewolves she put down at the end of a silver blade. They'd made love until the morning sun shining through the window blinds cast shadow stripes across their flesh. Charlotte had felt alive that night in a way she hadn't in fifty years.

And now that feeling was gone, forever snuffed out by an over-muscled Pakistani man who was probably hammering himself into Anastasia over and over again even as Charlotte stood reminiscing in her room, and Ana . . .

Ana was *letting* him do it.

Charlotte spun around and hurled the bracelet as hard as she could at the window. For a moment it seemed to hover against the glass, shimmering in the afternoon sun. Then the bracelet struck the pane. Cracks radiated outward from the point of impact in slow motion as rage pounded in Charlotte's head. The cracks transformed into a spiderweb of fractures as the safety glass broke into a million pieces. The bracelet neither passed through the shattered pane nor fell to the floor. Instead it stuck partway through the window, suspended in a lattice of shattered glass, like Charlotte's broken heart. It was a suitable way to leave the last memento of Anastasia. Charlotte grabbed her valise and marched from the room, not bothering to shut the door behind her.

She wasn't sure she'd ever come back.

Her hunger had reached a critical level. She stalked into the Thralls Lounge, set her suitcase down, grabbed the first thrall she found, and latched on. The young woman must have been new, for she still stiffened when bitten and Charlotte could feel the woman's pulse fluttering under her lips. It excited her and she nearly took too much blood. She closed her eyes and made herself suck slowly, taking life from the thrall to sustain her own pseudolife, letting the minutes tick by without hurrying. The thrall's blood monitor issued warning beeps after what felt like only a couple of minutes. If Charlotte had continued to feed, it would have become a steady alarm and other Agents would have descended upon her to keep her from causing any permanent harm to their willing food source.

She detached and muttered "Thank you," through lips that felt thick and torpid. Most vampires never spoke to thralls, but Charlotte always thanked them. She wasn't so old that she had forgotten what it was like to be human, and to be used for others' pleasures.

"Y-you're welcome," stammered the young woman. She was already holding a sterile cloth against the wound as the duty paramedics arrived, bearing plasma, juice, and a wide array of pills to combat stress, pain, and anything else which might make her less than nutritious for the next vampire who chose to feed upon her. Having fulfilled her immediate duty, the thrall would be exempt from being a food source for a minimum of twenty-four hours. The paramedics escorted her to the discharge office where she would be compensated and driven home. It was a good way to make a living, if one didn't mind being fed upon.

Charlotte left and almost tripped over a human lying in the hallway outside the Lounge. The young man was far paler than a thrall should have been. "You shouldn't be out here," she scolded.

He didn't reply. In fact, he didn't even move. Charlotte knelt down beside him. He'd been fed upon recently, but no blood leaked from the open wounds in his neck. She realized in horror someone had overfed upon him. "Hey, help! Thrall down out here!" she called, hoping the paramedics in the Lounge would respond. She felt the side of his neck but no pulse fluttered beneath her fingertips. "Shit!"

Agents of the Collective were required to learn some basic first aid—not because vampires required it, but because sometimes when hunting werewolves, they might find humans still alive, and friends and family of humans whose lives were saved would be less-inclined to ask too many questions about those who'd saved their loved ones. Charlotte ripped open the thrall's shirt, stacked her palms on top of his chest, and started compressions.

A few seconds later, the paramedics rushed out of the Lounge. One had a portable defibrillator out and ready to use. It wasn't the first time they'd had to resuscitate a thrall. Charlotte gladly surrendered her position and watched as the paramedics brought the young man back to life, administering numerous injections and bottles of plasma. Some vampire had been very careless, and if she found out who it was, she'd be sure to give out an appropriately severe ass-chewing.

* * *

The Midnight Collective had its own armory, and the vampire in charge of it was a patient man everyone called Old Nick, because he'd been approaching seventy when he was converted in London during the Blitzkrieg by none other than Blackstone himself.

Charlotte dropped her bag at the armory door and stalked inside. "Nick? You in here, Nicky?"

Old Nick didn't turn around from his workbench. He raised one finger and made a shushing noise. Then, with the patience of a glacier, he bent his hands back to his work, making Charlotte wait with nothing to do but stare at the weapons hung along the walls. Pistols and rifles of every caliber competed for space with heavier weapons like rocket-propelled grenades and bombs filled with silver iodide to kill werewolves en masse.

Instead of impatience raising her ire, Charlotte found herself calming down as soothing waves of unseen energy radiated from the old man. He never used his power for anything except to make people relax around him. Charlotte suspected he just liked things quiet.

At last, Old Nick set down his project and turned to regard Charlotte from behind his octagonal glasses with the hinged magnifying lenses flipped up. "Agent Pastor, you're looking well," he said in a creaky soft voice. "How was China?"

"Messy," said Charlotte. "We lost one of their agents."

"Pity, that. And here you are again. Already leaving?"

"Yes, I'm afraid so. Time to gear up and get going."

"The usual setup?" Old Nick trundled over to a cabinet and started to pull items from a drawer.

"Two nines with six clips. Four silver and two lead. Two canisters of aconite spray and a couple gas bombs if you have them."

"I do. You'll be wanting a duty uniform as well?"

Duty uniforms were made from either PVC or soft leather. They were formfitting to allow the greatest freedom of motion for vampires in the field. They resembled the standard bodysuits worn by many superheroes, albeit not in such bright primary colors. Old Nick knew Charlotte preferred the leather. "Yes, please."

"Anything else you need, Agent?"

"No. Yes," said Charlotte as she considered the other, less attractive option of who might be underneath the mask of the Reno vigilante. She lowered her voice. There were security cameras and audio recording devices in the armory; they could detect vampires in spite of Hollywood arguments to the contrary. In addition, some vampires had extraordinary hearing, but what she was about to say was for Old Nick's ears only.

"I might be dealing with a rogue. I'll need something in case I have to take down a vampire."

Old Nick lowered his voice as well. "Anyone I know? A certain young Pakistani man with a predilection for Russian women, perhaps?"

Charlotte grimaced. "Does everybody know?"

Old Nick smiled at her like a grandfather. "The Collective is as tight-knit a group as I've ever known. Very few secrets stay that way for long."

"You'd think we were a bunch of unemployed housewives," Charlotte said in a voice loaded with acidic sarcasm, "instead of crack anti-werewolf operatives."

"That's true." Old Nick doddered over to the end of his workbench and touched something underneath the edge. Then he looked up at the security camera. Charlotte followed his gaze. The red light was off. "There," the old man said in satisfaction. "We've got four minutes while the system reboots."

"How did you do that?"

"It's technical. Best you not ask too many questions, Nightfall."

"I hope they won't be suspicious upstairs."

"Don't worry. I hit this at random times. They'll assume it's the same glitch they can't find."

"There's far more to you than meets the eye, Nicky."

Wrinkles formed around his eyes as he smiled. "Sometimes it's best if things down here aren't seen or heard." He held up a case. "Have you ever used a crossbow before?"

"No."

Nick smiled. "Really? After decades in the field and you've never found a use for a weapon of stealth?"

"Once I start shooting at werewolves, I really don't give a damn if they know I'm there or not." Charlotte opened the case and looked at the matte-black weapon with its folding stock and pulley system that could deliver a bolt with enough force to punch through two people standing back to back.

"I suggest you get some practice in with this one. You can buy extra shafts in any sporting goods store. The ones I'm giving you are hawthorn wood with a garlic-infused varnish." His smile vanished. "Put one between the ribs and the shock will knock down any vampire long enough for you to finish him off conventionally."

Conventionally meant beheading, something Charlotte had never had to do in all her years as an Agent. She'd only ever hunted down one rogue vampire, and not by herself, either. She'd been part of a team of five Agents. They'd cornered the rogue on the upper floors of a partially completed skyscraper. He had sent one Agent plummeting to her death in a two-hundred-foot fall that even a vampire couldn't survive and impaled another on a protruding girder. Then another Agent caught up to the rogue and slashed him open using gloves made from werewolf teeth, then beheaded him and left him to dissolve. Charlotte had been the safety valve, loaded down with garlic-foam grenades to slow any escape. She hadn't had to use them, which was just as well, for her hands had been shaking so badly she might not have been able to hook a finger through the ring to pull the pins. As dangerous as werewolves could be, vampires were far worse prey. Werewolves were just savage and brutal, but a vampire had more cunning, and years of experience at their disposal.

She hoped the mysterious vigilante wouldn't turn out to be a vampire. Her talent at taking werewolves apart with whatever weapons she had at hand would get her killed if she tried them against a vampire with any sort of combat-oriented powers.

A light flickered once on Old Nick's workbench. "Time's up, Agent."

Charlotte nodded. "Is my car gassed up? I'm thinking a road trip might do me good." Her car was a 1974 Corvette Stingray that she'd bought brand-new off the lot. She loved driving it but rarely had the opportunity in her line of work.

"It is. Reno's only a couple hundred miles away. Should take you about four hours."

She winked. "Not the way I drive."

Chapter Five

November 2012
Reno, Nevada

"Thank you for coming, Mr. and Mrs. Hu." Jackie walked into the foyer of her house, where Jenn waited with the Chinese couple. Mrs. Hu gave her a pleasant smile, showing clear braces on her front teeth. Mr. Hu's shoulders rounded forward, as if he'd spent many thousands of hours bent over a bench, but his eyes were bright behind old-fashioned horn-rimmed glasses. Jackie shook their hands solemnly. "I'm Jacquelyn Langdon. I'm sure you'd like to see your son. This way, please."

She led the couple into the spare bedroom where they'd set up Mark Hu's bed. Alix stood beside her, checking his pulse.

The Hus rushed to their son's side. Mrs. Hu took Mark's hand and brushed his hair back from his face, while Mr. Hu rested one hand on his wife's back and the other on Mark's shoulder. Jackie felt a pang of jealousy at seeing the closeness of the family. Even though it had been a couple of years since her parents died, the pain resurfaced at unexpected times. The closeness she had developed with Dominica, Alix, and even Jenn was a poor substitute for the love of a family.

"Mr. and Mrs. Hu, I'm Doctor Alix Duchesne, Ms. Langdon's private physician. She called me right away when she found your son."

"Please, call me Sheng. This is my wife, Dao-Ming." Sheng Hu had a strong accent but spoke with the facility of someone who'd spent most of his life in America. "Please, tell us what happened."

"I was driving through Old Town when I spotted two men trying to grab your son. I drove in and scared them off. Mark was unresponsive so I called Dr. Duchesne right away. We met back here and that's when the doctor determined that your son was exposed to an unknown drug."

"Animals!" Mrs. Hu cried. "What did they do to you, my poor boy?"

"He's in a coma," Alix said, "but all his life signs are strong and he's showing no sign of any brain damage. Given that his brain activity has been increasing slowly but steadily, I expect him to regain consciousness within the next day or two. I'm not seeing any indications of lasting effects. In my opinion, he'll recover completely, and quickly."

"If you like, he can stay here under Dr. Duchesne's care. Or we can arrange his transport to a medical facility of your choice. I'm happy to foot the bill either way." Jackie frowned. "I may write a lot about monsters, but it makes me angry to find them in real life."

Mrs. Hu looked up at her husband. "Please, can he stay here? I feel like he will be safe here." She had tears in her eyes but her expression was one of hope.

Mr. Hu nodded. "If it is all right with Ms. Langdon, Mark will stay here. We are in your debt, Ms. Langdon. You are an honorable woman."

"Make yourselves at home. You're welcome to stay here while he recovers."

The Hus conversed in rapid-fire Chinese. "I must be in the shop today. I have a contract to fulfill. My wife will remain here," Mr. Hu said. "May I come back later?"

Jackie nodded. "Of course. As long as Mark is here, you may come and go as you please. Any time, day or night. My home is your home."

Mrs. Hu smiled. "He will be so pleased to meet you. He's read all your books."

The Hus both bowed and thanked Jackie repeatedly until it was almost embarrassing. The familial love between them was smothering. She felt like she did in the hours before a transformation, locked in the cage, pacing back and forth. She needed space. "Please forgive me, but this is my prime writing time, and like you, Mr. Hu, I have a contract to fulfill. I've got a manuscript due in four weeks. I'll check back on you later." She fled, leaving the Hus with some privacy.

Jackie found Jenn in the kitchen, sitting at the table in the breakfast nook, wheeling and dealing on her tablet computer. "Everything all right? You're blushing."

"It's a little disconcerting to be the cause of so much adulation."

Jenn snorted. "I remember a book signing in Vegas where not one but two housewives fainted when you signed their books, as I recall."

"That's different. They were lonely. And I'm pretty sure one of them was mostly disappointed I wasn't a dude. Even with my picture in the back of the book." She pulled a container from the fridge that held chunks of beef so rare they couldn't rightly be called cooked. She pulled the lid off and popped a piece into her mouth. She closed her eyes, and chewed, letting the cool flesh sooth her restless spirit.

"Then you'll be happy to know your editor called and wanted to know if you could move the first draft of *Silvertongue* up two weeks. Marketing wants a July release to coincide with the season premiere."

Jackie ate another piece of meat. "Two *weeks*? I've barely touched the thing. I'm stuck."

"You're not stuck. You're spending your nights running around in tights, Jackie, and your days sleeping it off. It's great you've found a new hobby, but you need to remember that you're a writer first."

She felt a little better, having soothed the beast within, and replaced the container in the fridge. Jackie folded her arms. "Actually, Jenn, I'm a werewolf first. And besides, there are forces of evil afoot here in Reno."

"There are people who write novels every month. You can manage one a year." Jenn didn't back down. She stared back at Jackie, meeting her gaze.

Jackie wilted under Jenn's unblinking glare. "Dammit. How do you do that?"

"My family raises show dogs. You just have to know how to assert your dominance over them, and that goes the same for people. And werewolves." Her eyes twinkled and Jackie realized she was joking.

Jackie laughed. "Call Doug back and tell him I'll have *Silvertongue* to him by Christmas, and that's the goddamn best I can do." Of course, saying so didn't make it so. Jackie wasn't optimistic she could work out her plot issues so soon, but her editor didn't need to know that.

Jenn touched her earpiece.

"Wait, are you calling him right now? Jenn, it is the middle of the night here. I don't even know what time it is in New York. Please don't piss off my editor!"

Jenn crossed her arms and gazed at Jackie. "Doug, it's Jenn. I've spoken with Jackie and she has promised *Silvertongue* will be in your hands by Christmas, and that's the goddamn best she can do. It's also the goddamn best I can do because forces of evil are afoot here in Reno. We'll call you later with an update."

"You're impossible."

Jenn grinned. "No, I'm just very good. Listen, I know you're a little . . . stuck . . . with this one." Jackie noticed, with gratitude, that she hadn't used the word *blocked*, which she refused to ever speak in association with her writing. She didn't get *blocked*, because Writer's Block could last for years. She just got *a little stuck* instead. "Anyway, I was thinking. How about introducing some zombies in this one? Zombies are really big right now in fiction."

"The *Silverback* series is about werewolves," Jackie said. They'd had this discussion before. "I know about werewolves. I don't know anything about zombies."

"You know more now than you did at this time yesterday," Jenn retorted. "If not zombies, how about vampires? They're big too. Maybe they're just as real as zombies." Despite her bravado, Jackie could smell the fear and concern wafting off her skin. Jenn's scents tended to be cyclic, following along her own transformational cycle. She was more concerned than normal, and more than a little afraid. Both of their worlds had just grown larger with the knowledge that the dead could be reanimated.

Jackie shrugged. "Maybe, but I doubt it."

A text came from Dominica. *Come downstairs ASAP.*

"Jenn, make sure the Hus get some refreshments and see if they need anything while they're here. I told them I had to go take care of some writerly business and they can stay as long as they want."

With the Hus in the house, Jackie couldn't take the elevator down to the mine. She went back to the master bedroom and stepped into the closet. At the touch of a hidden switch, a floor panel slid aside to reveal the landing of a narrow spiral staircase with a brass pipe running down its center. Jackie lowered herself down onto the landing and shut the panel above her. Then she wrapped her arms and legs around the pipe and slid forty feet to the floor of the mine below.

Dominica looked up from her computer station on the raised platform beside the truck's round table. "There you are. What took you so long?"

"I have guests upstairs. And I came as soon as you called. What's up?"

Dominica leaned back from her workstation and thumped her feet onto the desk with considerable pride. "First of all, you don't pay me nearly enough, and I want you to remember that as I wow you with everything I've discovered about that canister you brought in last night." She looked as satisfied as a dog who just finished tearing apart a rawhide bone.

"Well?"

"First of all, I was able to pull some prints off it. It was handled by at least two people."

"Including the zombies?"

Dominica shrugged. "Hard to say. Depends on how long they were dead before being reanimated. Fingerprints are delicate structures and decay pretty quick after death."

"Go on."

"Anyway, I isolated what prints I could and uploaded them to your phone. You'll have to pull strings with the cops to get the prints run."

"You know I don't have any strings to pull. I'm trying to keep a low profile."

"Hence dressing up like a wolf to beat up bad guys. No attention-seeking behavior there." Dominica grinned. "May I suggest you find a drunken, down-on-her-luck detective that nobody will believe and forge a secret partnership with her?"

"You watch too many movies, Dominica."

"Buddy cop stories are the best stories."

"How about what was in the canister, wiseass?"

"That's where things get interesting, boss. It's a mixture of at least seven distinct powders driven by a standard propellant. The powders don't register on my mass spectrometer, so I can't begin to identify them."

"English, Dominica. I'm a writer, not a scientist."

"It means that whatever this stuff is, it can't be identified by conventional means. Armed with that, I did some research with some online sites specializing in black magic."

"Magic? You can't be serious."

Dominica put her feet down and leaned forward. "You remember the Archmage fiasco a few years ago up in North Dakota? Just Cause was mixed up in that. It was all about magic. Magic's a real thing, just like parahuman abilities are. You're a werewolf, boss, and you just fought zombies. You can't discount magic just because science can't measure it."

"Fair enough, I guess." Jackie had never considered that werewolves were anything but a strange genetic anomaly, like parahumans. Could they—could *she* be *magical* somehow?

"So, I found a forum of people who deal with magic potions and stuff and started asking questions. wound up having a long conversation with a Mambo down in Florida."

"Isn't that a snake?"

"That's a black mamba. A mambo is a kind of voodoo priestess. Nice lady. I was thinking zombies all the way, right? We all were. But she said, no, this wasn't a recipe for making a zombie. Did you know there are recipes? Anyway, I described the stuff and what it did, and she said it sounded like it was alchemical."

"You mean like people trying to make gold out of lead?"

"No, more like magic potions. Egyptian, specifically. We're talking real old school here. Dark arts. Pre-chemistry, boss."

Jackie blinked. In the past twenty-four hours, her world view had expanded much further than ever before, and it made her feel smaller than she was used to. "So, if they're not zombies, what are they?"

"According to my source, they're possessed, more or less."

"By?" Jackie was sure she knew the answer already; she just needed to hear it to help it become less unbelievable.

"Demons." Dominica wiped her face like it was coated with sweat, but Jackie knew it was just a nervous tic. "She said that when a corpse is treated with this mixture, it becomes a hospitable vehicle for a demon. Then all you need is a magic spell or glyph or something—I wasn't really clear on that part of it—and you've brought your own pet demon into the world, bound to follow your directions."

"Demons. Magic spells. If I hadn't seen the results myself, I'd say you were spending your days off chewing peyote buttons."

"Peyote is disgusting. Besides, I'd need days off to do something like that," said Dominica. "Speaking of which . . ."

Jackie walked over and stared at the eye holes of her wolf cowl, as if she might find answers in the empty spaces. "No, I need you here right now. We've got someone in town practicing alchemy, summoning demons, and going after young men in alleys. I need all hands on deck for this."

"I ran checks to see if anyone else has been reported missing. Two others in the last week, both women."

"Why haven't I heard about it?" Jackie asked.

"Probably because you haven't made a good contact at the police department yet. Also, because they haven't released information to the public."

"Missing women should be big news."

"It's Reno. It's a gambling town in a state where prostitution isn't illegal. People go missing here more than other parts of the country. A lot of them turn up a few days later, because they were partying too hard and wound up sleeping it off in some stranger's room." Dominica shrugged. "Lots of poor decisions being made out there."

"Or maybe they got taken by demon-possessed zombies," Jackie snarled, clenching her fingers. It felt like she had already failed.

Dominica shrugged. "I don't know, boss. Whoever it is wanted Mark Hu alive. Maybe it's the same people who took the missing women, but that's pretty thin. Not enough for a cop or a reporter to go on."

"It's enough for White Fang."

"Assuming we're right, and the women were taken alive like the zombie things were trying with Mark . . . maybe these victims have something the alchemist needs that can't be taken from a corpse?"

"Which could be anything."

"I'm not an expert in the dark arts by any stretch, and it could take me a sold month of research to figure out what this all means."

"We don't have a month. We probably don't have much time at all." Jackie yawned and checked the time on her phone. Night had given up to dawn, and she was feeling every minute of missed sleep. "I'm going to hit the sack. I'll be back up before dusk. Maybe we can get some fresh perspective on it then."

"You want to wait that long?"

"If zombies start grabbing people in broad daylight, it's time to call in Just Cause," Jackie said. "You should get some sleep too, Dee."

Dominica cracked open an energy drink. "I'll get there eventually."

Jackie snorted. Kids. "Since you're going to be up, I need you to run some checks for me."

"Yeah, I figured."

"Take what information you have or can get about the two women who've disappeared and correlate it with what we know about Mark Hu. Maybe a pattern will emerge."

Dominica shrugged. "If so, we'll find it. Hey, um, I could really use a day off, you know? Get out into the sunlight? Reacquaint myself with other humans?"

"I know, and I'm sorry. I need you on this now."

"There's this online boy I'd really like to meet in person. He plays *Call of Duty* and isn't an asshole about it . . ."

Jackie rounded on her, bringing some of the *scary* out. "There are *lives* at stake here, Dominica, and that's more important than you trying to get laid. If he's worth it, he'll understand. I'll make it up to you and give you some time off after we solve this case."

"You said that after the last case," Dominica grumbled.

Jackie heard her clearly, but she wouldn't be baited. "I'm paying you well enough to put a kink in your social schedule."

"Yes, boss," Dominica said through clenched teeth.

Jackie felt a little bad about jumping down Dominica's throat. The full moon was approaching, and its nearness had her on edge. Sleep would be the best way to unwind the knot of tension growing in between her shoulders. Without another word, she spun on her heel and headed for the staircase to her bedroom.

* * *

The sun sat low over the mountains to the west when Jackie next opened her eyes. She felt the lingering soreness in her bones from her bout with the zombies, compounded by the tugging of the Moon on her soul. It made her want to snarl and lash out. Instead, she wrapped a lightweight robe around herself and stepped barefoot onto the patio adjacent to her room. A cold fall breeze blew through the canyon, carrying the scents of the mountains. She closed her eyes and let the wind wash over her as if she were bathing in it. After several minutes, her bare feet aching from the cold, she turned back to the comfort of her room. She dressed in sweats, a hoodie, slippers, and went down to the mine.

Dominica lay stretched out on a couch, her feet up on the arm and a baseball cap pulled low over her eyes. Headphones covered her ears and her slow, regular breathing confirmed she was asleep. For a moment, Jackie thought maybe she should let her friend stay asleep, but they had work to do. She went to the kitchenette to make a pot of coffee. When it was brewed, she knelt beside the couch and held a steaming mug near Dominica's face.

"That's not fair," Dominica grumbled. "Why can't you buy the bad coffee? I could stay asleep for the bad coffee."

Jackie set the mug on the table beside Dominica. "You got anything on our undead friends yet?"

Dominica shook her head. "Lots of dead ends."

"Consider yourself yelled at for that joke."

"It wasn't intentional, I swear."

"Where were those two women reported missing?"

Dominica sent coordinates from her computer to Jackie's. Jackie opened a Google map of Reno on the large flat screen at one end of the computer bay. The mouse pointer kept sticking, and her patience was wearing thin as the full moon approached. "Dominica, how much did you say that eighty-inch touchscreen would run?"

"Right about twelve large."

"Put it on the shopping list. We'll get one with the *Silvertongue* advance."

"We'll probably want a couple. Maybe three. I know I could use one and I bet Alix could as well."

"I'm not made of money, Dominica."

"I thought that's why you were taking on the drug rings." Dominica cocked her head toward the truck. "They paid for that. And Alix's lab equipment."

Jackie shut her mouth with a snap. Dominica was right. She returned her attention to the map. Somewhere in there, someone was doing magic. The possessed corpses she'd encountered had been on foot, and she didn't think they could carry an unconscious victim very far without somebody noticing. Either they had accomplices nearby waiting with a car for the demonic beings to complete their mission, or their destination with a captive was nearby.

She moved the map to center on Old Town and marked the two disappearances as well as where Mark had been attacked. Somewhere along their routes, they must have been gassed and captured. She drew a circle that encompassed all three locations, increased the size of that circle by fifty percent and decided her target was somewhere in that region.

"Where are you?" Jackie muttered, staring at the map.

She couldn't just keep patrolling the same area, hoping to catch someone in the act of another kidnapping. If she was in the wrong place, that would be one more victim, perhaps, who would vanish. There had to be some way to narrow it down, but her brain felt scattered. It was harder to stay focused on complicated thoughts as the moon waxed towards its inexorable fullness. She had three more nights of useful activity, followed by one where she wouldn't be much good for anything, then a night in the cage, and at least one more night of recovery.

She had to make some progress on the case before the days of downtime. It infuriated her that she would have to interrupt her work. Was it any wonder she was late turning in her manuscripts? She'd grown to loathe deadlines, whether soft or fixed. She glared at the circle she'd drawn as if it were mocking her. "I'll find you."

Her phone buzzed with a text from Jenn. *Mark just woke up.*

"Dominica, I'll be back down in a while. Make sure everything's ready for me to head out. The clock's ticking for me here."

"Yes, boss. Don't forget that I wowed you with my mad skills."

"I'll see what I can do about a raise."

"I'd settle for a Friday night off sometime."

"We'll see."

Jackie walked into a scene of domestic bliss. Mrs. Hu clasped her son tight against her and sobbed while Mr. Hu stood nearby, his head bowed in a prayer of thanks.

"I'm fine, Mom. Just a little tired. Where am I? This doesn't look like a hospital." In spite of his insistence that he felt fine, Mark's face was drawn tight. His eyes were surrounded by circles so dark he resembled a raccoon.

"You're in my house." Jackie stepped forward and put on her best, least-threatening smile. "I'm Jackie Langdon."

"Mark Hu. Pleased to meet you. Why am I in your . . . Wait, *the* Jackie Langdon?"

"The same. I understand you've read a couple of my books."

"Oh my God! I've read them all. I love your work!" Color returned to his cheeks in an embarrassed flush.

"Thank you very much."

"Don't you live up in the mountains? How did I get here? I was walking home and these two guys came after me. I thought they were, you know, looking for someone to hurt." He lowered his eyes. "I'm Asian-American and gay. I check a lot of boxes for those sorts of people."

Jackie reached out to touch his hand. "I think I can understand what that's like, being afraid because of who you are."

The ghost of a smile crossed Mark's face. "You're not very Asian."

"No, but I am gay. I don't think that's a big secret. I've been on the cover of *Out* twice. I get my share of hate for that. I interrupted those men before they could do anything to you. I thought you'd fainted, so I brought you back here to get checked out by Alix. She's a doctor and a family friend."

Alix stepped over from where she'd been watching. "Alix Duchesne, Mark." She gave the young man a firm, professional handshake. "You were dosed with a drug that knocked you out. I think you're going to be just fine, but I'd like to keep you here for another day to make sure. If that's all right with you and your parents, of course."

"I don't know," said Mark. "No offense meant, but I'd kind of like to go home. Sleep in my own bed."

Jackie cleared her throat. She knew Alix wanted to run some more tests, and perhaps a gentle interrogation of the young man might help unravel the mystery of the zombies and why they had tried to kidnap him. "If it would help convince you to stay one extra day, I'd be happy to let you get a peek at *Silvertongue*."

Mark's eyes widened. "Is that . . . ?"

"The new *Silverback* book. It's dropping next summer. I'm not even finished with it yet."

"You'd let me see it? Really? Mom, do you mind if I stay?"

Mrs. Hu shrugged. Jackie could almost smell the disappointment coming off her. "You're a grown man,

Mark. You don't have to check with me." Then she smiled. "But I do appreciate that you did. I don't see why not. We can't stay, though. We have the Super Bowl order to finish. And now that we know you are all right . . ."

"We're providing the stadium-level pyrotechnics for the halftime show," Mr. Hu said. "A great honor for such a humble company as ours."

"I bet they'll be fantastic," Jackie said. "I'll be sure to watch."

Mr. Hu bowed. "I do my best."

The Hus thanked Jackie profusely, and bowed so much all over again that it made Jackie feel a bit seasick. She showed them to the front door and encouraged them to return whenever they wished.

Once the couple left, she turned around to see Jenn standing in the foyer, her arms crossed in front of her and her tablet dangling from one hand. "What is it?" she asked. "What did I do this time?"

"Your interview with SKY News. They're here."

"They're not supposed to be here until tomorrow evening, Jenn."

"Jackie . . . it *is* tomorrow evening."

"Shit." Jackie glanced back outside and realized there was a KSKY van parked off to one side of the driveway. She was so wrapped up in her own thoughts that she hadn't noticed. Some vigilante she was turning out to be.

"They are. They're waiting for you in the study. You're not going to wear that, are you?"

Jackie looked down at her sweats, UNLV t-shirt, and moccasins. "What's wrong with it? It's clean."

Jenn rolled her eyes. "You look like you just rolled out of bed. The color is all wrong for television and washes out your skin. And do I need to mention the shoes?"

"I like these slippers," said Jackie. "They're comfortable."

"They're ratty and hideous. I don't care that they're not going to be in the shot. The reporter's going to notice them, and that's going to reflect badly upon you."

"Maybe if she notices my choice in footwear, she won't realize that I'm basically wearing my pajamas."

Jenn's slight cough was as sarcastic as Jackie had ever heard. "She'd have to be blind." She thrust a dark blue button-down at Jackie along with a gray jacket, matching slacks and some stylish black pumps. "Put these on. Leave the collar unbuttoned. That way you look like you're working."

"I *am* working." Nevertheless, Jackie knew when to concede. She traded her t-shirt and sweats for the jacket and slacks and stepped into the pumps. "Better?"

"Much. The reporter's name is Amanda, and she's going to talk to you about your series. Try not to take her down to show her around the secret superhero headquarters, huh?"

Jackie chuckled and headed to her study.

The interview was brief, for which Jackie was grateful, and Amanda the reporter was perky, for which she was not. She pitched nothing but softball questions like *where do you get your ideas* and *what's your favorite Silverback book* and wrapped things up with *what do you like best about Reno?* Jackie offered her standard, pat answers to the questions, smiled a lot, and laughed when she should. After Perky Amanda and her videographer left, Jackie went to check in on Mark. She found him doodling on a sketchpad resting against his upraised knees. He looked up when she entered.

"How was your interview?"

"Predictable," Jackie said.

"Is that a good thing?"

"Yeah. I can do those kinds of interviews in my sleep, which is good because sometimes it's the only sleep I have time to get."

"You do look a little tired. Staying up too late writing?"

"More or less. But it's almost the weekend, and even writers need to take a day off now and then."

Mark's face fell. "Oh, shoot. What day is it? Friday?"

"Yes," said Jackie.

"Crap! I was supposed to meet my friend Suzanne. We were going to catch the dress rehearsal of the ballet. She's probably gone on without me."

"Why the dress rehearsal?" Jackie asked. "What I remember from my high school theater days is that the dress rehearsal is usually a disaster."

A bit of color inflamed Mark's pale cheeks once again. "I'm a student, Ms. Langdon. My options are kind of limited by my finances." He yawned.

"Please, call me Jackie. I hate that you're going to miss it. Perhaps you'd let me escort you to the ballet tomorrow. I have a social function to attend in the early evening, which I'm really not looking forward to. Leaving early for a performance would be a perfect excuse." It would also give her a chance to find out more about Mark and perhaps identify why he was targeted by the zombies.

"Really?"

"It would be my pleasure."

Mark leaned back against his pillows and yawned. "God, I'm so sleepy all of a sudden. But I'd love to go with you tomorrow."

"I'll let you get some rest." Jackie went to the door. When she looked back, Mark's eyes were closed. She closed the door most of the way and went to find Jenn.

Her assistant was in her office, working on what looked suspiciously like a book tour itinerary. "Jenn, I'm going to need two tickets to the ballet tomorrow evening, and yes I know it means I'll have to leave your little party early."

"It's not a *little party*, as you call it. It's a five-hundred-dollar-a-plate charity function for the Timberline Foundation."

"You said that I was going to hate it. I like the Timberline Foundation. They're doing good work." The Foundation was dedicated to protecting wilderness environments. Among other things, they worked to reintroduce wolves to areas where herds were overgrazing and causing excessive ecological damage. Jackie could get behind any organization working to care for her lupine brothers and sisters. "I just wish it wasn't tomorrow. Not with this zombie thing."

"You committed to attend. You're writing them a donation check with the money you took from those Russian smugglers you busted last month. Besides, there are plenty of folks who would like to make the acquaintance of a famous author."

"That's not why I'm going . . . Hmmm. Russian." An idea occurred to her.

"What is it, Jackie?"

"Time to put on my *real* work clothes. White Fang needs to make a social call."

Chapter Six

November 2012
Reno, Nevada

Charlotte covered the two-hundred-odd miles between San Francisco and Reno in just over two and a half hours. That included a stop for fuel and feeding upon one poor California highway patrolman who decided to take a chance on pulling her over despite the catch-and-release flag on her profile in his computer system. Decades ago, Blackstone had made arrangements with someone in the FBI to ensure Midnight Collective agents could conduct their business without interference from local law enforcement.

This guy hadn't gotten the memo, and when he swaggered his fat cop belly over to Charlotte's window and said, "What's a pretty little thing like you doing with a car like this?" she had no problem dragging him behind a billboard for a quick couple of pints.

Charlotte delighted in the patrolman's struggles as her fangs elongated and she drove them into his exposed throat. Poison flowed through her teeth into his bloodstream, causing him to become torpid and complacent. She pulled her fangs free of the paired wounds, placed her lips over them, and fed. Life-giving blood flowed into her body. Dead cells came to life to exchange stored toxins and waste for fresh oxygen and nutrients. Processes of life, suspended within vampires between feedings, began anew. She took a deep, rattling breath as she sucked, this time because her lung tissues craved oxygen to mix with the blood within her. She felt vital and alive. Her body tingled with the wild, untamed flavor of the patrolman's blood.

He tasted sweet, like donuts.

Energized after feeding, she attacked the highway with fresh determination and cut a blazing trail through the Sierra Nevada mountains. Her 'Vette roared and inspired her to take the curves far faster than was safe, but the fat tires soaked up all that punishment and seemed to beg for more.

Her skin stung from exposure to the few minutes of sunlight she'd suffered, reminding her to be more careful. Sunscreen would help, but only for a few minutes, and wouldn't do any good in Reno's higher altitude anyway. Sometimes when she spent a lot of time behind the wheel, safely sequestered behind polarized glass, she forgot about the discomfort of sunlight.

She cruised down Interstate 80's final hill into Northwest Reno and took the first exit she came to. There, she selected a motel that didn't look too seedy, paid cash, and hung the *Do Not Disturb* sign on the door. Being undead, she didn't sweat or excrete or do any of things that made humans stink, but she drew a tepid bath anyway and lay in the tub for a few minutes, allowing herself to relax and focusing upon every square inch of her skin to remind herself how to feel. After a while, the water made her skin feel odd and rubbery. She toweled off, not bothering to dress, and lay naked on the bed to sleep the rest of the day away. Her final thought before falling into the typical vampiric dreamless slumber was how grateful she was that bedbugs, should they infest the room, would leave her alone.

Charlotte awoke when the sun set. She took a few minutes to pretty herself up. Investigations always went smoother when she gave men a pretty face and cleavage to look at. To that end, she dressed in her best tight leather pants and matching jacket, lace-up bustier, red lipstick, and a shiny black wig. Maybe she'd prowl through Reno's bar scene. She needed something to make her feel better about herself, and meaningless, anonymous sex might be just the thing.

Her pistols went into holsters concealed on the inside of her jacket. One held regular bullets, the other silver.

A quick internet search on her laptop turned up some likely areas to find street-level crime, and she drove her 'Vette to that part of town. Heavy clouds hung low over the casinos and skyscrapers of downtown, reflecting the city lights. Even in the chill autumn air, the flesh trade was brisk business. Charlotte parked the 'Vette in an empty space on the street and watched the evening vices unfold. Even though the air was cold, a couple dozen shadowy men and women lurked in doorways, clustered around bus benches, or sat in parked cars talking to pedestrians. Some were young, but the lifestyle made them all seem older. Rough living took its toll on their skin, and Charlotte could see numerous sores and needle marks. Some of the prostitutes looked strung out. Others were drunk. Most of the smiles stopped at the corners of mouths, and their eyes showed only pain. Despite the lack of perfection among those selling themselves, deals were still struck with clients and then a car would pull away from the curb with a new passenger. Another vehicle would take the empty spot and the negotiations would begin anew.

A police cruiser rolled by. Hands came out of pockets to remain conspicuous and empty. Streetwalkers moved away from parked cars. Everyone found interesting things to look at on the ground or across the street until the prowling cruiser moved on to the next block.

A dealer had to be somewhere amid all the prostitutes, selling to civilians and employees alike. It didn't take long before Charlotte spotted a young white boy with a flannel jacket over a hooded sweatshirt and a ball cap on sideways. With well-practiced casual moves, he accepted folded cash from a tall man and slipped him a small baggie tied shut with a rubber band.

That boy was her mark.

She waited with the patience of someone who'd already lived a full lifetime and had many more to go. The pedestrian traffic dwindled and it became apparent that he wasn't going to transact any more business in his current location. He left his spot. As he walked past Charlotte's car, she rolled down her window. "Hey, what have you got tonight?"

He looked at her, took in the wig, lipstick, and cleavage, and ambled over with interest written all over his face. "Whatchoo lookin' for, shawty?"

Charlotte cringed on the inside at his clearly false ghetto accent. She held up a hundred-dollar bill. "Information."

The unusual request made the young man look around again, as if he were expecting trouble. He lowered his voice and asked, "You five-oh?"

"No. I'm a private investigator. You know anything about the wolfman vigilante?"

"White Fang? Naw, I don't know nuthin'. I don't want nuthin' to do with it."

Charlotte smiled. Now she had a name. And this young man knew more than he wanted to share. Well, she was an expert at getting people to give up information they'd rather keep a secret. In a blur of speed, she exchanged the hundred for one of her pistols, pointed right at the boy's heart. "I'd hate to waste all that pretty blood running through your veins, but I'm not afraid to do it and find someone else to ask. Keep your hands where I can see them and get in the car."

"Aw, sheeyit." The boy started to make a move for the front of his pants.

"Don't do it," said Charlotte. "Last warning."

"All right, all right, you crazy bitch. Jesus."

"Jesus isn't going to help you now. Open the door."

The young thug got in and sat down, keeping his hands up near his head. "What happens now? You gonna shoot me?"

"Not if I don't have to. We're going to take a little drive and have a little chat. And when we're done, you're going to get out of the car and walk away with my hundred-dollar bill. I'll drive off in another direction and everybody's happy. And just to keep you honest . . ." Charlotte tucked away her own pistol and grabbed the butt of the one the boy had in his waistband before he could so much as blink. She drove the muzzle against his lap. "Now, I don't like being distracted while I drive, so I think you should stay very still and answer my questions. What's your name?"

"V-vin."

"Really? Because you don't look like a *Vin*. What's your real name, kid?" Charlotte started the engine and pulled the 'Vette out into the street.

"It's Marvin. Hey, watch it!"

Charlotte ran a red light. Horns honked and tires squealed as she slipped the car through the space between a bus and a cab. "Lying is distracting to me. How about you stick to the truth from now on, Marvin, so I don't have to . . . *chkchk blam!*"

Marvin shrieked.

"Pee on my seat and you're a dead man."

"I won't. You're crazy!" Marvin's eyes looked like they might pop out of his head and make a break for it. It made Charlotte want to laugh.

"White Fang. What do you know about him?"

"I don't know! He just goes around town, beatin' up my people."

"You mean drug dealers."

"Anybody, man! Anybody he thinks is breakin' the law."

Charlotte steered through a busy intersection. Marvin's terrified breath whistled through his teeth. "Aren't you breaking the law?"

"Look, I ain't holdin' a gun on folks, makin' them buy shit. If they don't get it from me, they'll just go get it somewhere else. I got it, so I might as well sell it and make some scratch. I got a kid to feed."

"Very noble of you, Marvin. You're a shining example of fine parenting. What does he look like?"

"My s-son?"

"White Fang, Marvin. Focus, please." A truck's horn blared as Charlotte cut in front of it.

"I ain't never seen him. They say he's a big dude, though. Real muscular-like. And strong. Maybe he does a lot of 'roids, yanno? I heard that shit fucks you up real bad. Makes you crazy. Aw shit, man, you ain't gonna kill me, are you?"

Charlotte turned a corner onto a quiet industrial street and stopped the car. "Not at the moment. See that I don't have a reason to. Tell me more."

"He's got a wolf's head that he wears over his own head. And an upside-down triangle thing on his chest that's white. That's like his . . . his brand, right? Like his superhero logo."

"You're doing well, Marvin. Keep talking." She'd struck gold already with Marvin. Maybe she could wrap up this assignment in short order and take a real vacation. Someplace tropical. Hell, maybe she'd even go back to Jamaica. Her early success made her feel powerful. Even with the highway patrolman's blood still coursing through her veins, Charlotte's appetite grew. Feeding would keep the feeling going even longer if she gave in to the urge.

"They say he's really bad-ass. Bullets don't stop him, like he's got armor or somethin'."

"He killed anyone?"

"I dunno. I haven't heard that he did. All I know is he's got some of the higher-ups scared. Folks sayin' the Mexicans lookin' to take out a contract on him. That's all I got, swear!"

"Two more questions and then we're done, Marvin. They're both easy ones. Who's above you? Who do you report to and how I reach that person?"

He told her. "But please don't say nuthin' that it was me. I'm just tryin' to feed my kid."

"And you're going to take the hundred dollars I'm about to give you and go buy some groceries, aren't you?"

"Yes, I promise!"

"Last question, Marvin. Do you use what you sell?" She was only asking to ask, she told herself. Not because she was gauging his feeding potential. Not at all.

"Just a li'l weed. That's all. Everybody does that. I don't touch that harder stuff. Meth, smack, crack, that shit will fuck you up bad."

"Good boy. See that you stay clean and you'll live a whole lot longer." Charlotte removed her hand from his pants and made a pistol appear in her other hand. She flashed the hundred in front of his eyes. "Take it, get out of my car, and walk away." And do it before I jump on you and drain you half-dry, you delicious, frightened little boy, she thought.

He hesitated, then snagged the bill and lunged for the door handle. He slammed the door shut too hard behind him, which set Charlotte's teeth on edge. She hated when people mistreated her car. She watched in her rear-view mirror as he hurried up the street, away from the crazy bitch in the Corvette.

"Just let him go," she said aloud. "He gave you what you needed. He's free to go. That's what you told him."

Her fingers tightened around the wheel as he stepped further away. "Fuck it. I am what I am," she told her reflection in the mirror, and got out of the car.

She didn't need to feed. She'd taken two pints from the highway patrolman just hours ago. She just needed to feel something, to cut through the numbness pervading her undead body. She could have fucked him —she'd have felt *that*—or she could have torn his throat out and punched his heart through his ribs. The act of killing would let her feel alive, at least for a little while.

Or she could feed.

Hating herself for her bullshit, Charlotte hurried along the side of the buildings facing the street, where Marvin wouldn't see her if he turned to look. When she got close enough, she jumped from the wall and tackled him mid-stride. He squealed in surprise. His pistol skittered across the sidewalk to splash into the gutter. Thrills ran through her body for the second time that day. It reminded her of the old days, when vampires still hunted thralls.

She made herself stop after only draining a pint. It wasn't easy; it never was. Vampires who hadn't been able to control their feeding had been responsible for many cullings throughout history. Agents of the Midnight Collective worked hard to prevent more human uprisings against vampirekind. Weakened humans would heal and get on with their lives. Dead ones would attract the wrong attention. She'd promised to let Marvin walk home and if she took any more than that first pint, he'd be unable to move and freeze to death where he lay. She stopped suckling and laid her tongue over the open wounds. The glands around the edges of her mouth secreted a soporific coagulant. His bleeding stopped within seconds and his eyes rolled back in his head. He'd awaken within an hour with lingering soreness and the exhaustion that came from blood loss, but otherwise be unharmed.

Charlotte dragged him to the side of a nearby building and set him against it. Feeling generous, she tucked another hundred into his wallet for his trouble. She hoped it would be there when he woke. This block had been quiet and nobody had come by to interrupt her feeding. With luck, he would remain undisturbed while he recovered from it.

"Thank you, Marvin," she said. She got back into her car and left him, heading for the heart of the city and the next rung of the ladder that would eventually lead her to White Fang.

Chapter Seven

November 2012
Reno, Nevada

Jackie, fully attired as White Fang, crouched on a rooftop of the warehouse district in the town of Sparks, Nevada, watching the transaction on the dark street below. The stink of the nearby water reclamation plant permeated the air, giving her a headache and a tickle in the back of her throat. A chill breeze blew down from the mountains, carrying wispy high clouds across the face of nearly full moon. The binocular lenses Dominica had built into the cowl didn't work as well as she would have liked, so she'd slid them back up into the forehead of the mask and squinted into the night. Just outside the ring of the streetlight, three thick-necked men with goatees and shaved heads stood outside a large black SUV. Two of them examined baggies of coke or meth or heroin or whatever the drug was that week. The third stood with his back to them and kept his eyes on the truck driver, whose eyes bulged beneath his trucker hat as he waited to see if his product passed muster. His semi idled behind him, kicking out regular puffs of black smoke into the cloudy night.

Jackie didn't recognize the thugs as part of Andrej Rachmaninoff's mob, but the Russian's organization was large. She did get a good enough glimpse at the SUV's license plate to text the number to Dominica, who texted back in a few minutes that it was registered to Global Imports, Rachmaninoff's company. Global Imports was, on the surface, an importer of rare and unusual goods. Whether it was Satya incense from India or original master pressings of Led Zeppelin vinyl records, Rachmaninoff was the best man to find those items and bring them to those who could pay his rates. Beneath that legitimate business front lay a complex fencing operation and a distribution network of designer drugs popular among athletes, long-haul truck drivers, and high school kids looking for a new way to get a buzz going.

People in the underground industry referred to him in whispered tones as *The Conductor*, and to cross him was to invite trouble of the worst kind. More than one body over the years had washed up on the banks of the Truckee River, throat opened from ear to ear in what had become known as a Russian Smile.

The two thugs examining the briefcase conversed in Russian.

"Hey, man, I gotta get back on the road," the truck driver said. "I got a schedule to keep, you know? Speakee English?"

The third thug shifted his bulk. "Shut your fucking mouth," he said in a nearly impenetrable accent. He added something in Russian, which made the other two men burst out laughing. Jackie made a mental note that if she was going to spend a lot of time working on taking down The Conductor's organization, she was going to have to learn the language.

It was nearly time for her to act. The werewolf under her skin felt like howling to announce the hunt, but Jackie bit her lip and watched.

Apparently satisfied with the transaction, the two men took the briefcase and climbed back into their SUV, still chuckling over whatever the third man had said. The last man handed the truck driver an envelope from inside his coat and turned to go.

"Hey . . ." The trucker sounded braver now that he'd been paid. "How do I know this is all here?"

"Count it, *litl golovastika*, but on your own time. Not mine."

The moment had arrived. Jackie took a running leap from the rooftop and landed atop the trailer. She rolled, sprang onto the hood of the semi and let out a fierce growl at the two men.

The startled trucker got tangled up in his own feet and sprawled onto the pavement. With remarkable alacrity, the thug reached into his coat and pulled out a semi-automatic pistol that looked tiny in his great paw. He squeezed off two shots at Jackie before his partners in the SUV began to comprehend what was going on.

The bullets starred the truck's windshield but Jackie had already jumped from the hood to the nearby warehouse wall, and then instantly pushed off to come at the thug from an unexpected sideways direction.

She tackled him and they rolled across the damp pavement. A well-aimed kick broke the thug's wrist and his smoking gun spun across the ground.

Jackie drove her fist right into the man's open mouth. Teeth shattered into bloody fragments. She hurled the stunned man against the warehouse wall hard enough to dent the corrugated aluminum siding.

Shouting in Russian, the other thugs jumped from their SUV and sprayed bullets toward her, unmindful of their hapless companion in their desperate attempt to kill the wolf vigilante. Jackie hit the ground as the thug slumped to the pavement, bleeding from several holes, including one above his ear that had probably killed him.

The scent of blood in the air made the wolf within her want to howl, to terrify her prey before tearing out their throats. It was all she could do to prevent the heat and thrill of combat from triggering the transformation. Bullets whistled over the tips of her cowl's raised ears as she raced on all fours toward the remaining thugs. As they adjusted their aim, she dove beneath their SUV.

The thug on the driver's side backed away from the SUV.

His partner wasn't fast enough. From beneath the truck, Jackie grabbed the man's ankles and yanked. He shrieked as he fell backward. His pistol bounced away as his knuckles banged against the pavement. He screamed as Jackie dragged him beneath the truck by his feet.

His struggle was for naught. Once his head was within reach, Jackie grabbed it and banged it twice against the SUV's frame. The first blow knocked him out and the second was just to be sure. Jackie's teeth felt sharper than they should have. The wolf was close to the surface. She rolled out from underneath the SUV to find the third thug and as she stood, a bullet burned a hot trail across one of her legs. The sharp pain tore a yelp from her throat that was more animal than human.

Jackie turned and she saw the bulging eyes of the truck driver, shaking hands holding a pistol far too large for him. He'd spilled her blood, and Jackie couldn't keep the wolf at bay any longer. The transformation took hold. Visions of tearing out her assailant's throat and dining on his entrails filled her head as her spine curved and her face lengthened into a snout.

Jackie fought to contain the monster. If she changed now, her plan would be ruined. She'd hunt and kill remember nothing outside of her nightmares. *No, I must not change! Force the beast back, shove it back into the darkest recess and slam a bar across the door!*

She sprang high into the air as the trucker fired again. The bullet whizzed below her feet as she flipped forward to land at arm's length from him. She wrenched the pistol from his trembling hands in one smooth motion, ejected the clip, and popped the remaining round from the firing chamber. She wagged a threatening finger in the trucker's face. The smell of fresh urine wafted upward from his crotch.

"J-Jesus," whimpered the man.

"Not even close," she growled through the voice modulator. She drove a swift uppercut into his chin, his head snapped back, and he collapsed to the asphalt. She cast the empty pistol aside and went after the last thug. The heavyset man ran puffing down the street, his pistol clutched in one fat hand and trying to push buttons on a cell phone with the other. Jackie went up the side of the warehouse to run across the roof, overtaking the fat Russian in only a few seconds. He turned to look but saw nothing behind him and slowed his flight, face flushed and dripping with sweat, breath wheezing out of his lungs in great clouds of steam.

Although she'd healed from the bullet would, Jackie wasn't anxious to get shot again. She needed to make the Russian use up his ammunition. Inspiration came in the form of a handful of rooftop gravel, which she tossed down near the sweating thug. He jumped and fired two shots in that direction. Another handful of gravel got him to waste two more shots. Panting in fear, he hit the *send* button on his phone and raised it to his head. Jackie let a bit more gravel trickle down the side of the building to bounce off the Russian's head just as a voice from the phone said "*Da?*"

He whirled and fired three more bullets followed by the click of an empty chamber. Jackie leaped from the rooftop to land beside him and slammed a solid fist into the man's gut. He bent double, dropping his phone and empty weapon. She grabbed his meaty shoulders and drove his face into her knee. His nose crunched into shreds and he went down as hard as if he'd been shot dead.

Jackie could have killed them all in seconds. That would have ended their criminal careers with more certainty than anything else. But as the old story said, *dead men tell no tales.*These men would be hurt, afraid, and alive.

And they would talk, and thus would White Fang's legend grow.

"*Vassily? Chto ne tak?*" demanded the speaker on the phone.

Jackie picked up the phone. "He'll call you back." She ended the call, popped open the back of the phone, and removed the SIM card. Both phone and card went into pouches on her belt for Dominica to examine later.

The Russians' SUV sat abandoned in the road, doors hanging open and engine running. The electronic alarm dinged over and over as the cry of approaching sirens swelled. The police wouldn't find anything but the unconscious Russian gangsters and the trucker with their incriminating bags of drugs and more stories to add to White Fang's legend. She took the briefcase full of baggies from the SUV and set in the middle of the road. To make sure Reno's Finest didn't miss it, she lit a flare from a belt pouch and dropped it beside the case. Those drugs, at least, would be off the street, and maybe the gangsters would do some time behind bars. At the very least, they would do a little time in the hospital, and they might think twice about making future drug transactions in dark Reno alleys.

Damn, it felt good to be a vigilante.

Jackie climbed into the driver's seat of the SUV and pulled the doors shut. She was panting despite the chilly, autumn air. Her heart hammered a brisk tattoo, making her eyeballs throb, distorting her vision a little with each beat. She'd be exhausted later, once the hunt-thrill wore off. Fortunately, the full moon was only a few days away, which gave her more energy than normal. She drove away from the scene of the crime, careful to avoid the incoming police. Once she was several blocks away, she parked and examined the SUV's onboard GPS system.

The text was in Cyrillic. "Of course, it is," she murmured. "There's an app for that, right?" She removed her phone from its protected pouch and tapped at the screen carefully with the clawed tip of one gloved finger. She'd broken several touchscreens before learning how gentle she had to be with them. She scrolled through the apps until she found the Cyrillic photo-translator. After snapping a picture of the GPS screen, the app provided a useful-enough translation of the text. A couple of subsequent translation scans and she found the language controls to turn everything into English. She touched the *Home* button. "Don't mind if I do," she said as the screen laid out a route back to Rachmaninoff's compound in the hills to the southwest. She smirked at his address. He was practically her neighbor.

Jackie switched to a different app on her phone— one Dominica had created. It used the carrier signal from cellular towers to activate the remote control guidance systems of her truck. Although she wasn't very good at operating it manually using only the phone interface, the truck's onboard computer and sensors were up to the task of following various programs. She ordered it to follow half a mile behind her and at a comparable speed. By tracking her own phone's GPS, the truck would be right where she needed it. It would even follow the rules of the road.

Jackie shifted the SUV into drive and pulled away from the curb, clearing out well ahead of Reno's somewhat-less-than-finest. It only took a few minutes to get to the Interstate, heading west toward the Sierras, shadows towering in the distance. She found the right exit and soon headed up into the hills. The Russians' SUV made short work of the hairpins and switchbacks. The growing autumnal clouds seemed close enough that Jackie could have reached up and touched them if she'd just rolled down the window.

Rachmaninoff's palatial residence sat on a steep slope where he could look down upon the city as he counted his ill-gotten gains. He'd bought up adjoining properties when he moved into town back in the mid-Nineties, razed them all, and had a mansion built that resembled an Eighteenth Century Russian castle. Designed by an eastern European architect, the mansion sported foreboding granite edifices, arched windows, and stone gargoyles at regular intervals along the sharply sloping roof. Jackie would need a distraction so she could enter the grounds and scale the building, but then it would be simple enough to climb and look through windows until she spotted Rachmaninoff.

She parked up the street from the Russian's house and abandoned the SUV, heading into the trees. On the breeze, she smelled the gun oil and sweat from his guards, and the dogs patrolling the perimeter with them. She hoped she wouldn't have to fight any of them; they felt like kin to her.

She slipped through the trees, moving through the shadows until she was at a dark section of the wall. A normal human would have needed a ladder to reach the top, but Jackie wasn't normal. She vaulted over it, a shadow moving against other shadows.

She found herself in the remains of a garden, full of dead perennials. She crawled through the garden, minimizing the rustling with slow, deliberate movements. In the shadow of a big tree, she crept across the lawn until she rose with her back against the trunk. She was only a few yards from a wing of the house. Drawing upon her animal strength and speed, she sprang across the open space in two great bounds and a moment later climbed the wall, hidden well by the shadows.

Jackie found plenty of purchase for her gauntlet claws and the matching studs mounted on the toes of her boots. She checked window after window as she traversed the wall, but they all displayed darkened rooms beyond. *Where is Rachmaninoff?*

She caught a sharp tang of cigar smoke on the cool breeze and heard a brusque voice spitting rapid-fire Russian somewhere around the corner of the house. She ascended the rest of the way to the roof to better move around the perimeter without being spotted from below. At the rear, she found a large balcony overlooking the valley to the north, and pacing it was Andrej Rachmaninoff, wrapped in a heavy robe. He spoke intensely into a cell phone, a cigar clutched in one fat hand. His chin was unshaven and his mustache magnificent.

Jackie peeked over the edge of the roof to make sure nobody else was on the balcony, perhaps tucked into a discreet corner, but Rachmaninoff was alone. The heavyset Russian finished his conversation and dropped his phone into a pocket of his robe. He raised his cigar back to his lips and took a puff, smoothing the flyaway gray hairs from the sides of his head.

Jackie dropped down beside him and pulled the cigar from the his surprised lips. "Filthy habit."

"Wh-what . . ." Rachmaninoff stammered. Jackie grabbed his head and jammed one hand over his mouth, the wolf cowl close to his face.

"I'm here for information. Nothing else." Her voice modulator grated into Rachmaninoff's ear. "You answer my questions, and I'll leave you alone for now. Try to raise an alarm and I promise you will regret it for the remainder of your pain-filled life. Nod if you understand me."

Rachmaninoff nodded. Instead of eyes widening in fear, his narrowed with suspicion. It made Jackie feel odd. She'd become so used to people being afraid of her that it threw her off balance when she discovered someone who wasn't. Rachmaninoff was sizing her up. When she looked into his eyes, she saw a man who could be every bit as imposing as her. For the first time since she'd taken up the vigilante mantle, she suspected she'd met her match.

Still, she couldn't squander the opportunity by considering whether she'd found an archenemy. "I'm going to say some words. If you've imported them recently, you nod. If not, shake your head. Galbanum gum."

Rachmaninoff nodded.

"Civet tincture."

Another nod.

"Socotran dragon's blood resin."

Nod.

"Ambergris."

Nod.

"Dhofari frankincense."

Rachmaninoff's bushy eyebrows drew together and he nodded once again. Jackie knew he recognized all these odd ingredients. "There's more, isn't there? All weird stuff. All purchased by the same party?"

Rachmaninoff nodded once again.

"Very good, Andrej. Now give me a name and I'll be on my way." Jackie removed her hand from over the Russian's mouth but left the other clenched on the back of the man's neck with her tungsten claws pricking into his skin as a none-too-subtle reminder of who was in charge. She felt his muscles tense in preparation for making a move and dug her claws in deeper, making him hiss in pain. "Try anything and I'll tear your spine out through your neck. You know I can do it. Answer the question, Andrej."

"The buyer arranged everything through email and paid for the transaction using a blind electronic funds transfer. I don't have a name." Rachmaninoff glared at the Jackie. "So fuck off."

"Not so fast, Andrej. Someone had to deliver those ingredients to a physical location. Where did they go?"

Rachmaninoff shrugged. "I'm an importer. I can't be bothered to keep track of every single delivery in my network, wolfman."

"This stuff was unusual enough you'd have overseen it personally. I can guess what it cost to bring it into the U.S. and avoid customs hassles. You know where it went."

Rachmaninoff smiled, his lips nearly hidden by the massive mustache. "You have me, my friend. The delivery went to the Silver Legacy parking garage. My man met the client's man, transferred the merchandise, and that, as they say, was that. If I could be of more help to you, I assure you I would." He paused. "You've done me a great service, wolfman, by showing me the holes in my security. I will attend to them right away. Perhaps you might like to come work for me, yes? I could use a man with your unique talents." His eyes roved up and down her frame. "You . . . are a man? Suddenly I'm not so sure."

"You couldn't afford me." Jackie shoved him away, her senses singing warnings. She couldn't have more than a minute left before things got far more exciting than she wanted.

"You'd be surprised at what I can afford." Rachmaninoff spotted his smoldering cigar where Jackie had dropped it, bent to retrieve it, and looked at the bruised tobacco with real disappointment.

Jackie growled, "You couldn't afford the damage I'd do to your organization." Out of the corner of her eye, she spotted some movement beyond the glass balcony doors.

Rachmaninoff put his cigar back in his teeth. "And I doubt seriously you can afford the damage my organization will do to you."

Jackie took a step back, gauging the distance to the edge of the balcony out of the corner of her eye. "A man with your talents can make a lot of money on the right side of the law. Think about it, Andrej. You're a smart man. Too smart for petty criminal enterprises. Keep it up and I'll have to pay you another visit sometime soon. I got in here once. I promise you I can do it again. And next time, I won't be so polite." She whirled and bounded over the edge. She hit the ground, rolled, and came up running for the fence at the back of Rachmaninoff's property.

"Goddammit, shoot that son of a bitch!" shouted Rachmaninoff behind her.

Jackie covered the distance to the fence in seconds, but in that time, Rachmaninoff's men reacted with admirable speed. The *chuff* of silenced pistols firing and the crack of bullets hitting the fence echoed in her ears.

Despite the guards' enthusiasm, their marksmanship was lacking. Jackie vaulted over the fence. The terrain beyond was more vertical than horizontal. Jackie trusted her animal side and slid, bounced, and bounded until she reached a road. She triggered the *Recall* button for her truck and trotted along the shoulder to meet it as it rolled up the road, lights off, engine barely purring.

She slipped inside. Armed with the information she'd learned from Rachmaninoff, she called Dominica.

"Yeah, boss?"

Secure behind dark tinted windows, Jackie pulled off the cowl so she could wipe sweat from her brow. "See what you can do with security footage from the Silver Legacy parking garage."

"I'll have to hack into their systems. That'll take some time."

"Can you do it?"

"Sure. Give me enough time and I can do anything."

"Uh huh." On the way down the winding road, Jackie spotted a pristine black classic Corvette parked in one of the gravel pullouts. She slowed the truck enough to admire the clean lines in her headlights before continuing on. Probably a couple of rich kids had pulled over to make out. It was what she'd have been doing when she was still in high school, if she hadn't been a werewolf.

"What am I looking for?"

"Rachmaninoff's people transferred the ingredients to the buyer's people in the parking garage. I want you to run the plates of vehicles going in and out of the garage against Rachmaninoff and known associates. When you find one, get the footage of it going in and out. Find out what you can about the buyers." If the buyer wasn't someone in the casino itself, it was a good starting point.

"Sure thing. You want me to maybe overthrow Singapore in my spare time, too?"

"Just do it, Dominica."

"Yes, ma'am."

"Don't call me *ma'am*."

"Yes . . . sir?"

"Don't push it."

The call to hunt was strong. The night had barely begun. Restless, she drove away from the mountains and back toward Reno looking for new trouble to break up. Muggings, breaking and entering, gang violence, drugs . . .

She wasn't picky.

Chapter Eight

November 2012
Reno, Nevada

Charlotte spent the rest of the evening working her way up the drug chain from Marvin.

Marvin told her about Javon, who worked in the garage of the bus station downtown. When she sashayed into the garage in her tight leathers, he might as well have been holding up a sign with his name on it. He looked her up and down from behind his sunglasses and ran a hand over his desperately out-of-date fade haircut to make sure it was tidy. "Hey, baby, how you doin'?" She put an arm around him and tucked one of her boobs under his arm to distract him.

"Real fine, sugar. Whatchoo doin' here?"

"Marvin sent me." While Javon was busy looking at her cleavage, she lifted the gun he had in a holster at the small of his back.

Javon blinked. "Marvin? That punk-ass cracka? Whass he want?"

"It's not what he wants." Charlotte raised Javon's pistol and tucked the end of it inside one of his nostrils before he could move. "It's what I want."

"Aw, shit. You a cop?"

"No, Javon, I'm not. Which means I don't have any problem shooting you. But I also don't have any interest in you being dead, either. Give me a name. Who's next up the food chain?"

"Bennie. Benito Martinez. Mexican Mafia, bitch. Mess with him, you bring down a world of shit on yourself."

"That's my problem, isn't it, Javon? Now if you tell me where he is, I might not tell him who sent me." She cocked the pistol for emphasis, even though it was a pointless gesture with modern weaponry. She still enjoyed doing it. There was a reason why directors put it into movies; the *chick-clack* of a cocked chamber had worked its way into modern consciousness as a sound that said *I mean business*.

"He got a building down on Mill Street. Looks like a bar with apartments overhead. It's a fuckin' crack house, man."

"What's it called?"

"Benito's. What the fuck you *think* it's called?"

A voice interrupted before Charlotte could continue her interrogation. "Hey, Javon, you holdin' tonight?" A young black man with his pants belted around his thighs and an off-kilter baseball cap sauntered around the corner of a bus. In a blur of motion, Charlotte whipped her own pistol out in a fast-draw even the fastest gunfighter in the world couldn't duplicate. The boy's eyes grew as wide as the bus headlamps beside him. He wasn't a fool, though, and put his hands up. "Peace, girl, I don't want none anyway!"

Charlotte smiled at him as pleasantly as if she'd recognized him across a crowded room. "Javon's a little busy right now. Why don't you come back later?"

"Yeah, okay." He paused and Charlotte wondered if she was going to have to shoot him anyway. "You don't wanna give me your number, do you?"

Charlotte almost laughed. She hadn't expected that. "No. Trust me, I'm all ninety-nine problems at once."

"Word." The boy went back around the bus. Charlotte kept an ear out in case he came back, but the only sound she could hear besides Javon's shuddering breathing was the boy's footsteps fading into the night.

"Now then, Javon. I'll be quite pissed if Bennie hears about me. If I find trouble waiting for me when I get there, I'll come back here and take it out of your ass. I got the drop on you once. You better believe the next time you won't even see me coming. Clear?"

"Y-yeah. Shit, I ain't gonna call nobody."

Charlotte leaned in and kissed his cheek. "Good. I'm glad we had this little chat. Think about changing your line of work, Javon. You don't have the nerves for this." She coiled her muscles and sprang onto the roof of the bus in one fluid motion. Then she ran along the top of it, leaped onto another bus, and traversed the rest of the garage without ever setting foot on the floor, a shadow moving through the darkness. She tossed Javon's gun into a storm drain and slid behind the wheel of her Corvette.

If grilling Javon had been straightforward, catching Bennie unawares was so easy that Charlotte was embarrassed for him. She'd climbed the side of his building and gone in through his bathroom window, which he'd opened to keep the air fresh while he was taking a dump. "Caught you with your pants down, Bennie," she said as she perched on the edge of the tub with a pistol in his face. The unfortunate smell of his wastes made her wrinkle her nose. "I'll make this fast. Who's at the top?"

He'd been most accommodating. *Viejo.*

With the sky lightening in the east, Charlotte returned to her motel room with a name and address to follow up on the next night and the little thrill in the small of her back that told her something was going to happen very soon. As the first rays of sunlight peeked around the edges of cheap polyester curtains over her room's single window, Charlotte stripped naked, rearranged the pillows to block any stray beams of sunlight, stopped breathing altogether, and fell asleep on the odd lumpiness of the mattress.

* * *

As the sun dropped below the Sierras, Charlotte arose from her death-like slumber with her first deep, shuddering breath in hours. Anastasia had teased her about the human foible. Thinking of Anastasia put her in a somber mood, and she struggled to push the woman from her thoughts and focus on the business at hand. She dressed in the leather duty uniform and packed her wig, lipstick, and some tightly rolled lingerie into empty belt pouches. Her mask went into the belt as well; she'd put it on once she'd arrived at her destination. She allowed herself an hour online to research everything she could about Roberto Viejo, local drug kingpin. He was a prominent leader in the Mexican Mafia. Like so many others of his stature in organized crime, his record was spotless and yet everyone knew his money came from nefarious means. Nobody had ever been able to prove it, and he made so many donations to local charities that even the police tended to overlook him.

The aftermarket GPS in her 'Vette guided her out of town toward southern highlands where the ultra-rich lived. Viejo lived at the edge of a steep rock face, nearly a sheer cliff. She couldn't wait to climb it. Buildings were one thing, but digging her fingers and toes into rock would feel like coming home.

She found a place to pull off the road and parked the 'Vette far enough back that even a weaving drunk would be unlikely to collide with it.

The steep, grooved slope of the mountain stretched above her. Somewhere up there, atop a six-hundred-foot vertical climb, was the estate of her target.

Charlotte had picked up the activity back in the Thirties, when she was involved with a Brazilian vampire who loved climbing the Andes. He'd taught her about using ropes as well as free-climbing, and she'd discovered a knack for fitting her slender fingers into crevices that seemed far too small. That talent, combined with her greater-than-human strength and the talons she could grow at the ends of her fingers and toes, meant she had yet to find something she couldn't climb.

This would be one of the trickier ones. Although it looked solid, the rock was deceptive and crumbling in places and could send her plummeting without warning. She wasn't afraid of falling; she'd fallen plenty of times in the past. It hurt, but she always healed, and she still had extra blood in her body for the time being. If she fell and wound up partially buried, trapped in such a way that she couldn't get out before the sun rose, she would burn to death. It would be an unpleasant way to go.

She would have to be cautious.

Charlotte slipped off her gloves and boots. She didn't need them for protection, and they wouldn't be of any use to her during the climb. She concentrated on her fingers and toes, willing the talons to extend from the tips. Jagged, inch-long spikes emerged from each finger and toe. It was an uncommon ability among vampires, albeit one attributed to all of them in legend and myth. The first time she'd hunted for a thrall, they'd emerged on their own, much to her shock. Since then, she'd learned to control when to push them forth. They hurt coming out, but the very act of their emergence was also a relief. The talons had the appearance of bone but were sharp as broken glass and hard as quartz. They clicked on the rocks as she found her first finger and toe-holds and started to climb.

She dug her fingers into a slender crack. A rock broke apart beneath her feet and she dangled for several dangerous seconds, held only by her finger talons wedged into the crevice. She spread her other hand wide and slapped it hard against the cliff face. Rock splinters flew as her talons penetrated, making her own piton. She kicked her toe claws into the rock as well. She hung there, spread-eagled against the wall, muscles quivering with nervous tension. The extra blood she'd consumed the day before was serving her well in the stress of the climb.

She hauled herself up, making better time through a section of sturdy, weathered rock. Experience had taught her not to look down, but at intervals she'd look up to check on her progress. She was pleased to see she'd covered about half of the vertical climb already. Once she made it to the last fifty feet, she'd be to the most dangerous part. The rock was crumbly along the edge of the cliff, and honeycombed by sparse weeds and stunted trees, clinging to cracks and ledges. One wrong move this high up and she could bounce all the way to the road. Showers of pebbles came loose every time she placed fingers or toes. She had to test her weight against every outcropping and ledge before moving even a few inches. As her progress slowed to a crawl, she felt her ire rise. She made herself take a deep breath. She moved ten feet to her right and found a sturdier section of rock.

Then she wasn't climbing but ascending a slope on her feet. The estates along the rim all had sturdy, six-foot fences along their edges to prevent inquisitive children or drunken party guests from tumbling over the edge. Charlotte spotted Viejo's house right away from the online pictures she'd studied in her motel room. His villa crowded up against the fence, the better for him and his guests to have an uninterrupted view of the valley spread out to the north. Charlotte went up his fence and then the side of the house in a matter of moments. She could hear a party inside, and from the sudden, explosive cheers and groans, she figured the attendees were watching some sporting event.

That suited her just fine. It meant she'd have some time to herself in the private parts of the house. She found an upstairs window unlocked and climbed into a guest bedroom, pulling the leather cowl over her head.

Her talons stayed sheathed so she could move without them clicking on the floor. She searched until she found what must have been Viejo's bedroom. It was a testament to male virility and wealth, from the king-sized four-poster bed with the overhead mirror to the sex swing and stripper pole mounted to one side, to the eighty-inch plasma television hanging on the wall. The silk sheets on the bed were rumpled and stained with the juices of lovemaking. The room reeked of aftershave, incense, marijuana, and dirty girls.

Charlotte saw the computer and smiled. It was password protected, of course, but the Collective had tools to get around that. She plugged a thumb drive into a USB port and tucked it behind the tower. The unit would crack through his security, clone his hard drive and email, and send it all to her laptop using Viejo's own internet connection. Somewhere in there, he might even have a dossier on White Fang. In the old days, she'd have had to spend hours rifling through paper files.

With her initial mission objectives successful, it was time to implement the next part of the plan. She slipped the package of lingerie from her pocket and skinned out of her climbing suit. She balled it up and tied it together with its own belt, then set it beside the bed so she could grab it in a hurry if necessary. Dressing in the lingerie was something she did mechanically, with decades of practice in the art. Hooks were hooked, straps were tied, bangles were tweaked. When she turned to a mirror, she was stunned for a moment because she didn't see her reflection there. Mirrors in the Collective headquarters used conventional polished aluminum backing, so it was always a bit of a shock when she ran across an older mirror that used silver. A quick glance through the suite confirmed they were all the expensive silvered sort, so she used the reflection of a windowpane to put on a wig and paint her face to look like a high-class call girl.

Once satisfied she'd achieved a sufficient level of sultriness, she slipped into Viejo's bed to wait for him.

She didn't have to wait long.

A feminine voice giggled in the hall outside the bedroom, encouraged by a mumbling man's voice. The door opened and Roberto Viejo stumbled into the room. He was a hefty man with his hair shaved to stubble on the sides and back of his head, save for a long braided rat-tail caught with a tiny diamond clasp. The stains on his UNR Wolf Pack jersey smelled of hot wing sauce. A drunk blonde woman wearing cutoff jean shorts and a string bikini top giggled as she pawed at his crotch.

Charlotte sat up in the bed, letting the sheets fall to her waist. "There you are," she said in her best sultry voice. "I wondered when you'd come up here. Get rid of the whore, Roberto, and come to bed."

Viejo's reaction was predictable. He gaped at Charlotte and jumped when the blonde woman slapped him. "You bas . . . bastard," she slurred. "You said I was sp . . . special." She flounced away.

Viejo stared at Charlotte's nearly naked form for a few seconds before he pulled a gun from the pocket of his workout pants. "Who the fuck are you?"

Charlotte climbed out of the bed to stand nude before him, partly to distract him and partly to show she had nothing to hide. "Easy, *hombre*. If I'd wanted you dead, I'd have killed you long before you saw my tits. I'm here to talk. Nothing more."

Viejo's gun didn't waver. "How'd you get in here?"

"You wouldn't believe me if I told you. Now put that thing away before somebody gets hurt."

He didn't move and narrowed his eyes. "I know who you are. You're that crazy bitch been messin' with my boys. Word's out about you. You gonna start some shit here? Because I didn't get where I am by bein' no pussy."

"Look at me, Roberto. Where could I keep a gun?" Charlotte stood with her hips cocked askew. "I'm only messing with the ones who won't answer my questions without some proper motivation. Now, I'm not here to cause you any trouble. I just want to find out about White Fang, and I'm betting you're the man to tell me about him."

"That crazy fucker in the wolf suit? I got a real score to settle with that *puto*. He's cost me a lot of money with his little war."

Charlotte smiled. "I'm here because a . . . cartel I represent has similar concerns about him. They've sent me to deal with him."

Viejo laughed. "You? By yourself?"

"I got in here by myself, didn't I? Past all your boys and their guns and the bullshit you think makes you secure. I guarantee you that if I can get in here, so can anyone else with my skills. And not everyone is going to be as willing to talk things over with you as I am."

"You're serious? All you want is White Fang?"

Charlotte winked at him. "That's all, sugar. Dish on him and I'll leave you to your . . . other diversions."

Viejo snorted. "You might think you're badass, but White Fang, he brings that shit to a whole new level. He took down an entire distribution center. Ten guys with real guns, not this pussy shit I'm holding. And he took them apart. They said they shot him and he kept on coming. He's gotta be a parahuman, right?"

"I can take him."

"If you can, you got some *huevos grandes* hidden somewhere in that tight body. He's one bad motherfucker, that's for sure." He lowered his voice and his gun at the same time, apparently having decided Charlotte was no immediate threat to him. "I ain't never seen him myself. I figure he's too afraid to come here lookin' for trouble, because he'll find it." He laughed. "Hell, I got the goddamn Russians right next door to me and they don't fuck with me. I'm untouchable."

"You keep on believing that, Roberto, and see how far it gets you."

"What the fuck are you talking about?"

"It would appear we've got a common interest in seeing him off the streets. Perhaps we can work together. Tell me everything you know about him."

"Ain't much to tell. He's a big dude. He wears this tight-fitting black one-piece, right? With gloves and boots that have claws in 'em. He's got a mask that looks like a real wolf's head. It goes up over his head and the fur goes down his chest and back. The front is white. Real easy to see. Like a target."

"Maybe that's the idea. Maybe he's not bulletproof. He wants you to shoot where he's armored, not where he isn't."

Viejo's eyes narrowed. "You're pretty smart, huh? Maybe you do got a chance against this guy. He's got a big-ass black truck, too. Sometimes he has it with him, and sometimes he don't. That's about all I know."

"How long has he been hassling you?"

"Maybe a year."

"Does he ever disappear? Skip a couple nights a month and not be seen at all?"

Viejo shrugged. "I don't know. We don't see him every night as it is. He's a fuckin' superhero. He's probably rescuing kittens from trees and shit."

"Next question. How can I find him?"

Viejo's laugh was short and explosive. "Goddamn, girl. Don't you think if I knew that I'd already have sent someone to bust a cap in his ass?"

"Indeed. Perhaps you can introduce me to some other people in your line of work who might have better suggestions than you."

Viejo shuffled into the room, hitching up his low-riding pants. "You want to meet some people? I got just the thing. There's this charity thing I'm goin' to tomorrow night. Bunch of rich and powerful assholes. If this White Fang dude ain't one of them, sure as shit someone in that group is funding him. It ain't cheap, doin' what he does." He folded his arms. "He may have stolen a lot of money from me and mine, but that don't mean he started out rich. I been waitin' for this event for months. Somebody there's got to know somethin'."

"Sounds perfect. I'll need a ticket."

"Ain't no ticket, lady, but I'm allowed a plus-one."

"I'll wear something fancy."

Viejo gave her the time and place to meet him at the charity event then stood too close to her, leering.

Expectant hope was plain on his acne-scarred face. "Not going to happen, *pendejo*," she said. "You're really not my type."

"You might be surprised, *señorita*. I'm an Aztec warrior in the sheets."

Charlotte's sharp ears detected the muffled sounds of badly silenced gunshots through the windows. She glanced outside and spotted a commotion in the yard of the next estate. Just as she looked up, a shadowy figure raced across the grass and made an impossible leap over the rear fence to disappear. It might have been White Fang, or it might not. Either way, she took it as an omen that her investigation was on the right course.

She turned to Viejo and smiled. "You're so anxious to get laid? Go find your little blonde whore and explain to her that I'm just a business partner."

"You always dress like this for business?"

Charlotte smiled. "Surely, Roberto, you understand that to land a deal, you need a great hook to interest the buyer."

Chapter Nine

November 2012
Reno, Nevada

On a normal morning after a night spent patrolling, Jackie would go to bed just before sunup and sleep until lunchtime. With Mark Hu still in her home, thought, she felt she should be there and awake in the morning, so she cut off her nighttime vigilante antics by one o'clock and headed back to the house to catch a few hours of sleep.

Following her interrogation at Rachmaninoff's, she spent some time in Sparks, east of Reno proper. There, she broke up a drug deal with flash-bang grenades and well-aimed punches and kicks. In the end, she left six dealers disarmed with broken noses, wrists, and one with a dislocated jaw. They'd done nearly as much damage to each other trying to shoot her while she flowed around them, slashing and striking. She gift-wrapped the unconscious criminals with all the duct-tape she had in her truck, left enough baggies for evidence and burned the rest with a flare. She drove home with a briefcase full of cash on the seat beside her. Jenn would launder it through one of the dummy corporations she'd set up, make a few charitable donations, pay White Fang's staff, and put the rest toward Dominica's tech. When her alarm went off at seven, Jackie glared at it and looked around the room in suspicion. She couldn't remember the last time she'd seen seven AM. She stumbled into the bathroom to check the knife wound. The scab was already flaking off, leaving fresh white skin. She prodded the spot. It was a little sore but nothing that wouldn't go away with a good breakfast.

Alix Duchesne was already in the kitchen, working on a pot of coffee when Jackie strolled in, comfortable in sweatpants and a *Velma's Glasses* t-shirt. "How's our patient?"

"He's awake. Poor thing stayed up late reading that manuscript you gave him. He's been sketching this morning."

"Zombies yesterday and sketching today?" Despite her tone, Jackie wasn't surprised at the revelation. She'd thumbed through Mark's portfolio and seen he had a lot of talent, preferring to draw either dancers in motion or closeups of faces.

Alix frowned. "He doesn't remember a lot about what happened, but he's still upset about it. I'm pretty sure he's avoiding sleeping because of it." She refilled her coffee, taking it black the way Jackie did.

"Trauma is a real bitch," Jackie said.

"It's something you two have in common."

Jackie snorted. "I don't have any trauma."

"Yes you do." Alix took another sip. "Dressing up in a costume and doing what you do is not normal behavior under any circumstances."

"How do you know what's normal for werewolves?"

"I don't, but I'm your doctor, and I call it like I see it. Mark's a victim of violent circumstances. You are too, on a monthly basis. Neither of you have control over those events. I can recommend a couple of good therapists."

"Maybe later," Jackie said, intending nothing of the sort. She filled a large mug of coffee for herself before the doctor drank it all. She took a healthy sip, unconcerned about the high temperature. The momentary burning pain subsided right away thanks to her healing ability, and the influx of caffeine was more important, anyway. "I'm going to see how Mark is doing."

"Denial isn't just a river in Egypt," Alix said as Jackie left the kitchen.

Jackie went to the guest bedroom and knocked.

"Come in," Mark said.

Mark looked much livelier than he had the day before. He'd abandoned the bed for a chair beside it, but had his bare feet crossed upon the bedspread. He wore athletic shorts and a long-sleeved t-shirt his mother had brought him. His eyes still had a shadowed cast about them that a single night's rest wouldn't cure. Despite that faint haunted expression, he had a pencil tucked behind each ear and another clutched between his lips as he drew with a fourth. "Good morning, Ms. Langdon."

"Please, call me Jackie. *Ms. Langdon* makes me think of my mother."

"Is she as nice as you?"

Jackie cleared her throat. "She's . . . dead. Both she and my father died in an accident."

Mark's smile vanished. "Oh, I'm so sorry!"

"It's all right. It happened a couple of years ago."

Jackie shook off the somber feelings always caused by mention of her parents and changed the subject. "Dr. Duchesne says you're cleared to go home if you'd like to. How are you feeling?"

"I'm okay, I guess. I had some pretty shitty dreams when I did sleep. Drawing helps."

"You're very talented."

Mark blushed. "I'm just a student."

"May I see what you're working on now?"

Mark turned his sketchbook to show her.

A shadowy, wolfish figure rose behind two hooded men with dead faces. The uncanny accuracy of the scene startled Jackie. She forced herself to control her response. "That's great work. Makes me think of Silvertongue." Silvertongue was the central character of her work-in-progress, the one she'd promised to have to the publisher by Christmas.

"How did you like *Silvertongue*? Alix said you stayed up late reading it."

"It's really good," Mark said. "But it's sad."

"It is?"

"Silvertongue's got no clan. He's a true lone wolf. Is that how you see yourself?"

Jackie's mouth went dry. *Does he know?* She cleared her throat. "What do you mean?"

"Well, you live all alone up here, right? I mean, without a family."

"I guess you write what you know," Jackie said at last, falling back on a trope.

"You have such an amazing sense of what it would be like for a werewolf to live among regular people," Mark said, adding some bold lines to his drawing.

Jackie forced a smile. "I was quite the outsider growing up."

"Tell me about it. I'm the gay son of Chinese immigrants. I got shoved into more lockers in school than is even funny."

"I wish I'd gone to public school," Jackie said, suddenly realizing it was the truth. "I was home-schooled. I missed out on a lot of people time." She sighed. "I guess I am kind of a lone wolf." She shook herself. "You ready to head home?"

"Yes." Mark gathered up his portfolio. He paused to look at the sketch he'd shown to Jackie before packing it away. "I think it was him that saved me," he said in a solemn tone.

"Him?"

"The wolf man."

Jackie's smile was genuine. "I'm glad he did."

* * *

After dropping Mark off at his parents' shop, Jackie called Dominica from the car. "How's your research coming, Dee?"

"Not too shabby, boss. Some answers, some questions I'm still working on."

"What are you still working on?"

"Correlating Mark with the other two missing people. Not a whole lot to go on. Two women and a man. A fast food cashier, a cabbie, and an art student. Two Caucasians and an Asian-American. The cashier's nineteen, the cabbie twenty-four, and Mark's twenty-one."

Jackie turned off Mill Boulevard to head downtown toward the Silver Legacy casino, the tallest building in Reno. The parking garage off to one side was where Rachmaninoff's man had transferred the unusual ingredients to the buyer. Maybe Jackie could find some evidence there to advance her investigation.

"Any chance they knew each other? Went to the same schools or churches?"

"There's always a chance, but I'm guessing any contact they might have had with each other was purely incidental."

"That's not helping."

"Sorry, boss. It's all I've got on the victims so far."

"How about the Legacy? Anyone in there who might be the likely recipient of such bizarre ingredients?"

"You know, it's funny, because there is. Ever hear of Conrad Gault?"

"I know that name. What's he known for?"

Dominica began, "*There is truth, and there is beauty, and then there is—*"

"*—Deception,*" Jackie finished. "Gault is the Deception perfume guy?" Deception perfumes were very popular in both their mass-marketed, inexpensive styles as well as the custom blends created by Gault in his lab. He'd selected Reno because of its easy access to pure, fresh mountain water. Although the low-end perfumes used simple distilled waters and alcohols, all his exclusive blends were advertised as using the uniquely pure waters of the Sierra Nevada Mountains. His decision not to live among the trendy elites of the coast, or in Europe, had gotten him labeled a maverick in the industry. Jackie had never had the opportunity to meet the man. Despite Jackie's own wealth, Gault was still several levels farther up the social strata.

"The very same. And here's where it gets interesting. Almost all the ingredients in this list are used in perfumes or cosmetics. Or used to be. Most of them use artificial chemical substitutes now."

"A perfumer would know about all those esoteric ingredients and where to obtain them."

"Right, boss, but even though he has a permanent two-floor suite in the Legacy, there shouldn't be a lab there. I checked. The casino would never allow it. His actual lab is in Elko, most of the way across the state."

"So, assuming it's him, why have the stuff delivered to his residence instead of his lab?"

"That's kind of what I was thinking too."

"Unless the ingredients are so rare and bizarre it would raise red flags even with the people at the Deception facility."

"They're a pretty odd mix of substances. I can't even begin to imagine what some of the import tariffs on them might have been like."

"I'm sure they were smuggled into the country." Jackie looked up at the Silver Legacy's tower and wondered what secrets were hidden at its pinnacle. "Anyone else in the hotel who might have a reason to get all those rare items?"

"This isn't Vegas. The really big high roller types don't come here."

"Maybe that's exactly why they chose Reno. Lower profile," Jackie suggested.

"It doesn't even have to be someone in the Legacy at all. The garage could have just been where they made the transfer."

Jackie shook her head. "I like the casino as a location and Gault as a suspect. It's central to the area bordered by the three abductions and it's secure. So, we've got Gault with the knowledge and ability to create this alchemical powder. What we don't have is a motive."

"No, not yet, boss, but I like Gault as a suspect too, so I took the liberty of doing a little more digging into his recent history." Dominica paused. Jackie thought it might be to savor the moment. "He's been traveling abroad recently, ostensibly to find new scents for the next Gault fragrance."

"Let me guess . . . Egypt."

"Funny how that works out, huh? And get this. On his way back from Egypt, he stopped in the Caribbean."

"Known for, among other things, voodoo and black magic, right?"

"Boss, he's got a bunch of red flags on this, starting with all the requisite knowledge and background."

"Indeed. I'd love to get a look inside that suite."

"What are you going to do, climb up forty floors of sheer glass panes?"

Jackie stared up at the Silver Legacy with its sheer vertical faces. Columns of dark windows against the pale walls giving it a vertical striped appearance. She was game to try such a thing, but even her unnatural healing ability wouldn't save her from a tumble of hundreds of feet. "White Fang can't get up there, but I'll bet novelist Jackie Langdon could."

"That Timberline Foundation thing you're supposed to go to tomorrow night? That Jenn was all up in arms about? Gault is on the guest list. Might be the opportunity you need." Jackie could picture Dominica leaning back in her seat with a look of immense satisfaction across her face. "Your Russian buddy will be there too."

"Rachmaninoff?"

"The same."

"What a coincidence."

"Small world, boss. Maybe he can arrange an introduction to Gault for you."

"He doesn't know Jackie Langdon."

"I hacked his Amazon account. He's bought all of your books."

Jackie snorted. "He's a fan?"

"Doesn't mean he read them."

"My ego thanks you."

Chapter Ten

November 2012
Reno, Nevada

Charlotte chuckled as she finished her research and closed her laptop. The Timberline Foundation wasn't the kind of thing she'd expect Viejo to be involved with, but then, politics and organized crime made for strange bedfellows.

The event was in the Whitney Peak hotel, two blocks south of the Silver Legacy. The Whitney Peak was a wide building with a narrow cross section and a historic climbing wall running all the way up one side. Although tradition demanded she arrive fashionably late, Charlotte visited the hotel early, at sunset, so she could get the lay of the land. She dressed in jeans and a polo shirt with a freight company logo and a hooded parka over it all, ostensibly to keep her warm but really to protect her from the dying rays of the sun. With a sealed, official-looking envelope in her hand, nobody gave her more than a cursory glance as she cased the building.

Later, back in her own hotel, she painted herself into her little black cocktail dress. She spent extra time on her makeup and wig, then tucked her smallest pistol and an extra cartridge of silver bullets into her clutch. She felt sexy and dangerous. Normally, when she geared up, it was to clear out a werewolf den. This subtle, super-spy stuff was new to her, and she felt like she'd found a new mountain to climb. She couldn't wait to scale that summit.

She'd agreed to meet Viejo outside the hotel and damned if the heavyset Hispanic man wasn't hanging around out front of the Whitney Peak. Even dressed up in an expensive Italian suit, Viejo still looked like a gangbanger. His hair was slicked back, his ears sported diamond earrings, and he carried about him a subtle air of menace. The valets gave him a wide berth.

Charlotte pulled up to the front of the hotel in her Corvette, put it in park without shutting it off, and took her time climbing out. She wanted everyone out front to notice her arrival. Being remembered as the leggy brunette with the sweet car would be to her advantage if she had to get into any kind of fight. Without the car and the long wig, she'd be just another forgettable black girl.

A pimply faced valet, who'd beaten out his fellows, stepped up to her with a cheesy grin. "Park your car for you, ma'am?"

"Please. And be careful, I just had her waxed." Charlotte handed a fifty-dollar bill to the awestruck young man, letting him wonder from where she'd produced it.

He thrust a claim ticket into her empty hand. "I'll treat her right, ma'am," he said, his voice cracking.

She wondered how he'd taste. Young, vibrant, delicious, she was sure. Pimples and cracking voices didn't bother her; not when she could practically feel his hot blood coursing down her throat. She made herself turn away. If she ingested any more blood before using up that which she'd already taken, she'd become drunk on it. A drunken vampire was a danger to herself and everyone around her. And a danger to the entire species, she reminded herself.

"I was beginnin' to think you stood me up," Viejo said. "Man, I thought you were fine naked, but I think I prefer you like this."

Charlotte gave him a tight smile. "You clean up pretty well yourself, Roberto. Not my type, but at least I'm not ashamed to be seen near you." She slipped her arm around his. "Let's go inside and mingle." Viejo looked down at her arm as if unsure what to do with it. Charlotte sighed. It had been at least thirty years since she'd met anyone who knew how to properly treat a lady. She stretched up to whisper in his ear. "Touch my ass and I'll break your fingers one at a time."

They entered the Whitney Peak's lobby. The staff had cleaned it up from the afternoon gaggle of tourists. A cheery fire burned in a large brick fireplace, suffusing the room with its warm glow. Dark leather chairs and sofas were arranged in a semicircle around it, occupied by people in fancy dress discussing important matters of state, industry, and gossip. The governor was there, and the mayor of Reno. Charlotte spotted a Nevada state senator and his wife, who had eyes mainly for one of her husband's aides. Everyone who was anyone in Reno was there to be seen handing checks to the Timberline executives.

Old-fashioned incandescent lights filled all the nouveau chandelier fixtures, adding to the cozy atmosphere. The gray stone walls and wooden trim of the lobby made Charlotte feel as if she were in a high desert lodge.

Two beefy men stood on either side of the entrance to the ballroom, flanking a rope barrier and offering pleasantries and polite smiles to anyone who approached. They checked names against a list, checked them off, and welcomed the guests into the presence of Reno's rich and famous.

Viejo waited, shuffling from foot to foot while the men checked their list. At last they found his name, meaning he'd put in a thousand dollars for him and his guest ahead of time. One of them unclipped the rope. "Thank you for your contribution to the Timberline Foundation, Mr. Viejo," said the man in a deep voice. "Enjoy your dinner."

"You don't seem like the charitable sort, Roberto," Charlotte said as they walked away. "What's your interest in Timberline?"

"I don't give a fuck about Timberline. I'm here to make connections. These are the people with the cash. And rich fuckers are always looking for a way to spend it. And they like to party, girl, like you wouldn't believe." They entered the grand ballroom and even a jaded Charlotte had to admit it was lovely.

Numerous chandeliers made the grand ballroom even brighter than the lobby, and decorative brickwork along the walls created a warm, rustic feeling. Dozens of small round tables with white tablecloths featured silver service and tasteful floral centerpieces. A jazz combo played a non-threatening Latin tune, heavy on marimba and piano. Charlotte thought the sax and trumpet players looked bored to tears. Some couples danced in a half-hearted fashion, though the music wasn't quite right for it.

"Ugh, this is some bullshit here." Charlotte had been to parties like it before, inevitably dreary affairs full of self-important assholes desperate to impress other self-important assholes.

"It is quite bullshit, young lady," said a man nearby. He had a thick Russian accent. "But this is what passes for high society function in this little town." He presented a hand to Viejo, but his eyes wandered across Charlotte's curves. "I am Andrej Rachmaninoff."

"Viejo. Roberto Viejo." They shook hands.

"At last we meet, Mr. Viejo. All this time we have been neighbors, and not once have I had the opportunity to chat with you while washing the car or mowing the lawn."

"Yeah, well, I'm a pretty busy, man. I know your rep, though. I been meaning to look you up."

Rachmaninoff smirked. "Perhaps you could Facebook me, no?" A discreet waiter appeared at his elbow. The Russian turned his head to acknowledge the man. "Martini. Two olives." He sucked with defiance on a large unlit cigar, for which Charlotte was grateful. She couldn't bear cigar smoke. Nevertheless, she looked him over with care. He was too short and heavyset to be White Fang, so she crossed him off her list.

"Sir?" the waiter asked of Viejo.

"Uh . . . Dos Equis. In, uh, in a bottle."

Charlotte smiled at the man's discomfort at being so far out of his element. She turned to the waiter. "Club soda with lime, sugar."

"Tell me, Mr. Viejo," Rachmaninoff said. "Who is this charming lady you've brought?"

"She's . . ." A bamboozled Viejo stopped as he realized he didn't even know her name.

"Charlotte Pastor." She shook Rachmaninoff's hand. "I'm a reporter. I understand Reno's got a fellow who dresses up like a werewolf to play superhero. Know anything about him?"

Rachmaninoff's face turned thunderous with such speed that Charlotte took a step back in surprise. He muttered something in Russian under his breath. "You want to know about White Fang? I'll tell you about him. He's a bastard and a menace. He ought to be locked up for . . . for trespassing and making threats."

"Threats to you, Mr. Rachmaninoff?"

Rachmaninoff cleared his throat. The waiter reappeared at his side with drinks on a tray. The Russian grabbed his martini and downed it in a single gulp. "Another," he said, chewing on the olives.

Viejo took his chilled bottle of beer and took a pull from it. "I heard he paid you a visit, *señor*. That true?"

"You're well-informed, Mr. Viejo."

"We're neighbors, ain't we? That *puto* has been puttin' a real dent in my business, if you know what I'm sayin'."

"Subtlety is not one of your stronger points, is it, Mr. Viejo?" Rachmaninoff set his empty glass on a passing waiter's tray and lit his cigar, flagrantly transgressing the hotel's nonsmoking policy.

"Subtlety is usin' a nine when you coulda used a forty-five." Viejo shrugged and lit a cigar of his own.

Charlotte choked back a snort of amusement. She hoped Rachmaninoff wasn't an undercover law enforcement agent, because he was drawing out Viejo like a professional.

"It seems to me that we might have something in common, my friend."

Viejo clapped the Russian on the back. "*Cabron*, you and me got a lot to talk about. I hate that White Fang guy as much as you, if not more."

"Perhaps we pool our resources, yes?"

"Count me in," Charlotte said. "I'm here to meet White Fang."

"White Fang? Sounds right up my alley," said a feminine voice. Charlotte turned to look at the newcomer. She was tall, with a black and gray suit disguising well-defined muscles except to Charlotte's practiced eye. Her short black hair was slicked back. Her movements were a predator's, hidden beneath a disarming smile.

Charlotte smiled despite the clanging of her internal alarms. She'd hunted enough werewolves to recognize the hidden indicators of the wolf within the human—the constant subtle twitches of nostrils and ears, the almost imperceptible furtive glances. Most people would never pick up on such things, but to Charlotte, there might as well have been a big neon sign reading *Werewolf* floating over the woman.

She could have gone after the woman right then and there with the weapon in her clutch bag if that had been her assignment, but the consequences of doing so in front of all these people would be too steep. Instead, she'd try to catch the woman in a more private place later.

"Sorry for eavesdropping, but White Fang fascinates me." The woman extended a hand. "Jacquelyn Langdon, author of the *Silverback* series." She motioned to the young Asian man beside her, standing close as if he were a thrall. "And this is Mark."

"Pleased to meet you both. I'm Charlotte Pastor." Charlotte knew of the *Silverback* books, although she'd never read one. In her line of work, there never seemed to be enough time to read for fun, and even if she had the drive to do so, the last thing she'd want to read about was more damned werewolves. She eased herself in between Viejo and Rachmaninoff. She hoped their cologne and cigars would help to mask her scent, since werewolves could identify vampires by smell. If Langdon was truly her prey, she'd have to be careful. Would the rest of her clan be so brazen as to have infiltrated Reno high society? She glanced around the room, trying to pick out other possible werewolves.

Rachmaninoff took Langdon's hand, paused as if considering whether kissing it would be gauche, and then proceeded to do so anyway. "My niece is a great fan of your work, Ms. Langdon. The last time she visited, all she would say is *Silverback* this and *Silverback* that. I bought her your entire series for her birthday."

"Well, I can't fault her for her taste in reading." Langdon pulled a small case from her pocket and removed a sticker shaped like a wolf's head with a signature scrawled across it. "Give her this from me."

Rachmaninoff laughed. "She will be most overjoyed, I'm sure."

Someone opened the door to the ballroom and a cool breeze blew across the back of Charlotte's neck. She gritted her teeth, knowing that the air current was carrying her scent right toward Langdon.

Langdon smiled and turned to Viejo. "You do much reading, Mr. Viejo?"

"No," was Viejo's brusque response.

Charlotte gave Viejo a gentle tug. It wasn't safe here. Too open, too many people. Although, unless Langdon had the entire hotel staff and guests in her pocket, it wasn't likely she'd try anything either.

Langdon wrinkled her nose, as if she were sniffing the air. Her eyes wandered to Charlotte and she frowned for just a moment, an odd expression of recognizing that something was *wrong*.

Charlotte kept her face a stone mask, but she knew she'd just been made. She went on alert, expecting immediate trouble. She realized she hadn't breathed in a long time—minutes, perhaps—and forced herself to expand and contract her lungs.

"What kind of work do you do, Mr. Rachmaninoff?" Langdon asked. Her eyes kept straying toward Charlotte as if she couldn't understand what her senses were telling her. Could it be she had no experience with vampires?

"Please, call me Andrej. I import rare commodities."

"Now that sounds fascinating," Langdon said. "I bet you have some stories to tell. Bring in anything cool recently?" Once again, the woman's eyes fixed upon Charlotte and a slight frown creased her forehead.

Rachmaninoff puffed himself up with the pleasure of being asked to talk about himself. It was a brilliant psychological ploy on Langdon's part. Charlotte didn't know a werewolf could be so subtle. He'd imported artwork and sculptures for several of the high-society types in the room, and delighted in pointing them out. "And most recently, I even brought in some special ingredients for Conrad Gault. Are you familiar with his perfumes, my dear?"

Langdon laughed. "I'm wearing *Deception* right now, in fact."

Of course you are, Charlotte thought.

Langdon continued. "I'd love to meet him. Isn't he here tonight?"

"I believe so." Rachmaninoff smiled.

A hand settled across the upper curve of Charlotte's ass. She turned to glare at Viejo, who bore the expression of a kid caught with his hand in the cookie jar. "Move it or I'm cutting it off and taking it home as a souvenir," she said.

"Hey, I'm just tryin' to be nice," said Viejo, hands spread in apology.

"And I'm just trying to keep from killing you where you stand. Go find some whore if you want tail, because you're not getting it from me."

Viejo moved his hand away.

Rachmaninoff said, "I'll see if I can find Conrad. Perhaps he will join us at our table."

Charlotte turned to Langdon. "Being a writer must be fascinating," she said. "I bet you meet all kinds of interesting people and do a lot of neat things."

"It's not nearly as glamorous as people think," Langdon said. "It's a lot of time sitting alone in a quiet room."

"Surely you must get out from time to time. Explore the sights, sounds, and smells of the world." Langdon's nostrils twitched again at Charlotte's words. *Good.*

"I do travel occasionally, but Reno is my favorite place."

"How's the night life here? I mean, it's no Vegas, but so few places are anymore."

"Nights here are like anywhere else. Entertaining or dangerous." At the word *dangerous*, Langdon's companion Mark twitched a little, and moved almost imperceptibly closer to her. *She's protecting him, but from what? And he doesn't know what she is, or he does . . . and doesn't care.*

Charlotte moistened her lips with her champagne. "Which do you prefer, Ms. Langdon? You seem like someone who doesn't mind a bit of danger."

Langdon's nose twitched again and she covered it with an immediate smile. "Danger can be entertaining, and entertainment can be dangerous."

The band finished its tune and an emcee took the stage. "Thank you, thank you very much. Can we have a big hand for tonight's entertainment?"

The audience gave up their dutiful applause as the musicians bowed. Everyone turned to face the emcee.

"I want to thank you all for your generous contributions to the Timberline Foundation. Many of you have included far more than the five hundred dollars tonight, and we are extremely grateful for that.

As you know, pine beetle infestation is one of the largest problems facing the mountain west today . . ."

Charlotte tuned out the emcee's spiel and stared at Langdon's back. Her suit was tailored to minimize instead of emphasize her musculature. Charlotte didn't find it difficult at all to imagine the woman in a tight-fitting body suit with a wolf's head mask. What had driven her to take an altruistic, vigilante route instead of hiding and hunting humans? It was unusual, un-werewolfish behavior.

" . . . So if you'd all like to take seats, we'll begin our dinner in a few minutes," the emcee said.

Rachmaninoff waved at Langdon and her companion from across the room to join him.

"Come on." Charlotte took Viejo's hand. "We're going to sit with them too." She pulled the confused Hispanic man after her.

The two couples crossed the floor to one of the most gorgeous humans Charlotte had seen in decades. Conrad Gault wore a stylish black suit and black silk shirt with a tie the color of congealed blood, which she found to be an attractive accessory. Curly dark hair framed his chiseled face and stubble decorated his chin. Charlotte imagined how his blood would taste. Truly a choice vintage compared to the flavorless thralls in the Midnight Collective headquarters.

"Conrad Gault, this is Jacquelyn Langdon, the well-known author," said Rachmaninoff. "And my . . . neighbor, Roberto Viejo."

Gault smiled, showing perfect teeth. "*Bonjour, mes amis.* I am pleased to meet you. I've read your works, *Mademoiselle* Langdon. Fascinating insights into the private life of the werewolf."

"And I'm wearing *Deception* tonight, so I suppose we're even." Langdon laughed. "May we join you?"

Gault inclined his head. "I would be honored."

Charlotte didn't bother to ask for permission. She turned to Viejo. "I think you should leave," she said softly.

She didn't have Nick's gift to compel others to follow commands, but she laced her words with enough subtle threat that Viejo couldn't mistake it for anything else.

Viejo shuffled his feet. "I, uh, gotta take a leak." He made for the exit.

Charlotte rearranged her face into a practiced pout. "I think I just got ditched."

Conrad Gault pulled out a chair for her. "That is a crime, to be sure. A lovely young lady such as yourself should not go unescorted. Please, sit with me."

Charlotte did so. "Very kind of you, Mr. Gault. You seem like an interesting bunch of people."

"And you seem just as interesting, Miss Pastor." Langdon's gaze smoldered.

Chapter Eleven

November 2012
Reno, Nevada

Jackie couldn't figure out why, but Charlotte Pastor made her uncomfortable. It was like she was picking up a hint of a scent that almost didn't register at all, even to her super-sensitive nose. It reminded her of the dark, sour odor of meat left too long out of the refrigerator, or drying blood tinged with fear and violence. Despite the faint charnel smell, Pastor seemed as far removed from death as anyone could be. She laughed with Mark, made eyes at Conrad Gault beside her, and joked about writing with Jackie.

The beast within Jackie yammered and howled, anxious to be released for the kill, but it wasn't the normal hunger that drove her werewolf side. It was . . . *afraid*. Fear was nothing new to Jackie, but her fear normally centered on the fear of discovery, or of harming those she'd come to love. This was a more primal fear, a fight-or-flight response. Could Pastor be another werewolf? In all the years of research she'd done, both for her books and in her personal quest for knowledge, she'd never encountered anything more than rumors of others like her. There had to be more; she was living proof of the traits being passed along through generations, like parahuman powers. Was this her body's way of warning her of a new competitor in the hunting field? Or was she something entirely new?

Two weeks ago, Jackie would have laughed if anybody had told her zombies were real, but now she knew better. Perhaps other unnatural, fantastic creatures existed in the world. Could Pastor be a faerie or vampire? Or did those even exist?

She tried to put aside her suspicions about Pastor and focus on Gault. She was determined not to leave the table without an invitation into the man's Silver Legacy suite. Still, her discomfort remained, for it seemed every time she glanced in Pastor's direction, the woman's eyes were on her. Had she connected Jackie and White Fang? Or was it something more sinister?

Focus on the target, she told herself. Stay on task. The nearness of the full moon and Pastor's unexplainable aroma made concentration difficult. Her head buzzed as if it were full of bees. She pinched the bridge of her nose to try to make it stop.

"Jackie, are you all right?" Mark touched her hand. "You look like someone just walked across your grave."

"What? Oh . . ." Her eyes dropped to her appetizer plate in search of inspiration. She'd devoured a shrimp cocktail with a creamy dill aioli sauce. "It's the shrimp sauce. It must have real cream in it. I'm a bit lactose intolerant. I'll have to take something when I get home." She smiled as pleasantly as she could and, out of sight of the others, dug her fingers into the sides of her chair until she felt the wood splinter. This would be her last night in the field for a while. By tomorrow evening, the moon would be only a day from full, and she'd have to stay home. She turned her attention back to Gault, trying to put Pastor out of her mind. The perfumer smelled of a musky, herbal concoction that even Jackie's sensitive nose couldn't identify. "So, do you do a lot of traveling, Mr. Gault?"

"Indeed, I do, *Mademoiselle* Langdon. Travel is a mind-broadening activity."

"I couldn't agree more," Pastor said. "I just returned from a trip to China, in fact." She fluttered her eyelashes at Gault. Jackie wanted to roll her eyes, but the Frenchman was buying what she was selling.

"I love China," said Gault. "A beautiful country, rich in history and secrets. I have recently been in Egypt myself. Also rich in history."

"And perfume ingredients, I'd bet," added Jackie. "You must find some really strange things in that part of the world to mix into your scents."

"It is not so simple as that." Gault took a sip from his champagne flute. "Many ingredients are rare and importing them is a costly process. I prefer to have my chemists find the essential formulae and recreate them in the labs." He smiled. "Perhaps you would like to tour the facility sometime, *oui*?"

"I'd like that very much, Mr. Gault."

"Call me *Conrad*, please. I get enough of the formality on a daily basis that I enjoy hearing my first name, especially when delivered by a beautiful woman's mouth."

"Then make it Jacquelyn." Jackie caught Pastor once again watching her. She lowered her voice and leaned closer to Gault. "Chemical equivalents are all well and good, Conrad, but consider the difference between a best-selling novel and one that can't earn out its advance. Both novels use the same words, the same language, but there's something indefinable in the bestseller that makes it so much better and more appealing to a reader than the other. You're telling me that your chemical equivalents are as good as the original source material?"

Gault laughed. "Very good, Jacquelyn. You're absolutely right. Some things cannot be recreated successfully, no matter how hard we try. I do mix up small batches of fragrances myself, using traditional ingredients. Those are for use as gifts. I could never sell them." He lowered his voice as well. "Some of the ingredients are rare enough for me to require the services of Mr. Rachmaninoff."

"I knew it!" Jackie slapped the table. Mark jumped, startled at Jackie's outburst, and accidentally knocked Pastor's clutch onto the floor. Pastor bent for it but Jackie was faster. She picked it up and handed it back to Pastor. "Allow me."

Pastor's smile was pleasant, teeth dazzling white. "Thank you, Ms. Langdon."

"My pleasure." Jackie smiled back and turned back to face Gault, and that's when the smell hit her.

Bright, shiny, poisonous metal. Nitrocellulose. Nitroglycerin. Steel. Oil. Brass. Silver. *Oh, so much silver!*

Pastor had a gun in her clasp, and an unusual amount of silver as well. She wasn't wearing any silver jewelry at all. Jackie could only think of one valid reason why she would have silver with her and not be wearing it, and why she would also have a gun.

Silver bullets.

Charlotte Pastor knew Jackie was a werewolf and was there to kill her.

Jackie's first instinct was to leap across the table to attack Pastor, followed by an equal desire to flee from the grand ballroom. She forced herself to remain calm; neither of those options would have a beneficial outcome. She needed a diversion, some reason to leave the table in a rush. She discarded her first idea of spilling her drink on herself. It would look far too clumsy and contrived. An accident, then. She picked up her glass, raised it to her lips, and closed her teeth upon it.

The glass shattered around her mouth. "Oh, shit!"

Mark gasped in surprise as Jackie set down her broken glass. "Oh my God, are you okay?"

A swirl of blood twisted through the golden single-malt Scotch remaining in the broken glass. Jackie grabbed a napkin and held it up to her mouth as blood threatened to drip onto her expensive suit. "I'm fine. I'll be right back."

Jackie hurried from the table. She glanced back once to see if Pastor was following, but Mark had already engaged her in a conversation. Good job, she thought. Mark was on Jackie's team and didn't even know it. By the time she left the ballroom, the bleeding had already stopped. She tossed the napkin into a trash can and instead of heading for the bathroom, went to the front desk.

"Yes, ma'am, can I help you?" the young man asked.

"I need to speak to hotel security right away," said Jackie.

A minute later, a distinguished-looking older man with a pronounced limp came to the desk from a nondescript side door. "I'm Lewis Philips, chief of security. What seems to be the trouble, ma'am?"

Jackie spoke in clipped, urgent tones. "I'm Jacquelyn Langdon, the author of the *Silverback* books. There's a woman named Charlotte Pastor at my table in the ballroom who's been stalking me for some time and I just discovered she has a gun in her possession. I'm worried for my safety, but I can't leave, because my friend's at the same table. I'm afraid for his life too if this woman gets trigger-happy."

"Can you describe her for me?"

Jackie described Charlotte Pastor. Philips relayed the information into a walkie-talkie. A moment later a voice replied, "She's still in there. We've got her on camera."

"We will escort her from the grounds, Ms. Langdon. Unless she's committed an actual crime, that's all we can do."

"That would be fine," said Jackie. "I'd feel safer if you did so."

"Of course, ma'am. The safety of our guests is a primary concern."

"I'll return to my seat. She'll be less likely to do something with me right there."

Philips smiled at her. "Don't you worry, Ms. Langdon. We're very discreet about security matters like this in the Whitney Peak."

Jackie walked back into the ballroom and sat back down at the table, pleased to discover her plate of food had arrived in her absence—a twenty-ounce porterhouse, thrown on the grill just long enough to get some black marks, given a dirty look, then dropped onto the plate. Just the way she liked it.

"Are you okay, Jackie?" Mark asked.

"Yes, just a minor cut. I'm fine." Jackie noticed her glass had been replaced and refilled as well. Good service here, she thought.

"I can't believe you're going to eat all that," Mark whispered. "And it's practically still mooing."

"Miss Pastor?" Two hefty security guards in hotel jackets stood behind the table. Their entrance had been so quiet that Jackie hadn't even noticed their arrival.

Charlotte looked up at the two thick-necked men with their crew cuts and jackets straining to contain solid muscle. "Yes?"

"There's a problem with your vehicle. Will you come with us, please?"

"My car? What happened?" Charlotte picked up her clutch and stood.

"You'd better come see for yourself, Ma'am." The security guards escorted her from the room with discreet professionalism without conveying the slightest sense that they were removing her.

Jackie smiled to herself. *Damn good service here.*

She returned her attention to Gault as the Frenchman ate pieces of buttery, flaky salmon crusted in herbs and washed every bite down with a sip of champagne. "So, Conrad, I'd love the chance to see your secret workshop. Maybe I could work it into a book somehow."

Gault smiled. "There is not much to see. A workbench, some burners, some flasks. Boring, *oui*?" He raised his champagne glass to his lips.

"Doing it old-school, huh? Ever think about making anything else?"

Gault nearly choked on his champagne. He coughed and wiped his mouth with a napkin.

"Are you all right?" Jackie felt like she'd scored a solid point. Gault couldn't have been clearer in his response if he'd admitted full guilt.

"I'm fine."

If Jackie had been closer to werewolf form, her hackles would have raised as a huge man approached the table, even larger than the two security guards who'd escorted Pastor out a moment ago. His blonde hair was caught back in a ponytail and a trimmed beard lined his cheeks, chin, and upper lip. His charcoal-gray jacket barely restrained his tremendous shoulders, and a prodigious gut pressed against a maroon shirt. Despite that belly, the man carried an air strength and power. The floor seemed to creak where he walked and the room flowed around him, as if he displaced things and people just by his presence.

He exuded a distinctive musky smell that almost triggered Jackie into an uncontrolled transformation. Something about him drove the monster inside Jackie's civilized trappings wild. Already on edge from Pastor's strange, spicy scent, she nearly lost it. Her fingers and nails started to thicken into clawed paws. Jackie clenched her teeth together, even though they didn't quite fit together the way they were supposed to when she was still human. If she lost control there in the hotel, she'd most likely be the last death in a bloody murder spree. The notion terrified her enough to drive the beast back within her darkest recesses.

The giant man glanced at Jackie and paused in his approach for a half a heartbeat. His nose wrinkled in an involuntary snarl, but he regained his composure right away. Jackie didn't miss it. The man's reaction was eerie in its similarity to her own.

The man placed one giant hand on the table, making it creak, and the other on the back of Gault's chair as he bent to whisper in the Frenchman's ear.

Gault looked up at the man for a moment. "Thank you, Sven." He wiped his mouth on his napkin and set the cloth over his plate. "Excuse me, *s'il vous plaît*. Something has come up that requires my attention. Thank you for indulging me tonight." He slid a card to Jackie. "Call my secretary to arrange a visit, Jacquelyn."

"I will very soon, Conrad."

Gault left the table with Sven, leaving Jackie and Mark alone.

"What is it, Jackie? What's the matter?" asked Mark.

Jackie realized she'd been clenching her teeth at Sven's back as she watched him cut a path through the crowded ballroom for his boss.

"Sorry. There was something about that man I didn't like. No idea what. Don't worry about it. I'm sure it's nothing a dessert and a ballet performance won't cure."

Mark smiled. "I'm looking forward to both."

Jackie smiled back, but she couldn't help glancing after Sven and Gault. She knew exactly what it was about the huge man that bothered her.

Sven was another werewolf.

Chapter Twelve

November 2012
Reno, Nevada

The two security men led Charlotte out to the circle drive where her car, undamaged and whole, sat in the valet drop-off parking with the door open. She turned to the men. "What is this?"

"Ma'am, I'm sorry, but I'm afraid you're going to have to leave hotel grounds."

Charlotte folded her arms and didn't move. "Oh?"

The men didn't back down. "Yes, ma'am. Whitney Peak policy clearly states that we can remove any person who is causing trouble for a guest."

"I'm a guest, aren't I?" She raised an eyebrow and cocked her head slightly, calculating the most likely moves to get the men to respond the way she wanted them to.

They had other ideas. "No, ma'am. We've reviewed our footage and the man you arrived with left some time ago. We have no record of you registering in the hotel or for the dinner. If you'll leave our property, we won't have to notify the police."

Charlotte reached into her clutch and both guards stiffened. She realized too late that Langdon must have smelled her pistol and notified hotel security. She probably shouldn't have brought it, but that would have been too risky altogether. Next time she'd have to be more cautious. She removed a slender billfold and closed the clutch again. "Easy, boys. What were you expecting, a gun or something? Is that what this so-called guest told you? That I'm an angry black woman?" She opened the billfold and started taking out hundred-dollar bills. "So, what's a plate at the dinner cost, five hundred? Here's six. What's a room cost? Here's another two hundred. And here's a gratuity for each of you. Now, tell me again about how I'm causing trouble."

The security officers looked at each other. Charlotte held out a thousand dollars in cash to them as if money meant little to her. It truly didn't. Eighty years of investing had made her wealthy.

The officers were a credit to their employer. Neither of them made the slightest move toward the offered payola. "I'm sorry, ma'am," one said, "but you need to leave the premises immediately or we'll be forced to notify the police and press criminal trespassing charges."

Conrad Gault walked out of the hotel alongside one of the largest men Charlotte had ever seen. The blond-haired giant made Raheem the Pakistani vampire look petite. His golden ponytail hung over one shoulder as he handed a paper stub to a valet and then walked to the curb with Gault. Ponytail glanced at Charlotte and made *the* face, twitching nostrils and ears.

She jumped a little, taken aback. Could he be a werewolf too? He looked a couple inches over seven feet and Charlotte guessed he weighed in the neighborhood of three-hundred fifty pounds. If he were a werewolf, he'd be utterly terrifying when transformed. All that mass, transformed into a razor-toothed killing machine, would make him more formidable than any opponent she'd faced.

She wondered if a silver bullet would even penetrate that massive frame.

"*Mademoiselle* Pastor, is everything all right?" Gault asked. His giant stood behind him, arms folded and glaring at Charlotte without trying to be subtle about it.

"Just a slight misunderstanding," said Charlotte. "Nothing to fret about. But you're leaving as well?"

"*Mais oui*. I've had a situation come up that requires my personal attention."

"A fragrance emergency?" Charlotte winked at him.

Gault laughed. "Not precisely, but that is a fine joke. I will have to remember it."

"Who's your big friend?"

"Sven is my personal assistant."

"Ma'am," said one of the security guards.

"All right, yes, I'm going." She climbed into her 'Vette and started the engine. Then she rolled down the window. "Conrad?"

He leaned down. Behind him, Sven stiffened. The giant looked like he could tip over her car with one hand and not break a sweat.

She revved her engine a couple times so the guards couldn't overhear her. "Did Jacquelyn happen to say what her plans were for later this evening?"

"I believe her companion mentioned the ballet."

Charlotte smiled at him. "Wonderful. Have a nice evening, Conrad. It was lovely to meet you."

"Likewise." He pressed a card into her hand. "If you're going to be in town for a while, give me a call. I would enjoy having dinner with you in a less-crowded setting."

"We'll see." She touched the button to roll the window back up and pulled away from the hotel. In her rear-view mirror, she saw Sven bend to whisper something in Gault's ear before an expensive custom Hummer obscured her view.

Charlotte shook her head, angry as she'd ever been since taking on the role of a hunter. She'd been spotted by two werewolves in one night, and instead of bagging them, she'd been the one to leave in humiliation. "You're getting soft in your old age," she said aloud, then grew sober. The mystery surrounding Langdon had only grown deeper now that Charlotte had met her in person. She pulled her car out of the circle and out into the evening traffic, only to swing into a parking lot a minute later so she could think.

Langdon was a werewolf, no question, and she had deduced Charlotte came to town after her. Prey who knew she was being hunted was the most dangerous of all. And what about White Fang? What had led a werewolf to take on the role of a crime-fighting vigilante? She couldn't imagine the convoluted circumstances that would lead to that. If Langdon had a need to put on a costume and put her abilities to use, why not join Just Cause?

The genetic test, of course. Parahumans were identified as such by the existence of a certain genetic structure common to nearly all of them. The exceptions were medical anomalies. People who had powers and didn't have the Musashi gene were rare enough to warrant lots of scientific inquiry. Unlike vampirism, which was a supernatural condition transmissible via a combination of bite and blood contamination, lycanthropes were genetic offshoots of humanity, and lycanthropy was a dominant gene. Given the current anti-parahuman bent in the American political and social environment, if humans learned about lycanthropes—and how to identify them genetically—it could bring about the kind of culling that might not stop with werewolves.

Langdon was only the tip of the iceberg. Sven was far more worrisome. She couldn't imagine him not being the head of a large colony of werewolves, and yet he was clearly subservient to Gault. What was Gault to have a pet werewolf waiting on him hand and foot? Werewolves gravitated to power, and colonies were invariably led by a strong alpha. Could Gault himself be an even stronger lycanthrope than Sven? If he was, he had a frightening level of self-control, for he had spoken with Charlotte at length and showed no sign whatsoever that he'd identified her as a vampire. That in turn raised an even more problematic question.

What if he *wasn't* a werewolf?

She shuddered to think what it might take for a human to be considered an alpha by *any* werewolf, never mind one of Sven's obvious power. She'd never heard of such a colossal beast, and that bothered her because monsters like him couldn't stay hidden for long. If Blackstone knew of Sven, he had neglected to share that detail with Charlotte. She wondered if Sven and Langdon knew each other or were in the same pack. A far larger colony could live here in this backward cow-town than anybody in the Midnight Collective had imagined. Should she call for backup?

No, she was being foolish. She had no evidence of a large pack in the area. At dinner, she had the sense that Gault and Langdon had met for the first time. That made it unlikely Sven and Langdon knew each other another, Because if they had, Sven would have asserted his dominance over Langdon and that would have been the end of White Fang.

What had Langdon been after with Gault? Charlotte had caught the pattern in the line of questions. Gault imported some rare and unusual ingredients, which in and of itself wasn't unusual for a fragrance designer, but the materials had apparently been delivered to Gault's residence instead of the labs in his factory. He'd been mixing up a special concoction at home. Something . . . secret.

She consulted the GPS on her smartphone. The ballet might afford a better opportunity to catch Langdon, and she owed the writer for the sneaky trick with the broken glass and hotel security. Although in retrospect, Charlotte had to give up grudging respect to the werewolf. It was a clever and devious way to be rid of her when Langdon could have as easily opened her throat and let her die where she fell.

For that reason alone, Charlotte wouldn't kill Langdon the next time she saw her.

Charlotte had hoped the Pioneer Center for the Performing Arts might be an older facility, with pools of shadow between lights, but it might as well have been daylight. A gaudy, golden geodesic dome stretched over the building with lights shining upon it to highlight it even more. She parked in the lot across Center Street, at the east end farthest from the facility. With the grace of practice, she slipped out of her little black cocktail dress without leaving the cramped seat of her car, pulled a cami over her head, and wiggled her hips into jeans. She then stuffed the wig into a plastic shopping bag and pulled a knit cap over her short hair. She finished off by replacing her heels with tennies and shrugging into her leather jacket. At last, she slipped the pistol out of her clutch and into her jacket pocket, where she could keep her hand on it.

She walked across the lot toward the PCPA with an unhurried pace. She was certain she'd arrived before Langdon . . . assuming Gault had given her good information. If she'd still been human, her pulse would have quickened at the crowd of people milling about the plaza before the entrance, waiting for the doors to open. Many enjoyed hot cider or coffee from the food carts doing brisk business in the chilly evening air. In order to better fit in, she bought a coffee and occasionally remembered to hold it up to her lips As she leaned against a convenient pillar that gave her a good view of the plaza. She should spot Langdon with plenty of time to act.

After another twenty minutes, the crowd thinned as people started to head into the Center to find their seats and Langdon still hadn't showed. Charlotte was beginning to think she'd been played for a fool. Or else Gault had been incorrect. Or perhaps Langdon and Mark had decided to skip the ballet altogether.

Then she saw them, Langdon wrapped in a long gray overcoat with a flowing white scarf, Mark in a ski parka with a shapeless knit cap. They approached at an easy pace, chatting like close friends. Charlotte could almost hear their laughter amid the buzz of other conversations surrounding her. She threw her cup of coffee into a trash can and approached the couple with her hands in her pockets, finger resting on the trigger of her pistol.

Langdon's nose wrinkled just before she found Charlotte in the crowd. "That's her," Charlotte heard her say, and moments later she was surrounded by a half dozen plainclothes police officers with their guns drawn.

She could have taken them all and won, but the Collective had protocols, and the primary goal was to cooperate with human law enforcement in order to avoid being identified as a vampire. Charlotte raised her hands and interlaced her fingers behind her head as she smiled at Langdon with grudging admiration. Werewolves were a cunning breed, but this went far beyond the crude traps they liked to set for hunters. She'd underestimated Langdon's ability to observe and plan, and it had gotten her in a world of potential trouble. Goddamn werewolves.

"Officers," she said in as clear a voice as possible so as to avoid any misunderstanding. "I have a weapon in the right front pocket of my jacket and my identification is in the inside left pocket. I have no intention of resisting and will cooperate fully." She hoped the Reno police weren't as trigger-happy as some she'd run across in other cities.

Fortunately, instead of shooting first, they cuffed her. She submitted to it without complaint or resistance. One of the officers withdrew the pistol from her pocket and another retrieved her pocketbook.

"Looks like you were right, Ms. Langdon," said the cop who'd confiscated Charlotte's gun. "Will you want to press charges?"

Langdon looked at Charlotte. "I expect so. I'll discuss it with my lawyer in the morning."

"She won't be going anywhere before then, I can promise you that. Maybe not for a lot longer if a judge won't set a bond for her."

"Thank you, officer, for looking out for our safety." Langdon smiled.

"Anytime, Ms. Langdon. Sorry for the interruption. Enjoy the rest of your evening."

"We will." Langdon and Mark walked into the ballet, leaving a handcuffed Charlotte behind in police custody.

Charlotte waited, impatient, for the catch-and-release code to turn up on her name. Langdon had played her twice in one evening, and that was more than anyone else had in decades. Charlotte decided that any goodwill she might have had just worn out.

"ID comes back clean with no warrants," reported a voice over the radio.

"Miss Pastor, you're under arrest for stalking and carrying a concealed weapon without a permit. You have the right to remain silent . . ." A female officer went through the arrest ritual. "Do you understand these rights as I have explained them to you?"

Stunned, Charlotte mumbled, "Yes." She didn't understand how this was happening. Why would they ignore a catch-and-release code? This wasn't some backwoods town where the people were all inbred and the Sheriffs had names like Bubba or Cletus and figured laws didn't apply to people who were the wrong color or gender. The Reno police should see the code on her file, apologize, return her weapon, and let her go. Instead, the female officer patted her down and escorted her to a police car.

Something was very wrong.

Charlotte could have burst the handcuffs apart, raced away, and climbed the nearest building in a few heartbeats, soaking up every shot the police took at her. Oh, how tempting it was! But she didn't dare blow her cover. In situations like this, when the entire weight of vampirekind rested on her head, she had to remain calm. An officer placed her hand on Charlotte's head so she wouldn't bang it on the edge of the door as she climbed into the back of the police car. The hard, plastic seat stank of disinfectant.

Two female uniformed officers took her to the county jail, where she was searched again and asked a series of questions by a civilian employee. She answered "no" to all of them; she didn't have any medical conditions, she hadn't been drinking or using drugs, she wasn't pregnant.

This kind of thing wasn't supposed to happen, especially not to her. She was one of the Collective's top agents, and she'd been bagged and tagged. It was so unprofessional she was surprised she hadn't been letting her fangs hang out on top of everything else.

Someone must have altered her records in the NCIC database. It was the only explanation, since the catch-and-release had been in place when she had been pulled over by the California trooper on her way to Nevada. Sometime between then and now, she had become a cipher and a criminal.

She asked for and received permission to make a phone call. She considered calling Blackstone first, but she'd have a lot of explaining to do to him, and it would make him angry. His confidence in her would be broken since she'd been bested by a single werewolf who hadn't even transformed. No, she couldn't call him. Not even to warn him that her NCIC profile had apparently been compromised.

Without warning, Ana's face popped into her mind. Couldn't she call her former lover for help? No, of course she couldn't. Ana had made her choice, and Charlotte had been left to twist in the sunlight. If their roles had been reversed, Charlotte wouldn't even have accepted a phone call from Ana, much less gone to help her. That was a dead end.

Then she had it, the one man she knew she could trust. She dialed the number. "Nick? I'm in trouble . . ."

Chapter Thirteen

November 2012
Reno, Nevada

The ballet was very good, and even though sitting still for so long was difficult so close to her time of transformation, Jackie enjoyed it. Some of the acrobatic feats achieved by the performers would have been difficult for a werewolf with superhuman strength, never mind a normal human. She wondered if dancing might not be a good hobby for her. She already had superhuman strength, stamina, and speed, but in the end White Fang was only a brawler, with unscientific and undisciplined combat techniques. She'd avoided the obvious solution of martial arts for fear of losing control and transforming during an aggressive training session. Acrobatic dancing might be a useful tool in her crusade, and she decided to have Jenn check into it.

At intermission, Mark was borderline clingy, standing well within Jackie's personal space. It wasn't chauvinistic protectiveness; if anything, Mark seemed genuinely frightened and had latched onto Jackie as someone who could defend him. "You okay, Mark?"

"I guess that thing with the stalker kind of freaked me out, especially after the other night in the . . . the alley. And you're just like, whatever. It's like it didn't bother you at all."

"Sure, it bothered me. I mean, it bothers me," Jackie said. "But it's over. She's gone, so I'm trying to get on with my life and enjoy the ballet."

"Why do you think she was after you?"

"I don't know." Jackie frowned as the lobby lights flashed to indicate the end of intermission. "But she went to a lot of trouble to track me down. I guess the *Silverback* series affects some people in strange ways."

The lights in the hall darkened. A spotlight picked up the conductor as he walked to his podium to polite applause. He raised his baton and the orchestra began the overture.

By the time the performers took their final bows, the clock was pushing midnight and Jackie felt the tug of a moon fast approaching full.

Tomorrow, she'd be in the cage.

Clouds of steam came from Mark's mouth as they walked back toward Jackie's car. "The moon looks beautiful tonight."

The evening chill had become frosty and Jackie smelled a hint of approaching snow. The moon sat behind high, icy clouds and lit them with its purifying, terrifying white glow. Jackie didn't glance upward. She didn't like to be reminded of what was to come. "Listen, I'm pretty tired. It's been a long day and I'm not going to be great company much longer. What say I take you home?"

"Yeah, okay."

The ten-minute drive back to the Hu household was quiet. Jackie turned her words over and over in her mind until they gnawed at her insides. She realized she didn't know how to have *friends*. Sure, she had Alix and Dominica and Jenn, but they *knew* her. The *real* her. She couldn't just share that with anyone. As Jenn had reminded her, she had security to consider. It was painful to realize everything she knew about how real friendships formed came from books and movies. How pathetic was that?

Jackie pulled her car in front of *Hu Makes Fireworks*. A light burned upstairs in the apartment over the shop.

"Mark, thank you for coming with me tonight. I'm sorry to be such a wet blanket."

Mark's smile was so kind and genuine that Jackie almost opened up to him right then and there. "It's okay, Jackie. I had a really good time tonight." He laughed. "Best date I've had in months . . . and it was with a lesbian."

Mark went to the door of the shop, turned back to wave once, and let himself inside.

Jackie took a deep breath and said aloud what she wished she could have said to Mark. "I'm a werewolf, and I'm afraid of accidentally killing you. Sorry in advance if I tear you apart when all you want to do is hug me."

She drove home, left her car in the driveway, and stumbled inside. Frustration, arousal, nervous aggression, and exhaustion all mixed together to make her feel like she'd been awake for two days. Her bedroom seemed too far away, so she fell onto a couch and curled up like a dog. She drifted to sleep plagued by dreams of bright white circles in fields of darkness.

* * *

Distant voices dredged her out of the murkiness of sleep into a morning with jarring sunlight blazing in through east-facing windows. Alix and Jenn had barged right into her house and were walking all over the place like they owned it.

"Good morning, Jackie. Rough night?" Jenn handed her a steaming mug of coffee and a terrycloth bathrobe. She felt loose threads against her skin, looked down, and saw that in her sleep she'd clawed her silk shirt to tatters.

"Where's my sunglasses? And close those goddamn blinds." She swiped the coffee from Jenn, who stepped back to avoid being splashed by Jackie's careless movements.

Alix adjusted the blinds so the living room became darker. "Jackie, we've talked about this. Do your meditation and breathing exercises. You've got to get your pre-transformation temper under control."

Jackie drained half her cup in one swallow. "You couldn't let me sleep in?"

"We did," said Jenn. "It's past nine."

"Don't see how anyone can sleep when the two of you are babbling." Jackie shut her eyes, feeling the caffeine start to leach into her boiling bloodstream to take the edge from her temper.

Jenn glanced at Alix. "How was the dinner and the ballet?"

"Odd." Jackie finished her coffee. "There was this woman at dinner. She smelled weird. Like she wasn't exactly alive."

"A zombie? Like those two you saved Mark from?" asked Alix.

"They're not zombies. They're possessed by demons. And no, she was still vibrant and seemed lively instead of decaying. But she had a gun in her purse with silver bullets."

Alix looked taken aback. "How do you know? And what's this about demons?"

"Ask Dominica. I could smell the bullets. She was there to kill me. Of course, she was. Why would anyone carry silver bullets except to kill a werewolf?"

"That's a little far-fetched, even for you," said Jenn. "Maybe she had silver jewelry in her purse or something."

"I could smell the powder in the bullets. Don't you think I've been shot at enough to know the scent when I come across it?" Jackie snarled. "She had a gun with silver bullets, and she was after me. I dropped hotel security on her at the Whitney Peak, but then she turned up at the ballet as well. Luckily, I notified the police before we arrived, and they arrested her. Wouldn't want anything to happen to their local writer celebrity."

"Where is she now?" asked Jenn.

"Still in jail, I guess, unless she got bailed out." Jackie shook her head, trying to clear an itch that wouldn't go away. She could feel the transformation looming. "There's something else. Conrad Gault has a pet werewolf." She couldn't deny it. To do so would only lead to more trouble in the future. "I guess I always knew there would be others, that I couldn't be the only one. This guy is huge, though. If he's well-trained, I don't know if I could take him."

"You may have to sooner rather than later." Jenn's expression had turned grim. She handed a *Reno Gazette-Journal* to Jackie.

Splashed across the front page was the headline: *Police stumped by multiple disappearances*. With a sinking feeling in the pit of her stomach, Jackie read further. It wasn't two women who were missing, it was eight people over the past week. The last two had disappeared while she was at dinner and the ballet with Mark, pretending to be domesticated instead of patrolling the streets. Police had released some details on the missing people in the hopes anyone with information might come forward. They had no suspects and were recommending pedestrians avoid traveling alone at night.

"Son of a bitch!" Jackie threw the newspaper onto the coffee table. "How did we miss this? Eight people. And going on for a fucking week!"

She stalked to the bathroom to splash water on her face. As her rage grew, she felt the beast threatening to come out early.

Jenn followed her. "Jackie, I know you wanted to keep White Fang an urban legend, but maybe it's time to get some allies in the police department. Unless you want to give up this ridiculous charade altogether, anyway. You're writer, not a superhero."

"This isn't about being a superhero, Jenn." Jackie pointed at Jenn, water dripping from her face. "It's about me trying to do the right thing. I'm a fucking werewolf. I could be baying at the full moon and tearing victims to shreds once a month because that's my nature. But I'm trying to be better than that, and if that means using what cursed abilities I have to make this city a better place, then that's what I'm going to do."

"So, what are you going to do?" Jenn asked. "Climb the outside of the Silver Legacy? Break into Conrad Gault's penthouse looking for kidnap victims?"

"If I have to, yes."

"You don't even know if they're there."

Jackie went to the elevator. Jenn and Alix followed, the sour smell of concern radiating from both of them. "I don't know they're not there, either. What I do know is that Gault smells like deception. The act, not the cologne. Plus, he's got a werewolf with him, and he's got the ingredients for Dominica's magic demon-possessed zombie potion. That's enough reason for me to make him my number one suspect." Her tongue wandered over her teeth. They felt sharper than they should have. It was close.

The elevator reached the mine floor. Dominica looked over from her console, ramen noodles hanging out of her mouth and some complicated strategy game playing out on her monitor. "Whuh?" She slurped in the noodles and swallowed. "Are we working?"

"We are." Jackie scratched at the back of her hand. The fine, pale hair there had grown longer, darker, and thicker. "Get me something on these eight victims and Mark. Anything to connect them. If they all drink decaf, I want to know. If none of them ever saw *Titanic*, I want to know."

Dominica looked taken aback. "Okay, boss, I'm on it."

"Jackie, what are you doing?" Alix interposed herself between Jackie and the White Fang suit.

"What does it look like I'm doing? I'm gearing up. Move."

"No." Alix folded her arms. "You're not going anywhere. It's too close to the full moon and you're a danger to others."

"I said move!" Jackie snarled. The beast was very close now but she wouldn't let it consume her. Not when she had important work to do. She reached out to move Alix aside and Jenn closed her hands around Jackie's arm.

"Jackie, stop it. You're out of control."

Jackie whirled and gnashed her teeth at Jenn, and Alix took the opportunity to plunge a syringe into Jackie's neck.

Jackie roared in fury and clawed at the plastic tube dangling from her neck. Jenn and Alix scurried away.

"Jesus!" Dominica sounded terrified.

"Bitches . . ." Jackie's words slurred, and she realized she was already seeing double. Tears of rage streamed down her cheeks. "Kill . . . you . . ."

"We'll do what we can, Jackie," said the blur that was Jenn. "And hopefully have answers for you after tomorrow."

Jackie's eyes fell shut, and she felt herself dragged across the floor. The sedative wouldn't last long as the transformation roared upon her, but it would hold her long enough for her friends to move her safely into the cage.

The last thing Jackie heard clearly was the rattle of iron as they locked her into the cage.

Chapter Fourteen

November 2012
Reno, Nevada

The rest of the night passed, and the following day, and Charlotte stayed in her cell as a parade of prostitutes, drug addicts, drunks, and perpetrators of domestic violence passed in and out. She was under the impression the police were waiting for Langdon to come in and file charges. It was too close to the full moon, and Charlotte intended to be long gone by the time Langdon got past her monthly transformation.

Sure enough, as the wall clock in the booking lobby pushed toward five o'clock in the afternoon, and Charlotte had been a guest of the city for the better part of a day, a desk officer unlocked her cell door, saying her attorney had arrived.

Old Nick awaited her in at the booking desk, wearing a rumpled suit and a dour expression. His unseen power flowed outward, making the police more agreeable with his suggestions. A half hour later, Nick escorted Charlotte out of the jail and into a long, black Lincoln Town Car with a rental agency's sticker in the rear window.

"Classy ride for an old guy," Charlotte said. The sun already hid behind the highest mountains to the west and the sky quickly darkened. Cold wind raced down from those distant mountaintops, bringing a chill to the late fall air in the city, although she had to make herself remember how to feel it. Somewhere nearby, someone in Old Town burned mesquite wood in a fireplace, adding its tang to the breeze.

"I asked for a sports car, but this was all they had available on short notice," Nick said. "Damn yuppies and their tastes." He threw Charlotte's file folder into the back seat. Papers scattered about, but he didn't even glance back at them.

"How'd you pull off the lawyer thing?"

"I *am* a lawyer. I've passed the bar in twenty-eight states. It was a hobby of mine for a while back in the Seventies."

"Nicky, what's going on? Why didn't my catch-and-release code show up on my ID?"

"I checked into it. Your file has been completely wiped. As far as it's concerned, you're just a name and a face. No special handling, no get-out-of-jail-free card. You're a civilian again."

"How could someone get to my file? I thought hunter files were supposed to be encrypted and secure."

Nick smiled as he drove the big car out into early evening traffic. "Nightfall, you're still thinking like it's fifty years ago. Any talented hacker can get through encryption with enough motivation and processing power behind them. Hell, I've heard rumors there are parahumans who can do it without a computer at all. Nothing is secure anymore if someone wants to get to it."

"Okay, so I don't know computer shit. *Why* would somebody burn me like that?"

"Made any enemies lately? Step on any toes?"

Unbidden, an image of Anastasia popped into Charlotte's mind, lips parted for a kiss, eyes half-closed. The image melded into the wide, leering face of Raheem the Pakistani. Ana would never have done such a thing. At least, Charlotte needed to believe that. She didn't think Raheem had cause to hate her to the point of ruining her career, and possibly her life. "I'm always stepping on somebody's toes, but never like this."

"Look, whatever happened, somebody has got your number. You've been cut loose and hung out to dry. No file means you no longer exist in the Collective database. Technically, I'm violating Collective policies even by speaking to you right now, never mind helping you. You're a rogue, Nightfall, and I don't have to remind you what that means."

The thought of a vampire hit team being dispatched to take her out would have made Charlotte's blood run cold if she'd had any. "That's ridiculous, Nick. Blackstone knows me. Call him. We can straighten this out."

"He's not in the office. I'm not even sure he's in the country. He left on business the day after you did. Maybe he could vouch for you, but I wouldn't count on anybody else."

"What about Ana?"

"She doesn't have any authority to override a rogue designation. Neither do I. Do you know anyone further east? Anyone with clout?"

Charlotte shook her head. She hadn't been to any Midnight Collective offices outside of San Francisco in three decades.

"That's it, then. You're staked out in the sun."

Charlotte frowned, and an ugly idea formed in her mind. She glanced sidelong at Nick as he drove. Had they sent *him* to do the deed? He didn't seem any different, still the good old crabby and cantankerous man she'd met all those years ago when she first joined the Collective. Of course, with his ability, he could have her smiling and nodding even as he pulled out a pistol and put a hardwood bullet through her heart.

"I can already tell what you're thinking." Nick ran a yellow light. "And no, I'm not here to kill you. I came because you called, not because they sent me. They might know I'm gone, but they don't know where I went. I may not be the oldest vampire in the Collective, but the day one of those punks outsmarts me is the day I take a long walk in the noonday sun."

"Oh, please, Nick, you're going to outlive us all, you canny old bastard."

"I don't know about everyone else, but if you're being targeted like I think, I'll certainly outlive you."

"Maybe if I bring them the head of White Fang, they'll feel different about it."

"You know where to find him?"

Charlotte's smile was devoid of humor. "He's a she, and I'm not completely incompetent when it comes to computers. Let me use your phone." He passed it to her and after a few minutes of creative internet searches, she found Langdon's address by searching the Washoe County property tax database.

"That's good work," Nick said, typing the address into the car's GPS. "Nice to know I don't have a complete novice in you."

"You have a gun?"

Nick snorted as if it were a foolish question. "Glove compartment."

Charlotte opened it and found a black case containing a Glock semiautomatic pistol, a shoulder holster, and a magazine of silverpoints. "This'll do." The police had confiscated her own pistol as evidence. They'd find the silver bullets an oddity, but since they had her pegged as a celebrity stalker, it might make sense to them that someone obsessed with werewolves would carry them.

Nick glanced at her as she loaded the clip and primed it. "Going to shoot first and ask questions later?"

"I'm a werewolf hunter. It's all I've done for thirty years, Nicky."

"Has White Fang killed anyone?"

Charlotte shrugged out of her jacket to strap on the shoulder holster. "Not as far as I know, although she's left a lot of pain in her wake." In fact, her research had turned up a lot of assaults and injuries requiring hospitalization. Broken limbs, lacerations, a truly staggering amount of dental reconstruction. The official police department policy was to *detain for questioning* if an officer happened across the nighttime vigilante. Charlotte had read enough news quotes and seen enough video clips to suspect that, to the lowly beat cops, White Fang had earned their grudging respect for her efforts to clean up the rampant crime, and perhaps they might look the other way given the opportunity to do so.

White Fang was a werewolf, but she wasn't a killer, and that contradicted everything Charlotte had ever learned about the species.

"Maybe she's not the threat somebody thinks she is," Nick said.

"What do you mean?"

"You were sent here to *deal with* her, right? That has to mean killing her."

"I'm supposed to use my judgment."

Nick snorted. "You can't fool me. You've already made up your mind."

"Have I?"

"Someone went to all the trouble of removing your files from the Collective registry. They made you illegitimate, a renegade. They wanted you to take down White Fang without knowing you'd been cut loose from the Collective. Then they'd flag you for an unsanctioned kill and you'd be hunted down yourself."

Although the Collective dispatched its hunters to slay werewolves, it did so with careful planning so as not to raise the interest of humans—or parahumans, now that they were a factor in daily lives. A rogue hunter leaving a trail of bodies in his or her wake was likely to attract the wrong sort of attention. The right person following that trail could blow the secret of vampires wide open, and then the entire world would be after them. When the Collective dedicated itself to protecting vampirekind, that occasionally meant culling their own to preserve their secrecy. Someone had laid all the groundwork for the Collective to cull Charlotte after she fulfilled her mission, and the only person who could vouch for her was missing in action.

"So, are you saying I shouldn't take her out? She's a werewolf." She pulled her jacket back on and zipped it up to hide the gun from view.

"Just because some Germans bombed London doesn't mean they were all bad people. I'm just saying go into this with your eyes and ears open, Charlotte. You're a smart girl. Don't be somebody else's fool."

"I'll keep it in mind, Nicky."

"What's your plan?" Nick steered around the winding curves as they ascended above the valley.

"It's close to moonrise, and tonight's the full moon," said Charlotte. "There's no history of animal attacks in this area—at least, not from what I could find in the news database. Langdon's got to be locked up somewhere. I'm guessing she's got somebody working with her. Maybe that young guy she was with yesterday. She couldn't go into the full-scale crimefighting business without a support staff. We're going to use your ability to talk to them. Then we're going to deal with White Fang. Then we're going back to San Francisco and find out who's got it in for me." Maybe White Fang was doing some good in Reno, and from the short time she'd spent in it, the city needed *someone* to do good.

She just didn't think a werewolf was the best solution.

"Sounds reasonable to me. Ah, here we are." The Lincoln's GPS directed them onto a gravel drive. Langdon's house would be at the top of the steep driveway.

Nick drove the car into the circle drive before the large house. Charlotte smelled the faint vanilla-orange tang of pine and incipient snow. It was late dusk with clear skies overhead. She listened for a moment to the whisper of wind through pine needles both nearby and the gentle roar from across the canyon. It would be a beautiful night, but a cold one. She'd have been miserable were she still alive.

She went up to the heavy oak door and rang the bell. Nick stood beside her, hands clasped behind his back as he looked thoughtfully up at the horizon, already aglow with the approaching moon.

A young woman answered the door. Charlotte appraised her with cool detachment. Bobbed blonde hair, glasses, lip gloss. She had the look of someone who habitually wore professional attire but had dressed down for the evening in yoga pants, a t-shirt for the band *A Week's Worth of Jane*, and fuzzy slippers.

The young woman looked at the two vampires on her doorstep. "Can I help you?"

"Yes, is this Jackie Langdon's residence? I'm a huge fan of her work." Charlotte gushed like a fangirl.

"No, I'm sorry, you have the wrong address." The young woman tried to shut the door.

Charlotte put her hand on it to keep it from closing. "I'm sure this is the right place. I need to speak with her."

The woman's eyes narrowed. "You're that woman who accosted her at the ballet. Alix, call the police."

"Hold on, love, let's not get all hasty." Nick's affable words carried his power across the doorstep. "Perhaps we could come in and talk this over first. We're not here to raise a fuss."

"Exactly." Charlotte felt herself in complete agreement with Nick despite being fully aware of his power. "We just want to talk to Ms. Langdon."

"Who are you people?" The young woman was resisting Nick's Jedi Mind Trick.

Another woman, larger and with a curvaceous figure, stepped into view beyond the young woman. She wore clean hospital scrubs and had her red hair caught up in a bun. She held a phone in one hand but hadn't yet raised it to her head. Perhaps she was more susceptible to Nick's ability. "Why don't you let them in, Jenn?"

"Well . . . all right. Come on in. I'm Jenn. This is Alix."

Charlotte and Nick stepped over the threshold into Langdon's house even though they needn't have waited. It was a myth that vampires couldn't enter a domicile without invitation. The house wasn't like any colony den Charlotte had encountered before. It was filled with expensive furnishings and tasteful art, cozy without being confining. The high airy ceilings made the place seem cavernous.

"Ms. Langdon is on deadline," Jenn said. "She can't be disturbed. So how can we help you?"

"I'm Charlotte, and this is Nick—" Charlotte broke off as she spotted some movement beyond one of the windows.

It was White Fang, staring into the house with her jaw hanging open in frank surprise beneath the wolf's-head cowl.

"Son of a bitch!" Charlotte launched herself across the living room and dove fist-first through the window. Glass crashed all around her as she hit the ground and rolled up to her feet with her gun out.

White Fang shrieked and ran into the trees, slipping and sliding down the steep slope.

Charlotte aimed her gun, but the vigilante had put too many trees between them, and she couldn't get a clean shot off. "Shit." She shoved the gun back into her holster and kicked off her shoes. With finger and toe claws spread wide, she gave chase.

They scrambled down the mountainside. White Fang half-ran, half-fell as she dodged around pine trees and boulders in the near darkness. Charlotte leaped from boulder to boulder, using the higher vantage points to choose her path. She sprang from the top of a short rise and caught a pine tree bole between her feet. She ricocheted from it immediately, crossing behind the flailing fugitive and just missed her. White Fang veered away, stumbling on the slope as Charlotte balanced on a rock the size of a car, and then hit her with a flying tackle. They rolled down and came to a stop against a dried-out pine tree that dropped a thousand needles on them from the impact.

Charlotte straddled White Fang, squeezing her with her thighs. She forced the vigilante's arms across together and held them with only one hand. With the other, she grabbed the cowl by its ears and ripped it off White Fang's head, realizing as she did so the woman wore regular street clothes.

To her surprise, underneath the cowl was not Jackie Langdon, but a young Hispanic woman she didn't recognize.

"Don't kill me! Please don't kill me!" the woman cried in fear and shock.

"You're not Langdon." Charlotte was surprised and angry with herself. She should have known it was a ruse the moment she saw the vigilante. The realization she'd been cut loose from the Collective had her more rattled than she thought.

"No shit, lady. What the hell are you?" The woman's eyes bulged out as she saw Charlotte's talons and fangs, which had unconsciously emerged in the thrill of the pursuit. "Don't kill me! I'm just the techie!"

"You're not really White Fang, are you?"

"No! God, no!"

"Why are you wearing her mask?"

"You're gonna kill me, aren't you? *Madre de Dios*!"

Charlotte stood and lifted the blubbering woman off the ground with her fingers twisted in the fabric of her bodysuit. "I'm not going to kill you, but you're going to take me to Langdon right now. Hurry. I want to see her before the moon rises."

The young woman scrambled back up the slope toward the house. Charlotte paced her, carrying the cowl like a trophy, nudging her with the tips of her claws every time she hesitated.

"You know the truth about her, don't you?" The woman recovered from her fear with remarkable alacrity when she realized Charlotte wasn't going to kill her. Perhaps being around a werewolf all the time had inured her to some of the more frightening aspects of undead and unnatural creatures.

Charlotte didn't reply, instead jabbing her once more with her claws.

"Ow! Shit. She's going to be pissed if you damage me. Without me, she's just a chick in a mask. And it cost a buttload to make that mask. Quit sticking your damn claws into it."

Charlotte closed a hand on the woman's shoulder from behind, holding her in place. She leaned in close and whispered, "What's your name?"

"D-Dominica." Her bravado evaporated once more.

"Well, D-Dominica, you may well be indispensable to her, but I bet you could continue your good work with a pint less blood than you started the day with." She traced a gentle claw down the side of Dominica's neck. "You follow me?"

"I'm sorry! I'll behave!"

"See that you do." When they returned to the house, Nick was doing his best with his ability to keep the other women calm, but they were too edgy to remain that way for long. When Charlotte and her captive entered the house, whatever spell Nick had woven was shattered like the window Charlotte had broken through.

"Oh my God! Dominica, are you all right?" Alix rushed to Dominica's side to check her for injuries, clucking in dismay with each scrape and cut she found.

"She's a . . . she's a vampire, I think," Dominica said with a sniffle. "She said I have to take her to see Jackie, or else."

"I think that's a very good idea," Nick said, confidence flowing outward in all directions.

Jenn shook her head, still fighting against Nick's power. "No. You need to leave. I'm going to call the police."

"Listen to us, Jenn, we're here to help," Nick said.

"Yes, listen to them," said Alix.

"They're here to help," said Dominica. "Ow! That's still attached to me."

"Sorry." Alix worked with tweezers to pull splinters from Dominica's side.

"Why were you wearing the mask?" asked Charlotte. "To fool me? Did you know I was coming?"

"No, we didn't know," said Alix.

"I heard your car pull up outside and so I left by the back door instead of the elevator, because it's real noisy," said Dominica. "I knew someone was hunting Jackie. I thought maybe I could—I don't know, throw you off the trail or something."

"You didn't really think this through, did you?" Nick asked.

"So, sue me. I'm still new to this nighttime vigilante thing."

Charlotte nodded. "Here's the truth. I was sent here to kill her. But now I'm thinking that might cause more problems than leaving her alone. I need to talk to her."

"You want to kill her?" Jenn leaped to her feet.

"Relax, nobody's going to kill anybody," Nick said.

"No killing," said Alix and Dominica in chorus.

"I'm not going to kill her." Charlotte must have succumbed to Nick's ability. She hadn't already made the decision to let Langdon live, had she? "Take me to see her. Quickly, before she transforms."

"You may as well." Nick wandered over to a wall to examine a painting.

"Downstairs," Dominica said. "Ow, what are you using, Doc, acid?"

"Alcohol, dear," Alix said. "Jackie is downstairs in the mine."

"What does it matter now?" Jenn rested her chin on her hands. "You already know what she is. It's all over. The whole thing's shot to hell. I may as well take you downstairs myself. I'm so fired for this."

They took Charlotte and Nick into a hidden elevator that went below the house into what had to be an old silver mine. Charlotte shivered at the idea of the werewolf living and working amid poison. "That's a scary ability you've got, Nick," she whispered, just loud enough for him to hear over the humming and clanks of the elevator.

"It's barely working on her," Nick said, inclining his head toward Jenn. "Never ran into so much resistance to it before. She must have a natural immunity to it or something."

"Immunity, hell. She's in love with Langdon."

"You think?"

Off to one side of the repurposed mine, Jackie Langdon writhed in a cage off to one side. A pelt of fine gray fur worked its way out of her naked skin. A stub of tail protruded from the base of her spine, which was wrenching into the characteristic curvature of a wolf. Her fingers compressed into toes while her hips bent forward. Tears of pain leaked from sulfurous yellow eyes and ran down an already lengthened face. She howled with the agony of her body's reshaping.

Charlotte had witnessed werewolves' transformations before, but it was the first time it had happened to someone she'd met, someone with whom she'd shared a meal. Werewolves as humans normally behaved similarly to their bestial counterparts. They were aggressive, boorish, vicious, and cruel. Langdon hadn't been any of those things. Everything about her indicated she was loyal, self-controlled, and honorable.

Was it possible she retained those traits in animal form?

For the first time, Charlotte thought about what it must really be like to be a werewolf, instead of thinking about the best way to kill one. To have one's personality and body stripped away, fully aware of what was happening, must have been horrifying. Werewolves lived with the monthly loss of their humanity. Was it any wonder they went insane, submerging their human personalities beneath layers of brutal instinct?

One of Charlotte's first coaches at the Collective had taught an unusual philosophy: killing werewolves was a kindness, a way to heal the tortured spirits of those men and women trapped in the decaying cycle of insanity. She'd discounted it as sentimental garbage, preferring simply to pull the trigger without considering the implications.

Charlotte realized her hand was inside her jacket, closed around the grip of her pistol. She was prepared out of habit to put Langdon out of her misery forever, but doubt filled her mind. She might be the most important member of her species ever—a werewolf that could live in peace among humans.

When Charlotte pulled her hand back out of her jacket, it was empty. Langdon's eyes met hers and Charlotte saw a spark of humanity. Langdon lunged forward against the bars. "Please," she hissed through malformed lips. "Stop Gault. The Alchemist. You have to stop him. He's going to do something . . . something terrible . . ."

Somewhere above, the Moon broke past the horizon, and Jackie Langdon completed her unwilling transformation. The beast battered herself bloody against the cage bars as she tried to get out. Again and again, she closed her jaws around the bars, snarling and spitting.

Charlotte watched the creature's fury as she struggled to get out. In her final moments of lucidity, Langdon hadn't begged for her life, or tried to bargain like so many had in the past. Instead, she'd pleaded for Charlotte's help. Even in the ordeal of losing her humanity, Langdon was still trying to be a hero instead of a monster. Charlotte turned to look at Jenn, Alix, and Dominica. They all looked miserable and sickened at Langdon's plight. Dominica kicked at the floor and wouldn't look at Langdon. Alix watched with clinical detachment, but her fingers drummed against her tightly folded arms with concern. Tears streamed unchecked down Jenn's cheeks as she chewed on her thumbnail. They must have seen the transformation several times by now, and yet their concern was evident.

A werewolf . . . who'd befriended humans and fought to protect them instead of hunting them for food and sport.

Amazing.

Charlotte raised her voice enough to be heard over the wolf's cries of fury. "Maybe you all had better tell me what's going on."

Chapter Fifteen

November 2012
Reno, Nevada

Strips of flesh tear away from soft white throats wet sounds of fresh meat fill head with madness belly with hunger so long since it could be assuaged by the slaying of meat to kill the thrill of jaws upon flesh the pain of teeth against bone steel bars harder than any bone to dash oneself senseless against until the blood falls like rain beating in heart beating in stomach beating in head from the fear of the cage soft creatures of meat and one of death watch like predators viewing another's slashing kill swatting through the cage bars at the flesh of the others unable to do more than bite the bars steel tastes sharp like fresh blood aching with the desire to maul and kill not just for food but for pleasure only flesh nothing else can satiate.

Hunger
Hunger
Hunger

Chapter Sixteen

November 2012
Reno, Nevada

"Look, it all sounds really far-fetched," Charlotte said. She and Nick had been regaled with tales of demonic zombie kidnappers, alchemy, and disappearing women. Jenn, Alix, and Dominica had talked over each other until Nick had to utilize his ability to calm them all down.

"Says the vampire in the werewolf's house." Jenn blew her nose into a tissue and deposited it into a wastebasket she'd set beside the couch. Her eyes were rimmed with red and her cheeks puffy from crying. Charlotte felt sorry for her; the young woman's love for Jackie was evident in every move and having to watch the werewolf's monthly torment was torture.

"It's not as far-fetched as you might think," Nick said. "When I was in my twenties, there was a lot of interest in matters of the occult in London. This would have been in the last several years of the Nineteenth Century for those of you keeping track. There was a great deal of talk about magic and alchemy and such at the time."

"Did anyone happen to mention making zombies with alchemy?" Alix asked.

"Reanimation of dead tissue was of great fascination to certain sects back then. They called them walking corpses, and they were prized for their unflagging ability to follow orders." Nick grew sober. "I saw some. They were frightening beings. Utterly devoted to whomever controlled them. They would have made a formidable army, had the sects stopped squabbling among themselves and united. We could have a very different world today, with legions of undead soldiers marching across battlefields. With proper chemical and ritual treatment, every dead human would expand the army. The alchemy prepared the body to become a mount for an enslaved demon, and the ritual summoned the nefarious creature and bound it within the flesh."

"Somebody retained that knowledge, and now apparently Gault has access to it," Charlotte said

"And he's using them to kidnap people. Does anybody want coffee or anything? I have to do something, or I'll go crazy." Jenn paced behind the couches.

Nobody wanted any. Charlotte could have gone for a pint of sexy blonde assistant, Latina techie, or redheaded doctor, but she kept that thought to herself.

"Jackie had the right idea about correlating the victims," Alix said. "Why these particular people? What do they—and Mark—have in common? They're all local to the Old Town area, but beyond that I can't see any pattern except that they were somewhere alone when taken. The youngest is eighteen. The oldest thirty. They're not all the same race. They're not working in similar jobs. Fast food. Housecleaning. Courier. Even a nun, of all things."

Nick looked up with interest. "A nun, you say?"

Charlotte turned to him. "You've got something?"

"I'm not sure. But it could be related. Let's say Gault is working powerful black magic. Something that needs special and rare components. He can get those in his line of work, but this summoning spell is much older, and requires a sacrifice."

Jenn stopped pacing and clutched the back of the couch. "What kind of sacrifice?"

Nick shrugged. "Virgin blood is reputed to be a powerful elixir. I've never had the pleasure myself, but I rather suspect he's not going to be the one drinking it."

Alix stood up from her chair and stalked to a corner of the room, her ears burning red.

Charlotte could tell that she was offended by the very existence of vampires. In a less-civilized world, she'd be the one strapping on a bandoleer of hawthorn stakes and a hammer. "You're giving shelter and succor to a werewolf, and you're passing judgment on me, Doctor?"

"Jackie can't help what she is." Alix glared back over her shoulder.

"And you think I can just stop being a vampire? It's not like heroin, dear." She mimicked the tone the doctor used earlier with Dominica. "You can't just kick the habit and go straight." Charlotte folded her arms, prepared to stare down the doctor all night if necessary.

"Did you *choose* to be one? Or were you raped?"

Charlotte winced. She'd been raped, a long time ago in Jamaica. Then she'd been raped again in a very different sort of way by a Swedish vampire named Hedda. In the end, though, she'd known more or less what she was getting into. If she'd said *no*, she'd always thought Hedda would have let her stay human. "It was my choice."

"It's not like you see it in the movies, lass. You don't just get bitten and then you're a vampire yourself. There's far more to it than that." Nick shrugged. "I'm a vampire, and I chose that as well. We require human blood to survive. I won't apologize for my existence."

"At least we've become civilized in the way we do it for the most part. Our thralls are volunteers. They get paid for their services and receive the best medical care. It's very humane."

Dominica glared at her as she fidgeted with a leather cord around her neck. "Awfully noble of you."

Charlotte felt stronger pangs of guilt than the old man. She wondered why it was so important to her to be accepted by these three humans. Their dedication to a werewolf, without fear or compromise, didn't make any sense. Did they see Jackie as a pet to be kept, like a zoo animal? Something to be respected and pitied?

No, that wasn't right.

They were her *friends*.

Charlotte realized she'd never really had any human friends in her life. One didn't form friendships so much on the streets of Kingston. You found someone to watch your back, and they'd watch yours, and that's as close as you ever got. Then, once she'd become a vampire, humans were distant thralls, whereas companionship came from other vampires.

How many times had Charlotte sat perched in the darkness, watching human families as they dined together, laughing and loving one another, or street revelers, celebrating nothing except the fact that they were alive? She'd spent so many years throwing herself into her work she'd never realized just how lonely she was. Here was a werewolf, a deadly killer, who had somehow managed to tame her inner beast enough to not only ally herself with humans, but to befriend them.

Charlotte wanted that, wanted it desperately. Maybe there was hope. But then she saw what hung from the leather cord: a pewter cross. Dominica looked as if she'd like to shove it into Charlotte's face. It wouldn't harm her, but Dominica didn't know that.

Maybe there wasn't any hope after all.

"You think the zombies are hunting virgins?" asked Charlotte.

"Gault's spared no expense in obtaining the ingredients to make walking corpses," Nick said. "If he's willing to do that, it's for something even bigger. Sacrificing virgins seems likely to me. Maybe you or I can't smell a virgin, but I'd bet a decade's interest that demons can."

"But to do what?" Charlotte picked at one of her talons.

"The oldest kind of black magic." Nick's voice was grim. "Evil spirits."

"I thought we were already dealing with evil spirits," said Alix.

"No, we're dealing with animals. Petty demons that aren't much better than the dead men they inhabit. You tell it to bring you a virgin female and turn it loose. It does the rest. A ritual involving virgin sacrifice would be used to draw upon a much more powerful denizen of the netherworld."

"You mean like the devil? Is there even such a thing?" Dominica asked.

Jenn snorted. "Bullshit."

"I don't know," Nick said. "But it stands to reason that there is a hierarchy of power there like everywhere else. Think of it like this. You flash a couple of dollar bills, you're going to attract street corner bums. You flash a couple of million, and you're going to attract a CEO."

"Whatever," Jenn mumbled.

Alix spun around to face the others. "I bet he's keeping them alive. You vampires understand that, right? Blood's best when it's fresh, right?"

Charlotte nodded. "Maybe they're drugged up like Mark was. And he's holding them until he has . . . however many he needs."

"Twelve is a likely bet," Nick said. "There are a lot of magical associations with the number twelve."

Silence flooded the room. Charlotte's thoughts whirled around as she considered the possibilities. "If he doesn't have all twelve victims yet, he's going to need more. He didn't strike me as the type to get his own hands dirty."

"Reno School of Medicine reported the theft of two cadavers four days ago," Alix said. "The morning after Jackie took down the first ones."

"He'll have more zombies out there, then," Jenn said.

"If we can find them, we can take them out and delay him further. He can't have an infinite supply of the ingredients to keep making them," Charlotte said.

Nick nodded. "With this many victims so close together, he's in a hurry. That means we don't have much time if we're going to do something."

"Back up," Jenn said. "All of a sudden you're *we* and *us*. Since when is this *your* party?" She glared right at Charlotte.

"I've been around long enough to know that as bad as vampires and werewolves can be, and believe me, I've seen some of them at their worst, lass, demons would be much worse. And not just bad for humans, either. A demon will slay anyone. We're all equal in their eyes. All prey."

"And you're not used to being on the other side of the teeth." Alix's tone was bitter.

"Not true. Werewolves hunt vampires as much as we hunt them," Charlotte said. "That's what I've been doing for decades. Protecting my people."

"So why help us now?" Jenn folded her arms. "I get why Nick is willing to. I'm waiting to hear from you, Charlotte."

Charlotte made herself take a deep breath. "Someone wanted me to fail in this mission. They wanted me to kill White Fang without any record of authorization, so I'd be considered a rogue and hunted down. That means I have a vested interest in keeping her alive. I've got my own skin to think about too. Besides . . . she asked me to help. I've never been asked for anything except mercy." She smiled a little. "It might be time for me to broaden my horizons."

"How are we going to catch zombies if they're looking for virgins?" Jenn asked. "Just start . . . asking around?"

Charlotte leaned back and inspected her nails. "Mark Hu was their target before. He must be a virgin. Maybe we can use him as bait."

"That's a horrible thing to say!" Jenn's face turned red.

Charlotte smiled. "Sometimes I'm a horrible person. And I'm also right. Maybe if we parade our pet virgin through likely areas of town, we'll attract your zombies. Call him."

"You're asking me to give up Jackie's secrets to him," Jenn said. "I can't do that without her permission."

"This is bigger than you or her. It's getting later and the zombies might already be on the prowl. You want the weight of another abduction on your mind?" Charlotte pointed a taloned finger at Jenn, who stared at the razor-sharp point.

"It's a good idea, lass," Nick said in a soft, persuasive voice. Charlotte could feel his power radiating through the room, making everyone calmer and more receptive to suggestions.

Jenn called Mark and made a convincing sales pitch about Jackie wanting to show some of Mark's art samples to her publisher. Mark sounded ecstatic over the phone, his voice loud enough to carry even without the speaker turned on. He said he'd be glad to get his portfolio together and meet with them.

Half an hour later, Charlotte and Jenn sat in Jenn's car and waited for Mark to leave *Hu Makes Fireworks*. Charlotte watched Jenn tap impatient fingers on the dashboard from where she sat in the darkened back seat and smiled. "You really wear your heart on your sleeve, don't you?"

Jenn turned to glare at her in the darkness. "What do you mean?"

Charlotte chuckled. "You're in love with Jackie. I don't even know you and it's as plain as the full moon up there."

Jenn spluttered and looked away. "It's not . . . I mean, it's none of your business."

Charlotte shrugged. "I know people. You don't spend as many years in this world as I have without understanding the human condition."

"Human. How can you even say that when you're a . . ."

"A vampire. You can say it. The embrace transformed my body and gives me abilities of legend. If I wasn't a blood-drinker, you'd say I was a parahuman, and what's so terrible about that?"

"You hunt people!"

"No, I hunt werewolves. People are . . ." Charlotte stopped. She'd been about to say people were just thralls, but it would have been rude. "I used to be a person before I was transformed. Now I have to remind myself to breathe so I don't forget how."

Seconds of silence ticked by. At last, Jenn said, "I'm sorry."

"Don't be. I chose this existence. If you're going to be sorry, be sorry for Jackie. Lycanthropes are offshoots of humanity. They're not made, they're born. She never had a choice about her life."

"I am sorry for her," Jenn said softly.

"Just make sure you're loving her for the right reasons. Pity isn't one of the right ones."

Jenn snorted. "I'm getting love advice from a hundred-year-old vampire who hunts werewolves for a living."

"It's a strange world we live in, Jenn." The door to *Hu Makes Fireworks* opened and Mark came out, wrapped in a heavy UNLV sweatshirt and a beanie with the Just Cause logo on it. He had a large portfolio under his arm. Charlotte drew herself deeper into the back-seat shadows.

Mark opened the door, looked in at Jenn, and then sat in the passenger seat. "Okay, I'm here. Where's Jackie?"

Jenn opened her mouth to say something, but Charlotte leaned forward into Mark's field of view. "The apology tour starts here and wraps up back at Jackie's place."

Mark made a frightened *eep!* sound and lunged for the door handle.

Jenn smoothly triggered the lock override with professionalism Charlotte appreciated. "It's okay, she's here to help."

Mark scrabbled at the door, still trying to get it to open. "That woman's crazy. She had a gun."

"Mark, please, you have to trust me. She's not going to hurt you."

Charlotte held her hands wide open. "No gun here. See? I'm here to protect you." She wished Nick was there with his calming abilities, but he'd stayed behind to watch over Alix and Dominica in case any other unexpected strangers came calling at the Langdon house.

"Pr-protect me? From what?"

"We'll explain everything. I promise," Jenn said.

"Where's Jackie?"

"Back at the house," Jenn said. "She's . . . uh, indisposed, but she asked us to come get you so you'd be safe."

"Safe from what?" Mark looked doubtful.

Charlotte sat back into the darkness again. "The men who attacked you the other night weren't men. They were reanimated corpses. They've kidnapped eight people, and you would have been the ninth if Langdon hadn't intervened to save your life."

"Reanimated . . . What? You're not making any sense."

"Zombies, Mark. Think of them as zombies. They're real . . . and so are werewolves and vampires," Jenn said. "I'm still wrapping my mind around it myself, but you've got to trust me." She started the car.

"Mark, I have a very important question to ask you. Are you a virgin?" Charlotte glanced around the street to keep a watchful eye out for anyone who didn't belong there. Anyone who might be shambling like a possessed corpse, or listening in on their conversation, like another agent from the Collective.

Mark's mouth fell open at the effrontery. "What kind of question is that?"

Charlotte met Jenn's gaze and nodded. Mark's embarrassment seemed answer enough. "We think the zombies are hunting virgins, to be used in a dark ritual. If you're a virgin, that means you're at a greater risk of being attacked again."

"How do I know you're not part of . . . of whoever it was who attacked me the first time?" Mark's hands twisted and turned in his lap as if he were seeking something to hold onto for comfort but could find nothing.

"Mark . . . I promise you, we're on your side," said Jenn. "What can I say that will convince you? We're not trying to harm you here. There are several other people whose lives are at risk. People who weren't rescued like you were."

"I don't know . . ."

Charlotte sighed. There was a time for diplomacy and patience, and that time had passed. "Look, you're a sweet young thing, and I think it's time you learned the truth about the world. There are monsters out here, and we're real." She popped out her fangs and finger talons. "I'm one. And Jackie's one too. Except she's not a vampire, she's a werewolf."

Mark's hands flew to his face. "No! That can't be."

Jenn pulled the car over underneath a streetlight. She turned around partway in the driver's seat so she could look right at Mark. Charlotte saw she had tears in her eyes. "Mark, it's a full moon tonight. Jackie's deathly afraid of hurting anyone when she's transformed. She makes us lock her in a cage. Otherwise, I'm sure she would be here right now too."

"What do you want me to do? Why come to me now, like this?" Mark looked like he was about to start hyperventilating.

What Charlotte wanted to do was punch Mark in his stupid human face for his inability to deal with a change to his worldview. Instead, she retracted her fangs and talons and tried to make herself as nonthreatening as possible. "Look," she said, trying for a tone that might sound reasonable. "We need your help to find these new zombies and stop them before they take anyone else. If we can destroy them, we'll delay the dark ritual at least a couple more days. That might give us time to stop it."

Mark raised an eyebrow and canted his head to one side a little. "You want me to be . . . bait?"

"We'll protect you. Two vampires are more than a match for any number of zombies. Yes, I have a partner. He's waiting for us."

"Why couldn't it have just been, like, regular parahumans? I could probably deal with that. Vampires are all, you know, made-up."

"That's by design, Mark. How would it look if we were openly feeding on humans? There's a bigger world than just humans and parahumans, but it's a world hidden in the shadows. Those shadows are threatening to spill out into your world. We need your help to stop it."

Mark looked at Jenn, then back at Charlotte. "Okay. What do you need me to do?"

"Sit tight for a bit." Charlotte opened her text messaging app. "Help's on the way." She sent a message to Nick: *It's on. Bring the car.*

* * *

Nick arrived fifteen minutes later behind the wheel of Charlotte's Corvette. He parked beside Jenn's car and handed the keys to Charlotte. "Thank you for trusting me with this lovely lady."

"Nice car," Mark said.

"Thanks. I bought it new." Charlotte opened the door.

"You're that old?"

"Dude, I'm a lot older than that. Will you get in, please? I'm not going to say I don't bite, but I'm not going to bite you."

"What about me?" Jenn asked.

"Stay in your car, just to be safe. Keep to main, well-lit streets. We'll call you when we need you," Nick said.

"I want to help!"

"You are helping," Charlotte said. "You're our backup."

"*I'm* the backup?" Jenn stared as Nick transformed to mist and drifted away, his edges blurring until he no longer looked like anything. "Who's *my* backup?" she called as Charlotte started the 'Vette and pulled away from the curb.

After an hour of slow cruising through the streets of Reno, Nick phoned Charlotte. "Two guys just got dumped out of the back of a van west of Keystone on Seventh Street. They might be our guys. I saw Holocaust survivors that looked better than these two."

Charlotte wondered how he managed to carry his phone with him in his body of mist as she checked her GPS. He must have coalesced to make his call. "That's not far. Nick, call Jenn and see if she can track down that van and get a picture of it." Mark gasped and grabbed for the dashboard to brace himself as Charlotte cranked the wheel over and hammered the accelerator. The Corvette power slid around a corner, wheels squealing. Horns blared from other cars as the black coupe slid into the darkness of residential streets.

She spotted the two men as they staggered stiff-legged down the street. At first, she thought they were drunk, but as she passed them, her headlights illuminated their pale faces underneath hooded sweatshirts. One man's nose had rotted away, leaving a gaping, greenish hole in the center of his face, while the other's jaw hung loose, held on only by the thinnest tendrils of sinew. "Son of a bitch, that's them all right."

"Oh my God!" Mark craned his head around to look at them. "I thought you were making it all up!"

"Really? You think I keep my claws and fangs in my pocket and just put them in to scare attractive young men?" Charlotte turned a sharp left around a building and made a U-turn to park near the corner. She shut off the 'Vette's rumbling engine and lights.

"This kind of stuff isn't supposed to happen in real life."

Charlotte touched Mark's arm. He shrank away from it, so Charlotte put her hand back on the wheel and stared straight ahead. She was trying hard not to see Mark as a thrall, but as a person. "I've been around a long time, Mark. I've seen some things you wouldn't believe. Things I can't ever forget. You're being really brave. I promise I won't let you come to harm tonight. If there's one thing I know I'm good at, it's killing."

"Can zombies even *be* killed? I mean, aren't they already dead?"

"Anything can be killed if you're motivated enough. Are you sure you want to do this? You can still back out."

Mark nodded. "I'm ready. I'm scared, but I believe that you know what you're doing. How are you going to stop them?"

"Probably with these." Charlotte displayed her talons. "Or with this." She patted the gun in her shoulder holster.

"You can't just . . . kill them now?"

"Not here. Someone could see. The whole point of this is we're trying to be subtle. You see that alley? Lead them in there and I'll do the rest."

"Okay." Mark took a deep breath and got out of the car. Charlotte had to admire the young man's courage. He leaned down to look in the window. "What do I do?"

Charlotte shrugged. "I don't know. Be virginal? What did you do the last time they were chasing you?"

"I just walked past them, I guess."

"Then walk past them. You'll be fine. I'm right here." Charlotte slipped off her shoes and waited.

Mark crossed the street and headed toward the two figures, hands in his pockets, head lowered. He got to within a few yards of the two zombies and they reacted to his presence. Their shambling took on a purpose and they moved faster. Mark froze. "Come on, don't just stand there, dumbass," Charlotte murmured, her fingers clenched around the steering wheel. "Move."

At last, Mark turned and walked back the way he'd come. He looked back over his shoulder and saw the zombies were following him. One dragged his leg as if it were broken. The other had already pulled a canister of spray gas from inside his dark hoodie.

Charlotte inhaled once, feeling the last bits of blood circulating through her veins. She'd need to feed soon to replenish herself. She stepped out of the Corvette.

It was time to be a hero.

Charlotte popped out her talons and fangs and scrambled up the side of the building in a half dozen springing leaps. The bracing night air invigorated her despite the low level of blood in her body. She needed to feed, and soon. Maybe Mark would be accommodating afterward. Or even Jenn, who seemed so anxious to do anything she could to help Jackie.

The crushed gravel of the rooftop crunched under Charlotte's feet as she crossed to the edge and looked down into the alley. The zombies shambled faster than before as they pursued Mark. Charlotte paced them, running along the building's raised lip. She didn't see Nick anywhere but figured he had to be nearby, probably in his mist form.

Mark reached the end of the alley, which was blocked with a chain link fence.

"Shit." Charlotte had hoped Mark would simply outdistance the zombies and then she and Nick could mop up things in the alley. Now she was going to have to keep one eye on Mark on top of everything else. She took two running steps to build her momentum and catapulted herself over the edge, arms and legs flailing like an Olympic long-jumper trying to gain that additional inch.

She hit the broken-leg zombie hard, one foot coming down on each of his shoulders, and felt his clavicle shatter beneath her heel. She dug her toe-talons into his dead flesh and used her forward and downward momentum to drag him through a forward roll with her feet and hurl him against a building hard enough to crack the bricks. Mark shrieked at Charlotte's sudden appearance and shrank back into the corner between a building and the chain link fence.

Fog flowed through the fence past Mark to enshroud the other zombie. It halted its advance as the mist flowed into its body through its mouth and nose. As Charlotte watched, the zombie quivered, then exploded, sending steaming flesh sizzling against the alley walls and rough pavement. Nick rose out of the mess, covered from head to toe with decayed flesh and slime.

"Damn, Nicky," Charlotte said.

"I'm going to need a bath," he said in dismay, then looked up and his eyes widened. "Watch out!"

Nick shoved Charlotte aside as a creature leaped onto him with an inhuman shriek. It still had flaps of the zombie's skin hanging off of it like tattered rags and Charlotte realized it was the remains of the one she'd thrown into the wall. The demon raised Nick in arms with muscles like steel cables and opened a toothy mouth that filled its entire head. Mark's scream of terror was overshadowed by the demon's triumphant cry.

Nick transformed to mist as the monster's teeth closed upon where his body would have been. It looked down at its featureless fingers in confusion for a moment, and then turned its attention toward the panicking Mark.

"No, you don't!" Charlotte wrapped her arms around the monster's neck and heaved backward. It wasn't as heavy as she'd anticipated, and she fell with it atop her. It shifted somehow and suddenly was facing her, like it had folded itself inside out. The monster's cavernous mouth yawned over her, large enough to engulf her entire head.

Something struck the creature's head and it tumbled off Charlotte. She rolled back to her feet and saw Mark, holding a board with shaking hands. "Get back. We've got this," Charlotte said with confidence she didn't feel.

The demon flung itself at her. It was faster than a vampire, faster even than a werewolf, and a moment later had her pressed against the wall. A tail snaked out from between its legs to swipe away Mark's board. The demon roared in triumph, but its roar cut short into a curious grunt. Charlotte glanced down to see a fist poking out of the creature's chest, holding what looked like a lump of black jelly. As she watched, the jelly disintegrated into powder and the demon followed suit, becoming a pile of stinking, sulfurous ash.

Nick stood behind the demon's remains, clutching one arm. It was blackened and withered. "Are you all right?" he asked Mark.

Mark was nearly hyperventilating but managed a weak nod. Charlotte wiped soot and dead flesh from her face. "How did you know that would work?"

"I didn't. I was just trying to get it off you. I guess even demons have hearts. Or something like them." Nick managed to look pleased with himself, despite the damage he'd done to himself in defeating the demon.

Charlotte had never seen that kind of injury done to a vampire before. "Does it hurt? Can I do anything to help?"

"No, I don't feel anything at all," Nick raised the branch-like appendage and looked at it. "I wonder if it's permanent."

"How can you be so blasé about it?" Charlotte touched his shoulder. Nick was the closest thing to a real friend she'd had in fifty years.

His eyes displayed a sadness she was only beginning to comprehend. "Because this is only the beginning. If we falter now, who knows what will be loosed upon this world?"

Chapter Seventeen

November 2012
Reno, Nevada

Jackie arose from the murky darkness with her heart pounding in fear. Had she done it this time? Had she broken loose and killed someone? She vaguely remembered Alix and Jenn with her at the cusp of the transformation. What if she had hurt them? The floor of the steel cage felt cold and hard against her naked skin. Her jaws ached from repeated attempts to chew through the steel bars. Lips . . . chapped. Tongue . . . raw. She squinted at the bright overhead lighting, trying to make sense of the blurred and fuzzy shapes around her. Color assaulted her eyes as they acclimated to the full range of colors humans perceived, instead of the limited tones she saw as a werewolf. Her gut twisted, hunger pangs taking precedence above all other discomforts.

"They said you would be hungry," said a soft, almost-familiar voice. "How do you feel?"

Jackie licked her chapped lips and rubbed her fists against her eyes. "That was a rough one." Her throat felt ragged from repeated howling and snarls, making her voice husky, as if she'd been screaming for hours.

A blurry form approached the cage and twisted the lock open.

It wasn't Jenn.

Jackie crouched down in surprise as she realized it was Mark Hu who stood before her, holding out a terrycloth bathrobe.

"I'm sorry. I didn't mean to startle you."

Jackie didn't know whether to be aghast, embarrassed, or terrified, so she settled on simple bemusement. "What are you doing here?"

"I'm waiting for you. Your friends . . . They told me everything." He pushed the robe at Jackie. "Thank you for saving my life. I know I thanked you before, but now I know you played an even bigger role."

Jackie looked around the mine. Everything was still where it belonged. Her truck was parked on the round table, ready to leave at a moment's notice. The computers in Dominica's retreat were all locked down in standby mode, the young technician nowhere to be seen. The science laboratory was likewise abandoned, with no sign of Alix. And of course, her trusty assistant Jenn was gone as well. "Where is everyone?"

"Sleeping off a busy night," Mark said. "I volunteered to get up early to watch for you since I was the only one who didn't really do anything. I just had to be the bait." He shuddered as if experiencing an unpleasant memory.

Jackie shrugged into the robe and knotted it. "Bait? What's going on?"

"Okay, well, we found two more zombie demon things last night. They were hunting virgins, like, um, like me. Charlotte and Nick tore them apart. It was pretty gross, but there wasn't any blood or anything."

"Charlotte . . . Pastor? And who's Nick?" A small table nearby held a stack of sandwiches and two large bottles of Gatorade. Her stomach twisting with aching hunger, Jackie grabbed a sandwich and bit into roast beef, swiss, and horseradish.

"He's a vampire."

"Vampires?" Jackie asked around a mouthful. She made herself chew and swallow. "Now there are vampires too?"

"The world is a lot more complicated a place than you may have realized." Charlotte Pastor walked out of the shadows and over to the. She wore a tight-fitting leather suit that stretched to her ankles and wrists. For some reason, she was barefoot. "Vampires are real, and apparently so are zombies. You're not the only werewolf, either. I've made a career out of hunting down monsters like you." She held an insulated coffee mug in one hand and sucked the crimson contents through a clear plastic straw. She saw Jackie staring at it with a mixture of horror and fascination. She chuckled. "Don't worry. It's not from any of your friends. Your doctor was kind enough to provide me with a pint from her storage. It's the vampire equivalent of a microwaved TV dinner. Tastes bad, not really nutritious."

Jackie stiffened. "Just how many of us—werewolves, I mean—are there? If hunting us is your specialty, there must be . . ."

"Tens of thousands," Charlotte said. "You're hardly an endangered species."

"And vampires? How many of you are out there hunting werewolves?"

"I don't know how many hunters there are, but I suspect our population is comparable to yours. We're the other fringe races, like parahumans. Those who evolved beyond humanity, or in your case devolved."

"Devolved?" Jackie felt vulnerable in her bathrobe and wished she had her costume handy, but she'd have to walk past the vampire to get it, and she didn't think turning her back on Charlotte would be healthy. "You're not making a very good case for yourself as an ally."

Charlotte blinked. Jackie could tell she'd struck a nerve.

"I'm . . . I'm sorry. You don't spend decades hunting werewolves without developing some pretty strong convictions about them. I can see what you've done here, with your friends, with this cage. I'm trying to open my mind, but believe me, it's not easy."

"Why hunt us at all?" Jackie wandered toward the computer station, as if to check on one of the screens, but mostly to move into a better tactical position. Charlotte moved too, keeping Jackie at a distance. If Jackie lunged at her, Charlotte would have time to draw the holstered pistol under her arm. It held silver bullets; Jackie could smell them, bright and metallic and poisonous. "What did we ever do to you?"

Charlotte's lips pressed together in a thin, dark line. "The first time I encountered werewolves was when a pack of them killed a dear friend of mine for sport."

"So, it's all a big revenge trip, is it?" Mark moved to stand beside Jackie. "Killing every werewolf in the world isn't going to bring back your friend."

"No, but it might keep someone else from sharing his fate."

"Do you think it'll make you feel better?" Jackie felt like she had some insight into Charlotte's psyche. Like Jackie, Charlotte was fighting a hopeless war in the hope of salving her own spirit. How was Jackie any different, taking on criminals big and small? How much difference could either of them hope to make against such insurmountable odds?

"I doubt it." Charlotte folded her arms. "But that's not why I'm here. Like I said, I'm trying to turn over a bit of a new leaf. There's something else going on here that's bigger than you or me. My friend Nick says the dark ritual that's ahead could have world-shaking ramifications. We're probably going to need far more help than we have to stop it, whatever it is." She looked down at her hand and frowned, as if giving careful consideration to her next action. Then she extended it to Jackie. "I'm offering you a truce until we resolve this situation. Maybe longer than that, as well."

Jackie looked at Charlotte's hand. It stank of silver, as if she'd had the metal on her person her entire life. Despite that, something about the vampire made Jackie want to trust her. Maybe it was because Charlotte was an outsider, like Jackie. Plus, she was willing to set aside a lifetime of hatred to risk allying with her sworn enemy.

Jackie could respect that.

She clasped Charlotte's hand, despite the distant howling of the beast in the back of her brain, which would much rather she slashed at it. With her transformation waning along with the moon, the beast couldn't do much more than yelp at her. Charlotte's hand was cool to the touch. "Agreed. Tell me what happened."

"We used what we'd learned from you, filled in some holes of what we didn't know, and tracked down the zombies. They came out of a van that was registered to Conrad Gault." Charlotte smiled. "Tip of the hat to you for that intuition."

"Good to know that much, at any rate." Jackie cracked open a Gatorade and drained half of it. "What else?"

"What else is that you need an industrial-size coffee maker down here." Alix emerged from one of the privacy huts tucked off to one side of the mine. She yawned and stretched, looking lost inside a triple-extra-large Just Cause hoodie.

"I'll have Jenn get right on that. Is she down here?"

"No, she's upstairs, waiting for the window guy."

"Why do I need a window guy?"

Alix poured herself a cup from the small coffee pot in the kitchenette and started refilling the pot with more grounds and water. "Long story. But I do have some interesting news about your zombies. Nick and Charlotte were kind enough to bring me back some larger lumps than you did." She walked over to her lab, opened the refrigerator door, and pulled out a large sealed glass jar containing a severed head floating in formaldehyde, which Jackie could smell despite the lids. Yucky bits of decaying flesh drifted from the stump of his neck. Mark turned a little green but put on a brave face and stayed beside Jackie.

Jackie polished off another sandwich and walked over to get a closer look.

"Jackie, meet Richard. Richard died in a car accident twenty-two days ago. He thoughtfully volunteered his body for science and until four days ago was a resident of the Reno School of Medicine where he'd been slated for dissection by medical students. Following his mysterious disappearance from cold storage, he appears to have been treated by an unusual mixture of chemicals that replaced his blood." Alix raised a long steel implement and used it as a pointer. "Now, what's most interesting to me are these crystalline structures around his nostrils. Ordinarily, I might dismiss this as frozen mucous, but Richard is quite dead and doesn't have any functional mucous membranes."

"So, what is it, then?"

"I don't know." Alix put the head back into the fridge. "But if I was going to make a wild-ass guess, they're what's allowing the zombies to track down virgins. Since we're way off the reservation and talking about magic here, I figure that zombies need a way to identify their targets."

"By smelling them with magic nose crystals? That's a reach," Jackie said.

"I didn't say it was a perfect theory, I said it was a wild-ass guess. These things do the magical mumbo-jumbo detecting and feed a scent to the zombie. I don't know the actual mechanics of it, and honestly, I don't fucking care."

"Gault would use scent as a primary identifier," Jackie said. "That's his specialty." She glanced over at Mark. "Did it work on you?"

Mark gave her an awkward smile and said, "I never met the right guy."

"Pity, that. I rather fancied the young men of the Orient in my misbegotten youth." A cloud of mist flowed out of the darkness and formed into an old man with a blackened, withered arm that hung motionless at his side.

Jackie startled at the man's sudden appearance, but his kindly, weathered face and pleasant smile, devoid of guile, put her at ease right away. "Nick, I presume?"

"One and the same. You've got quite an impressive setup down here, Ms. Langdon. I've been talking with your technical gal. She and I have a lot of similar interests. Perhaps there might be the possibility of a partnership in the future. Assuming, of course, you don't mind working with the enemy."

"*Are* you the enemy?" Jackie asked.

"It's all in your perspective," Nick said. "I'm old enough to have quite a bit of it. There's a bad storm brewing here in Reno. Black magic. Summoning of demons." He glanced down at his injured arm with a mixture of contempt and disappointment. "Evil things, lass, perpetrated by evil people." He glanced down at his injured arm with a mixture of contempt and disappointment.

"Evil like Gault," Charlotte said. "What do we do?"

Jackie finished a bottle of Gatorade and wiped her mouth with the back of her hand. "We've both got a standing invitation to visit him. What say we take him up on it?"

"You know as soon as we call him, he's going to set a trap for us," Charlotte said.

Jackie grinned. "I'm counting on it. Nick, let's talk about your misty self for a minute."

* * *

A brief phone call later and Jackie found herself riding shotgun in Charlotte's Corvette as they headed down the mountain toward Silver Legacy Casino. Despite the recent chilly nights, the midday sun was working hard enough to make heat waves rise off the asphalt. Nick, in mist form, rode in the car's small trunk. Watching him transform had been fascinating, and Jackie promised herself it would find its way into one of her books.

"I saw your car a few nights ago," she told Charlotte. "I was impressed. Still am. It's a beautiful ride."

Charlotte smiled. "Thanks. Got it brand new in Sacramento in December of '73. Early Christmas present for myself."

"That blows my mind. So, the whole vampires in sunlight thing is a myth?"

"Sort of. We get severe sunburns in minutes if our unprotected skin is exposed to sunlight. Sunscreen helps, and so does polarized glass. I could drive in my car all day and not be uncomfortable in that regard." Charlotte wove through traffic on the highway with little regard for speed limits.

"Anything else about vampires that I ought to know?"

"We really do drink blood. It keeps us alive, although not in the sense that you're alive. We can't make a vampire just by biting someone. It's a lot more in-depth than that. We can heal injuries rapidly, as long as those injuries weren't caused by a werewolf." She grew more sober. "Or a demon, apparently."

"What happens then?"

"To the teeth and claws of a werewolf, a vampire isn't any tougher than a human." Charlotte glanced over at her. "So, Sven with the ponytail? He's all yours."

"You can't shoot him with your silver bullets?"

"I can, and hopefully they will stop him before he takes a bite out of me. Speaking of silver, why in the world would you make your headquarters in a silver mine? You may as well be living in toxic waste. You could be breathing in airborne silver particles."

"Or I could get shot by a werewolf-hunting vampire. It's a dangerous world."

"That it is."

At forty-two floors, the Silver Legacy was the tallest building in Reno. Conrad Gault lived in a two-story suite that probably cost more than the GDP of some third-world nations. They sent Nick ahead to check out Gault's suite first while they waited in the elevator lobby a floor below. He vanished into a ventilation shaft. Minutes ticked by with only awkward silence between Jackie and Charlotte.

Nick returned shortly, looking as irritated as Jackie had seen him since they first met. "His suite is warded."

"What does that mean?" Jackie asked.

"It means he knows about vampires. You know the folklore that a vampire can't enter a house without an invitation? That's based upon magical wards. It's how mages protected themselves back in the day," Nick said. "An invitation unlocks the ward. I can't get in without one."

"That means he knows about vampires and werewolves," Charlotte said. "What are we getting ourselves into?"

"We're going to find out," Jackie said. "There are eight missing people and I'd bet my next advance he's behind it. Nick's our ace in the hole here. Even if we fall into Gault's trap, he can get us free."

"You're putting a lot of faith in me," Nick said. "I can't even enter the suite."

"What if we smuggled you in?" Jackie asked. "Do you take up a lot of space in your mist form?"

"I can condense myself pretty well, but where are you going to hide me?"

"Not me," Jackie said and nodded to Charlotte. "Her."

A few minutes later, young woman in a conservative black-and-white maid's uniform opened the door to Gault's suite. "Please, come in," she said. "Monsieur Gault is expecting you."

Jackie stepped across the threshold into the suite without a moment's hesitation. Charlotte followed right after her, pausing only for the barest fraction of a second at the door before plunging through. They found themselves in a sprawling room decorated in a Roman motif, with white marble floors and alabaster columns. Expensive LED lights built to resemble torches flickered along the walls in random patterns. Oriental rugs broke up the blinding white of the marble. Bronze statuary adorned the walls in between columns and potted plants, each of which had a grow light positioned over it.

"I will let Monsieur know you are here," said the maid. Her heels clacked on the floor as she turned and headed toward the second level of the suite. Charlotte opened her mouth and Nick's mist form flowed free. She'd been holding him in her lungs. He swirled around the ceiling for a moment before swooping into a ventilation grille and disappearing.

"Remind me never to do that again," Charlotte whispered. "He tastes weird."

"Hush," Jackie whispered back. The residence reeked of perfume and an underlying chemical stench, mixed with the raw pheromones of Gault's pet werewolf Sven.

Conrad Gault descended a wrought-iron staircase from the upper level, wearing slender black trousers and a crimson velvet jacket with gold buttons. He was barefoot, but if he'd been wearing boots, he'd have looked like a pirate. "Mademoiselles Langdon and Pastor, it is a pleasure to have you both visit me today."

"The pleasure is ours, Mr. Gault. You have a beautiful home," Charlotte said.

"Conrad, *s'il vous plaît*. You need not be formal with me."

Jackie felt mundane and sloppy next to her, for the vampire had slipped into an elite, cultured demeanor without any effort. Of course, she'd had decades to perfect her techniques.

"I was fascinated by your description of how you mix custom fragrances," Jackie said. "I'd really like to see how that works. It would be a great thing to add to a story."

"*Mais oui.* Please, let me give you the tour. Marie, bring refreshments for my guests. Sven will help you."

Jackie stiffened at the mention of the huge werewolf. She put on a smile she didn't feel.

Gault showed them through the impressive lower level of his home. The main living area was wide open and circular, with a thick central pillar that housed both a gas fireplace and gigantic entertainment center, replete with the latest, most expensive electronic gadgets. Couches of differing sizes and designs spread out around them, like the world's most comfortable and decadent movie theater. His dining room was well-appointed with silver service, an Egyptian linen tablecloth, and a centerpiece of fresh-cut flowers.

His library boasted hundreds of first-edition hardcovers with a blend of fiction and non-fiction. Jackie glanced across the shelves, wondering if her own works were somewhere in the collection. A foot-high stack of books crowded a lamp on a small round table beside an expensive recliner. The bookshelves continued into the study, but the orderly rows of hardcovers were replaced by haphazard stacks of scribbled notebooks, rolls of parchment and papyrus, folders, and ancient leathery tomes. It all encroached upon a computer desk with three separate monitors.

Beyond the study was the small chemistry lab where Gault mixed up his custom fragrances, using a unique combination of ancient tools and modern equipment. Jackie detected dozens of odors she couldn't identify individually, but blended together, they created a miasma of sublime and sensual scents. She looked at the shelves full of glass jars that contained everything from rock-like lumps to plants to what might have been animal parts. It was like a wizard's apothecary. "I never knew all this stuff was needed to make perfume."

"*Oui, ma chère.*"

Jackie caught a single whiff of the metallic, coma-inducing chemical blend across her nostrils like the smell of smoke on someone who was in a bar the night before. She smiled; her suspicions had been well-founded. "What are you working on now, Conrad?"

"Ah, one of my custom fragrances. I call it Dark Mystery. It has proven so popular with my close friends that I should probably just, how do you say, bite the bullet and do a full release. I must admit I am rather secretive about the recipe." Gault pulled two identical bottles off a shelf. "Take these samples of it, please. A gift, from me to you. I would be honored for you to wear my scent."

"Oh, no, we couldn't . . ." said Charlotte.

Gault smiled, drawing his eyebrows together. "I insist." He led them back to the main room and looked around. His demeanor hardened. "*Sacre bleu*, where is that woman? It is so hard to find good help these days. If you'll wait for me here, I'll retrieve your refreshments myself."

The moment Conrad left the room, a misty cloud flowed out from an unobtrusive vent and swirled around Charlotte and Jackie. "Upstairs," came a breathy voice from the cloud before it floated back into the shaft once more.

"Don't eat or drink anything he hands you," Charlotte whispered. "It won't affect me, but you still have a mostly human metabolism."

"You think I'm an idiot? He's just waiting for his moment," Jackie hissed back. "I'll keep him talking, you find out what's upstairs."

"How do I do that?" Charlotte asked, feeling awkward and unskilled in social graces amid so much obvious wealth.

"Say you need a bathroom or something. I'll keep him talking business." Jackie smiled. "Besides, I want to know who built that entertainment system for him. I want to hire whoever it is to do mine."

Charlotte snorted. "I'll work my own angle, thanks."

They returned to Gault's main room and made themselves comfortable on a couch. He rejoined them a minute later, bearing a tray of sliced fruits, cheeses, meats, and crackers, accompanied by a crystal decanter of pungent red wine. Gault poured them each a goblet of the wine and bade them to partake of the food.

"This place must cost you a fortune. What's upstairs, Conrad?" Charlotte looked at him through half-lowered eyes as she sipped at her wine.

He sighed. "A mess, I'm afraid. My dear grandmother had a remarkable collection of Parisian art. Upon her passing, the entire collection came to me. I'm still cataloging it all while I find a suitable gallery to display it. It's all quite dreary up there—packing crates and straw and the like." He leered at Charlotte. "Fortunately, I have a rather large and comfortable bedroom on this level."

Jackie glared at Charlotte while Conrad was looking at the dark-skinned vampire and motioned with her head toward the stairs. "Sounds like quite a chore. This is quite a lovely vintage, by the way." Jackie raised her wine glass to her lips and sniffed. She couldn't detect anything unusual within its bouquet, but remembered she was in the presence of a master perfumer. If Gault could create a scent like that Dark Mystery, he could just as easily create a more subtle odor to disguise something lethal, like perhaps a silver solution. To be safe, Jackie only wet her lips and then wiped them off unobtrusively.

Conrad turned away from Charlotte to smile at Jackie. "Are you a connoisseur, Jacquelyn?"

Jackie shrugged. "Not like you, I'm sure."

Charlotte returned Jackie's glare behind the perfumer's back. "Conrad, I'm sorry . . . I didn't see it before, but where is your bathroom?" She set down her goblet.

"You may use mine. Down the hall, past the stairs, and to the right of the bedroom."

"Thanks." Charlotte stood and headed that direction.

Jackie set her own glass upon the coffee table and smiled. "Now, Conrad, I want you to tell me all about this entertainment system you've got here. I'm suffering from a major case of gadget envy."

Gault smiled back. "It would be my pleasure."

Chapter Eighteen

November 2012
Reno, Nevada

Charlotte reached the stairs and paused for a moment, pretending to look at a painting on the wall but checking for cameras. She didn't see any surveillance devices, decided to chance it, and slipped up the stairs. Unlike the wrought-iron spiral staircase in the front room, this was a plain stair that ascended to a hallway ending in another door. She tested it to see if it was locked. The knob turned without resistance. Gault, or one of his lackeys, would probably catch on to her in a few minutes, and her only hope was to get as much information as she could. She fully expected she and Jackie would have to fight their way out.

Fighting alongside a werewolf, she thought, shaking her head in disbelief.

The heavy door opened into a small antechamber, like a closet or an elevator. The walls and ceiling of the chamber were lined with sculpted foam rubber soundproofing. The floor was spongy, like a similar material might be underneath the utilitarian brown berber carpet. The bland, ugly rug seemed out of place compared to the rest of the huge, beautiful suite. She slipped inside the antechamber and shut the first door. The second door looked the same as the first. She opened it.

She and Jackie had thought they would uncover evidence of Gault's involvement with the kidnappings, but nothing had prepared her for what she found in the adjoining room.

After the shocking white of the rest of the residence, this room was dark and smoky from real torches and smoking braziers along the walls, overwhelming the room's ventilation system and making the air hazy. The walls were paneled in dark wood and inscribed with unfamiliar symbols in black paint. A twelve-pointed star had been drawn on the floor in red powder, with glyphs in white powder set at each point. Twelve men and women hung from the chamber ceiling at her shoulder height, four more than Charlotte expected. They were naked, hanging from leather straps at wrist, ankle, and waist. Each was tilted back several degrees with their legs spread, presenting their genitalia to the center of the star. At first she thought they were dead, but then she saw a pulse flutter in one woman's throat. Green slime was spread around their nostrils, which Gault must have used to keep them comatose.

Something roiled at the center of the star. It looked like a flaming, glowing crack in reality, but no heat or sound came from it. Although its light was bright, the glow didn't cast a single shadow, as if it weren't really there. It shifted and twisted like a demonic lava lamp.

Beside her, mist coalesced into Nick. "He's farther along in this process than we expected."

"What the hell is that thing?" asked Charlotte.

"A gateway to Hell-with-a-capital-*H*, perhaps."

"Or *from* there." Charlotte shuddered. "This is way over my head, but there are only two reasons to open a portal thing—to send something to the other side or to let something from the other side come here. I don't imagine either is good, and I doubt these people come out of it alive."

"I agree. Let's see if we can get them down before something happens." Nick pulled a balisong knife from a pocket with his good hand and flipped it open with a well-practiced flourish.

"It's a little late for that." The familiar voice would have turned Charlotte's blood to ice if she'd had any in her body.

Charlotte whirled to see Blackstone walking across the chamber toward them. How had she missed him? On the heels of it came the realization that the ancient vampire was involved in this terrible ritual. They'd come to trap Gault, but had never considered he might have an ally as powerful as Blackstone. She reached for the gun in her concealed holster, even though the silver bullets in it wouldn't harm him in the least.

"Stop." The unfathomable power of Blackstone's voice froze Charlotte's hand halfway into her coat. "Don't move."

Charlotte strained, but her muscles wouldn't obey her. Beside her, Nick's grunt told her he was likewise paralyzed. The power in Blackstone's voice struck her at a fundamental level of her brain. "Blackstone . . ." Her lips felt like blocks of concrete. "What are you doing here?"

"Why, I was waiting for you, dear Charlotte. I knew you'd end up here sooner or later. You're far too smart not to have deduced Gault was at the root of all this, although I admit I'm fascinated to see that you've formed an alliance with one of your sworn enemies."

"They say the enemy of your enemy is your friend. I know where I stand with White Fang. And I *thought* I knew with you." Charlotte struggled to move but the commanding power of Blackstone's words had frozen her solid. "Why are you here? And why can't I move?"

"You never knew about my own special ability." Blackstone moved to stand before Charlotte. He traced a gentle finger down her jawline. She wanted to shiver but was unable to. "Dominance is a rare ability among vampires. It's served me well over the years when I've chosen to use it."

"Let me go, Blackstone," Nick said. "Treating with demons? It's insanity!"

"Is it? Did I miss you becoming an expert in ethics?" Blackstone looked at Nick with infinite sadness in his eyes. "I'm so very disappointed in you, Nicholas. After London, I thought we had an understanding."

"You may have made me what I am, but that doesn't make me your bitch. What's happened to you? This goes against everything you stood for when you created the Collective. You wanted vampires to live safely among humans. It's why you wanted to hunt down the weres and the rogues. To protect us. To protect those we share this world with."

"This is the kind of stuff that gets out," Charlotte said. "You're going to attract the attention of humans and parahumans, and they'll organize and hunt us down. It'll be the cullings of the 1920s all over again."

"Don't you dare tell me about vampires being hunted by our own food." Blackstone barked like an angry attorney. "I've seen more vampires die at human hands than almost anyone. The hunts of the 1300s. Roanoke 1586. Biarritz 1854. I'm ensuring this won't ever happen again."

"How?" Nick hissed. "You can't change humanity."

Blackstone laughed. "Who said anything about humanity? I'm removing the last weakness of vampirekind. The arrangement I've made will protect us forever from sunlight. Imagine it, Charlotte. How long has it been since you've been able to revel in the warmth of the sun's rays on your skin? Or enjoy a lazy summer afternoon on the beach? Ninety years?" His voice became hard. "It's been nine hundred years for me. *Nine. Hundred. Years.*"

"What do you mean, an *arrangement*?"

"There are beings beyond our universe. Powerful extradimensional beings, who can alter reality with a word. I've made a deal with one of them. A trivial ritual of blood sacrifice and representatives of undeath and unnature in return for a release from our shackles of darkness."

"You made a deal with . . . the Devil?" Charlotte couldn't believe she'd said the words.

"Not the Devil." Blackstone's smile was humorless. "Rather, a demon of somewhat lesser power, but one with a unique background. He made us."

"What do you mean, he *made* us?" Charlotte knew the longer she kept Blackstone talking, the more likely he was to make a mistake or give Jackie a chance to come to their aid.

"You think vampires *evolved* alongside humans, like these parahumans with which they're so enamored? That's preposterous. We are a created species, as are the werewolves. Imbued with the power of denizens of eternal darkness, consigned to live in Hell on Earth. Thousands of years ago, a demon bred with a human female and from her loins came the first vampire and werewolf, one of undeath and the other unnatural."

"That's crazy," said Nick.

"Crazy? Brothers fighting brothers has been a theme since history began. Cain and Abel. Thor and Loki. Kings Richard and John. Vampire and werewolf. It's taken me hundreds of years to identify the demon responsible for our creation. He who has made us can change us. All it takes is payment for services rendered." Blackstone gestured expansively toward the hanging men and women in the chamber.

"Blackstone, think about what you're doing, man! You're going to let a bloody great *demon* loose on the world!" Nick was aghast.

"Hardly, Nicholas. It will be safely contained here. It gets the virgin blood it desires, along with one each of its children. It pays us back, and then returns to its own realm. Everybody wins."

"Except the humans you're going to kill," Charlotte said. "The police are already looking for you."

"They're looking for a serial killer," Blackstone said. "And if need be, I will give them one. When the dust has settled, I'm still going to win."

"I'm going to kill you by inches." Charlotte strained at the invisible, psychic bonds preventing her from acting.

Blackstone touched his fingers to her lips. "Hush," he whispered, and she couldn't speak. "I knew you'd try if you found out. That's why I sent you here to Reno to hunt the werewolf vigilante. I couldn't trust anyone else in the Collective not to put a bullet in her the first chance they got. But you, Charlotte, you're curious. I knew that would lead you to ask more questions about White Fang. I cut you off from the Collective myself, knowing it would force you to seek assistance from other avenues. Given what research I'd done on White Fang, I suspected you might ally with her, and so I allowed the clues about Mr. Gault to surface. I've known you long enough to know you can't walk away from an open door. That inquisitiveness paid off handsomely, my dear. And now here you are, an unliving vampire and an unnatural werewolf. Siblings, as it were." He grinned, showing his fangs. "The final two pieces required for the ritual."

"You bloody bastard," Nick grunted. "Don't you dare do anything to her!"

Blackstone frowned. "Yes, there's still the problem of you being here. That was unexpected, and unfortunate. And quite frankly, Nicholas, I'm sorry. You're a good man, and I'll be saddened at your loss. But I'm sure our werewolf friend downstairs is growing quite suspicious. She'll need some words of encouragement from me. I'll leave the two of you in Sven's capable hands. Sven, come in here, please."

The gargantuan werewolf entered the room with a predator's leer stretched across his wide, Nordic face. His hair hung loose around his cheeks and instead of a business suit, he wore only a pair of blue jeans. Thick blond hair sprouted from the tops of his bare feet and covered his torso and shoulders like dry prairie grass. Charlotte struggled against Blackstone's psychic chains holding her fast. Like climbing a sheer rock face, she only needed to find a single crack to dig her fingers into, and that would lead to a path to the top, a way out of her imprisonment. If she could wiggle a single finger, or toe, that would be the crack.

Sven's low chuckle rumbled through the flickering torchlight. "Pretty new playthings. What shall I do first? Who wants to bleed?"

"I'm not afraid of you, werewolf." Nick oozed confidence.

Sven threw back his head and laughed. "Werewolf? *Werewolf*? I *ate* the last fucking werewolf I met. I'm worth a dozen of those pieces of shit. Two dozen, even." He stripped out of his jeans and kicked them aside, then hunched forward and started to grow. His body, already huge by human standards, thickened and sprouted a magnificent pelt of golden brown fur. Razor-sharp claws spread forth from his thick paws. His face widened, his nose lengthened and Charlotte realized Sven wasn't a werewolf at all.

He was a *bear*.

Sven-the-bear growled and snarled at Charlotte and Nick. He reached out a huge paw and slashed Nick's face. Nick hissed at the pain but refused to give the bear the satisfaction of crying out. Instead, he smiled back at Sven, his teeth visible through the tatters of his ruined cheek. "You numpty chav."

"Nick!" Charlotte struggled even harder against the compulsion holding her frozen. She still felt the weight of the pistol tucked into the concealed holster inside her coat. All she had to do was reach it, but her entire body felt encased in cement. "You have to mess with an old man? What's the matter, are you afraid of me? You're just a big pussy underneath all that fur. A pathetic little nothing."

The bear turned his burning gaze upon her, and fear stuck its cold, slimy tendrils through her spirit. Sven growled at her and licked his chops. Slaver dripped from the corner of his mouth, and Charlotte knew he was going to tear her apart and eat her. Her only hope was that Jackie could somehow turn the tables on the vampire or resist the domination.

Her hopes were dashed a moment later when a docile Jackie Jackie walked into the room between Gault and Blackstone. Blackstone must have used his domineering ability upon her.

"Sven, I hope you haven't damaged either of the vampires too much," Gault said. "We need one of them for the ritual."

The bear looked away from Charlotte and roared his displeasure at Gault. Then he lumbered back to where he'd discarded his clothing, transforming back to his huge, over-muscled human form. "You worry too much, Mr. Gault. I'm not going to lose control of myself." He pulled on his jeans and shot a savage, contemptuous grin toward the domineered Jackie. "I'm not a piece of shit werewolf or something."

"Shall we begin? All the requisite components are here," Blackstone said.

Excitement spread across Gault's face as he looked from the twelve people suspended from the ceiling, the powder patterns on the floor, and the three captives. "Yes, let us begin. I have many great things yet to accomplish."

Blackstone turned to Sven. "Keep watch over them. They shouldn't be able to move until I release them, but Agent Nightfall has proven herself resourceful in the past, and Nick is a sneaky old bastard." He smiled. "And everybody knows you can't trust a werewolf."

Sven tilted his head to one side, making his neck pop as joints and bones rearranged themselves. "They won't do anything. They wouldn't dare."

"We must purify ourselves for the ritual," Gault said. "We'll return in a few minutes and then begin." He and Blackstone descended the stairs once more.

"Jackie, are you all right?" Charlotte asked.

Jackie's head was down and her eyes were shut. She didn't move.

Sven shoved her and Jackie fell to the floor like a manikin. "She's just a dyke pussy. At least you vampires put up a bit of a fight."

"*Escute-me*," Nick mumbled.

Charlotte's eyes widened. She hadn't spoken Portuguese in forty years, maybe longer. Her brain remembered the words, though. He'd said *listen to me.*

"Huh?" Sven wrinkled up his face in confusion. "I didn't hit you that hard, old man."

Charlotte realized in relief the huge Nordic were-bear didn't speak Portuguese. She hadn't known Nick spoke it either, but as Blackstone had said, he was a sneaky old bastard.

"*Eu . . . eu estou ouvindo.*" *I'm listening.*

"Hey, knock that shit off!" Sven stalked over to Charlotte and cuffed her across the face hard enough to make her eyes lose focus.

"*Você tem que deixar eles me levarem. Então você tem que estar pronto. Eu vou te dar uma chance. Não desperdice.*" *You have to let them take me. Then you have to be ready. I will give you one chance. Don't waste it.*

"I said, cut it out!" Sven pounced upon Nick and dug his fingers into his shredded cheek.

Nick groaned.

"Leave him alone, damn you! Damn you to hell!" Charlotte cried.

Sven grinned at her. "Hell? Oh, you have no idea."

Behind him, the odd tear in reality popped and crackled like water droplets in hot oil.

Chapter Nineteen

November 2012
Reno, Nevada

A great battle raged within Jackie's body.

Perhaps the monster within her had sensed the impending threat from Gault and the black-haired man with him, for Jackie felt herself start an uncontrolled transformation as they entered the room. Before she could begin to fight off her change, Gault's new guest used some form of verbal hypnosis to control her.

Frozen and unable to act, she lay at one side of the ritual room where she'd fallen after Sven's shove. Her endocrine system screamed at her and her muscles quivered with frustrated impotence. She battled with her animal brain for control of her body. Only the paralysis kept the beast in check, and the interrupted transformation felt like it was tearing Jackie to pieces.

Across the room, Sven paced in front of Nick and Charlotte. Jackie hadn't even known were-*bears* were a thing. Could she take Sven? No question, the bear would be stronger, but she would be faster. Their battle would be brutal and bloody and certainly end with at least one of them dead and torn apart. The beast within her howled, eager to be released, to test itself against the monster before her.

Gault and the other man, whom Jackie understood was another vampire by his now-familiar scent, returned to the ritual room. They wore plain black robes and their heads had been anointed with fragrant oil. Gault carried an ancient, leather-wrapped tome.

He opened the book to a well-fingered page and intoned, "I, the Progenitor, take up the Station of the North." He stepped into a circle outlined in green powder just outside the circle of captives, facing the twisting, spitting entity floating in the room's center. "You, the Conspirator, take up the Station of the South."

"Blackstone, please! Think about what you're doing. We were friends once. Lovers. Doesn't that count for anything?" Charlotte struggled against her own unseen bonds.

Jackie's body yammered at her, trying to complete its change. She could feel the wolf, desperate to break free of the vampiric hypnosis. Knowing werewolves could kill vampires made her wonder if the beast might not be susceptible to Blackstone's power. If she let herself complete the transformation, she might kill Blackstone and Gault before Sven got hold of her, but she couldn't trust the beast not to seek the easiest prey—twelve helpless humans hanging from the ceiling.

Blackstone ignored Charlotte and moved into position in a blue-powdered circle opposite Gault.

"In the Station of the West, where the moon sets, the Unnatural," Gault intoned.

Sven lifted Jackie as if she weighed no more than a child and set her into a white-rimmed circle.

"And in the Station of the East, where the sun rises, the Undead." Gault's singsong voice took on a more urgent tone.

Sven hesitated. "Which one?"

"I don't care," Gault said. "Don't interrupt me again." Gault closed his eyes and began to chant in an ancient tongue. At intervals, he paused so Blackstone could repeat a few syllables.

"Take me," Charlotte said.

"No!" Nick shouted.

Sven grinned at Charlotte. "Sorry, Tits. It's your lucky day. I'll just have to take you . . . some other way." He grabbed Nick by the collar and lifted the old vampire easily with one hand.

"No!" Charlotte's cry was anguished.

Jackie felt the hormones that triggered the transformation flood through her body. Her glands clenched so hard they *hurt*.

As Sven set Nick down in the yellow powder circle, the old man started to cough and wheeze, as if the powder was causing him an allergic reaction.

Gault ceased his droning enchantment. "Silence him. I will not ask again."

Sven reached for Nick, but as he drew close, something popped in Nick's mouth and a glittering cloud erupted from him.

Sven gasped and staggered back, coughing and clawing at his face, disrupting the powder marks on the floor. The distinctive, sharp odor that was poisonous silver filled the air. Sven's face reddened and black spots appeared upon it where the silver had scarred him. He coughed and bright blood spattered out onto Nick's face.

Nick smiled, showing his fangs. "The thing about becoming mist is that you can hide things inside your body. Like a baggie full of silver dust, you stupid cunt."

Sven roared in fury. His jeans split apart as he became the ursine monstrosity.

"No! He'll ruin the ritual!" Gault screamed.

Sven lashed out at Nick and laid him open from throat to groin. The elderly vampire collapsed from the strangely bloodless wound without so much as a groan.

A grenade rolled out of his abdomen.

Suddenly, Jackie could move, and her own clothes shredded as her body became the wolf. All that was *Jackie* buried itself in the lowest levels of her brain, leaving the beast in complete control. She snarled her challenge at the bear and leaped at him, teeth flashing like knives.

* * *

As Jackie transformed into her werewolf form, Charlotte found she was freed from her paralysis. She dove for the grenade Nick had smuggled inside his body, yanked the pin, and hurled it at Gault and Blackstone. It skipped off the floor between them and struck the far wall with a resounding clank.

An explosion tore through the chamber. Wood paneling disintegrated into splinters, and the polarized glass windows behind it shattered. Sunlight poured into the room, catching Gault, Blackstone, and Charlotte in its burning rays.

Charlotte hauled herself into a shadow, shaking her head to clear it as choking dust filled the air. The clever old bastard had managed to get them all freed as he'd said he would, but at the cost of his life. Across the room, both Blackstone and Gault struggled to get out of the sunlight. Red blisters had appeared on their exposed flesh. *Gault is a vampire? How did I miss that?* He must have been freshly embraced.

They hadn't bothered to search her after taking her captive. Sloppy on their part, she thought, and drew her pistol. Then she realized the vampires had nothing to fear from her weapon. It was loaded with silver bullets; she hadn't expected to be fighting vampires. Her crossbow with the garlic-infused hawthorn bolts was still in her car, forty floors below, and it didn't look like she'd get a chance to retrieve it anytime soon.

"Go!" Blackstone shouted to Gault. "It's ruined." The explosion had scattered and blown away powder lines, breaking the circles. The crack in reality that had twisted in the room's center was gone.

Fire alarms hooted. Hotel guests were probably already fleeing the building.

The captive humans swung back and forth in their harnesses. A couple sported oozing shrapnel wounds that leaked thick, chemical-laden blood. Despite the explosion, none of them had awakened. Charlotte hoped none had sustained serious injuries. She felt weak and needed fresh blood, but she didn't dare feed on any of the captives because of their contamination.

Gault and Blackstone fled down the stairwell. Charlotte started to pursue them but stopped when she saw Jackie and Sven battling. Both wolf and bear were wounded but healing at unnatural lycanthropic pace. One of Jackie's forelegs dangled broken, having been crushed by a heavy blow. Blood sluiced down Sven's chest from a gash across his throat and he appeared to still be suffering the effects of silver poisoning in the form of open wounds leaking toxic black sludge.

Maybe Charlotte could even the odds.

She raised her pistol, took aim, and emptied her clip at the great bear. Silver bullets thudded into his hide and he roared in fury and pain. He sprang, not at Charlotte, but at Jackie. The bear bowled over the wolf, and both creatures tumbled out through a shattered window.

"Jackie!" Charlotte ran to the edge despite the afternoon sunlight bludgeoning her with its radiance. She feared they would still be falling down the face of the building, and no unnatural healing ability could save them from a forty-story plummet. Instead, she discovered they'd fallen onto an open terrace one floor down, and their battle continued anew.

The sun blistered Charlotte's skin and her pistol was empty. She fled back indoors and ran after Gault and Blackstone.

* * *

Wolf and Bear crashed to the cement terrace below the ritual room. Something broke in Wolf's side and made her yelp like a pup with a thorn in its foot. She scrambled back up to her three good feet to snarl at Bear, hackles raised.

Bear's fur was slick with his blood, some from the scratches and gashes Wolf had opened, and more gushing from wounds that stank of the poisonous metal. A great ugly stain spread from Bear's point of impact as the beast struggled to regain his feet. Wolf charged. She wouldn't be satisfied until Bear's organs were crushed within her jaws.

She lashed out for a killing stroke, but her wounded leg failed, and she tumbled to the cement. Bear was on her in a second, slamming a heavy paw into Wolf's side and making her broken ribs grate in excruciating pain. Bear roared and lowered his massive muzzle to tear Wolf's head off, jaws gaping wide.

Wolf whipped her slender snout upward and clamped her teeth down on Bear's tongue.

Bear screamed and shook his head, flinging Wolf aside like carrion. She struck the decorative cement railing at the terrace edge so hard her vision blacked out. She whimpered as her bones splintered. Bear found the strength to clamber to his feet despite his wounds, and Wolf felt the vibrations as the beast thundered toward her. Wolf whined as she tried to move, but her legs wouldn't bear her weight. Blood-scent filled her head as Bear charged.

Wolf used the last of her strength to fling herself to one side in one desperate lunge. She snapped jaws closed upon Bear's left foreleg as it passed by her, hamstringing it. The animal's heavy body smashed into and through the concrete railing and Bear fell with a receding roar of impotent fury, four hundred feet straight down.

Wolf whirled around, seeking someone else to slay in celebration. The crimson flooding her animal brain became white noise. Her legs wouldn't support her, and she fell to the cement, sides heaving as the pain of her body reshaping itself overtook her. The weak, soft human crouching in her hindbrain was trying to take over, pushing Wolf back into the cage of her mind. Wolf howled in frustration and fury, but what began as an ululating bestial shriek finished as a human's cry of agony.

Jackie gasped as she realized how badly the fight with Sven had injured her. Her unnatural healing ability had gone to work, and she felt the bones in her arms and sides knitting back together. Her entire body hurt. How much internal damage had she suffered? She'd never been so close to dying in a fight. It would have been so easy to just lie there against the cold concrete as the chill breeze blew across her naked skin.

But she couldn't do that. She still had work to do. Twelve innocents hung imprisoned and tortured for the benefit of some dark beast from the netherworld. Blackstone and Gault were both loose in the Silver Legacy. Charlotte would need Jackie's help.

She pushed her shoulders off the concrete, making fresh waves of pain shoot through her healing arm. Her side ached as broken ribs knitted. As she levered herself into a crouch, she realized she was healing faster than she ever had before. She'd have to ask Alix about it later. Or maybe Charlotte might know why.

Maybe, when it was all over, they could sit down and have a rational discussion like the couple of bizarre, unnatural creatures that they were.

Jackie eyed the hole Nick's grenade had blown in the side of the building and shook her head, knowing in her weakened state she couldn't make that vertical leap. She limped toward the terrace doors as fast as she could, hoping she wasn't too late.

Chapter Twenty

November 2012
Reno, Nevada

Charlotte hit the bottom of the stairwell with her pistol clutched in both hands. She'd reloaded with the only clip she had left, carrying standard lead bullets. Bullets, silver or otherwise, wouldn't do much to slow a vampire unless they struck someplace vital. If she could put a hole through a vital tendon, it might give her an advantage. She had no illusions about her chances, being outnumbered two to one. Gault may have been a fresh convert, but Blackstone was an ancient, powerful vampire, much stronger and faster than her. As if that weren't enough, he had that scary domination ability.

Gault was an unknown quantity. He must have been transformed in the intervening days since the Timberline dinner. He was still enough of a youngling vampire that his undead flesh hadn't yet become completely vulnerable to the sun. What abilities had he gained upon transformation? No two vampires were born the same, even when sired by the same parent.

She leaned out from the stairwell just enough to see down the hall, then whirled to check the opposite direction. Empty. *Which way should I go?* She chose the living room. If Blackstone and Gault hadn't already left, they'd have to pass by her to get out. With the building on a fire alert, the elevators would be locked down.

Blackstone and Gault could be hiding behind any of the large couches, the central support, or the pillars. Charlotte tried to cover every direction at once as she cautiously advanced into the main room. She paused to listen but only heard the distant growls and snarls of combat between Sven and Jackie.

At a soft noise behind her, she spun and fired blind. The gunshot echoed off the marble floor and the bullet buried itself in a column with an explosion of fragments.

"Dammit," she whispered. Another noise sounded behind her and she whirled again, finger quivering on the trigger. Again, nothing was there.

She closed her eyes for a dangerous full second. In that time, she allowed herself to relax, to become receptive to all external stimuli. When she opened them again, she saw Gault moving across the room. He must have the ability to become transparent. She was seeing him not so much with her eyes but the aggregate of her other senses.

She put a bullet into his face.

Gault tumbled head over heels from the impact and crashed against a wall. The bullet wouldn't kill him, but he'd be stunned from the sudden injection of foreign material into his skull. Charlotte turned away from him and something razor-sharp tore across her own face, blinding her for a moment. She fired in random directions until her gun clicked.

More pain ripped through her side. *A lycanthrope!* She screamed and lashed out blindly to defend herself. Her fist connected with bare flesh, not furred muscle.

Her vision cleared in one eye but the other remained blank and white. Blackstone stood there, his skin blistered where the sunlight had touched him. His fangs were bared and on his right hand he had a heavy leather gauntlet with gleaming claws made from werewolf fangs.

"Poor, dear Charlotte," he said. "Always so devoted to your work, so dedicated." He dropped into a fighting stance. "So pliable and easily manipulated. It's a shame you have to go this way."

"I'm not going any way, except out of here with your head in a bag," said Charlotte, taking a stance of her own. She would be at a terrible disadvantage against him when she could see from only one eye. In addition to the deadly gauntlet, he was bigger, faster, and stronger than her.

"Surrender," he said.

His dominance ability swelled against her, but she found reserves of strength to hold it off. The pain from her wounds kept her from focusing on his words and succumbing to his dominance. "Kiss my ass."

In all her years in the Collective, she'd trained against many vampires of differing combat skills, and was familiar with a variety of fighting styles.

But she'd never fought Blackstone before, not even in training.

He deflected her punches and kicks with his inhuman grace. His parries were beautiful, artistic. His ripostes were practical and violent. She got lucky and managed to snatch the gauntlet right off his hand but before she could use it herself, he swept her legs out from under her. As she fell, he straight-palmed her in the chest and sent her flying back into the central column. The expensive flat-screen television shattered into plastic splinters and the gauntlet flew away.

He flipped forward, his foot descending in a heavy axe kick. She rolled aside at the last moment or it would've shattered her spine. She entangled his feet in hers and twisted, bringing him to the floor. He crashed through the rack of stereo components. Before Charlotte could roll away, Blackstone kicked her in the face with the bottom of his foot hard enough for stars to flood the vision of her remaining good eye.

Her fingers found something heavy—the leg of the hardwood and glass coffee table. She yanked as hard as she could and broke the thick leg loose. In the same motion, she brought it around to smash across Blackstone's head. He collided with the corner of the stairs and stopped moving.

Before she could crawl after him, a hand clamped on her ankle. She kicked back in desperation, but the grip was unbreakable. She glanced back to see Gault hanging onto her, his eyes wide, his new fangs dripping venom.

Gault dragged her back. She tried to dig her talons into the floor, but they only scrabbled across the unyielding marble.

Then she was flying through the air, thrown by one ankle. She hit the wall hard enough to black out for a moment. Plaster rained around her and Gault stepped through the cloud of dust to grab her by her throat. He had the werewolf gauntlet on his other hand. He lifted her against the wall until her feet dangled. "Pl-please," she mumbled through the remains of her battered face. "S-sur . . . render." Charlotte could barely form the words through her mangled lips.

Gault paused before delivering his final, fatal blow. "You wish to surrender? To me?"

"No . . . You surrender . . . to me."

Gault's eyes widened and then he threw back his head and laughed. "Oh, *ma chérie*. That's rich. I'll remember those final words forever." His face hardened and Charlotte knew her time was at an end.

"Do it," she said.

The splintered coffee table leg burst through Gault's chest, driven by the fury and power of a battered, naked Jackie Langdon.

* * *

Gault slumped forward with the table leg sticking from his back, just to one side of his spine. Jackie felt sick. This was far worse than killing a zombie.

Gault twitched and fumbled at the piece of wood stuck through him. Foam bubbled from the corners of his mouth and he kept making a horrible "Uh . . . uh . . . uh . . ." sound.

Charlotte fell to the floor and Jackie knelt beside her. "God, you're really messed up," she said. One of the vampire's eyes was nothing but ruin amid the deep scratches and flaps of skin dangling from her face. Furrowed flesh showed amid the tatters of her clothing. The bloodless wounds unnerved Jackie, although she didn't know if it would be any better were Charlotte streaked with gore. The stink of death was more acute than it had been before.

Gault reached out an entreating hand to her. "Uh . . . uh . . ."

Charlotte clutched at Jackie, an intense gaze from her good eye. "Have to decapitate," she said through her torn-up lips.

"I . . . I can't. I'm not the monster you think I am." Jackie bowed her head.

Charlotte pulled her close and whispered in her ear. "I need you . . . to be the monster . . . that you are."

"Uh! Uh!" Gault's hands wrapped around the hardwood leg. With each little grunt, he tugged on it and it moved a quarter of an inch. Eventually, he would pull it out.

Jackie stepped away from Charlotte and looked at Gault. The man had helped to kidnap a dozen innocent women, with plans to slaughter them as a gift for a demon. No, Gault wasn't a man; he was a monster. Like setting a thief to catch a thief, there was only one way to kill a monster.

Jackie shut her eyes and released Wolf. It came to her faster and more easily than ever before. It didn't even hurt as the beast took hold and subsumed the woman. Wolf craved meat. Oh yes, her stomach cried out for the hot blood and entrails of a fresh kill. Not these cold, dead things laid out before her. But wait! One had the scent of an enemy about him. He wore the skin and teeth of a wolf on a limb.

"Uh! Uh!" shouted the enemy.

Wolf tore out the man's throat. No delicious burst of blood filled her mouth. It had to be there. She ripped deeper through dry sinew and tasteless flesh, flinging aside the chunks with disgust and contempt. Somewhere, she would find the warmth that all creatures had within them. The man wriggled. Wolf put her forepaws on the man's chest and head to hold him still. Her teeth found the spine deep within the enemy's neck. Spinal fluid would be a sweet delicacy if she could expose it. She bit harder, crunching through bone until her teeth met at the back of the neck.

Nothing!

Wolf nosed around the separate ends of the neck to see if she'd missed something edible, something to fill the yawning hunger. Nothing presented itself, so Wolf turned to pad away to seek real, living sustenance.

"Jackie!"

The stern tone made Wolf lower her head and tuck her tail between her legs. But . . . *she* was the alpha wolf, wasn't she? She spun around, hackles raised, and snarled at the woman on the floor.

Perhaps she had juicier flesh inside her.

Wolf smelled the woman's fear, but there was something else that made her hesitate. There was . . . warmth. Companionship. *Family!* Realization dawned upon her: the woman was of Wolf's pack.

Wolf's tail came up and wagged once, and her snarl became a friendly grin. The sudden self-awareness formed a spark deep within her, and that spark grew into a flame which consumed the wolf and bore the woman from the ashes.

Jackie fell to the floor, retching and gasping at the taste of death in her mouth. Gault's body lay off to the side, his head torn away and mangled, sightless eyes staring at the ceiling.

"You did it," Charlotte whispered. "Now Blackstone. By the stairs."

Jackie looked around, but Blackstone was gone.

Chapter Twenty-One

November 2012
Reno, Nevada

Jackie searched the entire floor as fast as she could, letting her nose be her guide. Blackstone was no perfumer. He had a scent and she could follow it.

She found Gault's housekeeper, dead with two puncture wounds in her neck. She was so pale Blackstone must have drained her dry. Jackie wondered if it would make the vampire more dangerous or slow and torpid. She returned to Charlotte's side. "I've got to get you out of here."

Charlotte's eyes were shut, and she was deathly still.

"Pastor? Charlotte?" Jackie shook her, unsure how to tell if the vampire was still alive.

A slight eyelid flutter, a tic of the muscles around Charlotte's nose, told Jackie the vampire lived.

She found her phone sitting on the end table, miraculously untouched in the battle. She touched a button. Alix answered after the second ring. "Alix, we found the kidnap victims. They've all been treated with the same stuff that was used on Mark. The hospital will need your expertise."

"Oh, thank God! We saw breaking news about an explosion at the Silver Legacy and someone falling from the upper floors. I was terrified it might be you."

"I'm a little shook up, but all right," Jackie told her. Alix relayed to the others that Jackie was okay, then promised to call a friend in the E.R. We saw breaking news about an explosion at the Silver Legacy and someone falling from the upper floors. I was terrified it might be you."

"I'm a little shook up, but all right. "Charlotte's in a bad way, Doc. You're going to need to work magic on her."

"Bring her back here. I'll do what I can. I wish there was a Gray's for vampire physiology, though."

"You're a rock star. You'll figure it out." Jackie hung up and took a deep breath. She was about to take a dangerous step into a much more complicated world.

She dialed 911.

"Nine-one-one. What's the nature of your emergency?" said a call taker.

Jackie didn't have her costume, so the voice modulator was out. She pitched her voice into the deepest growl she could manage. "This is White Fang. I've found the kidnapped victims. They're alive but require immediate medical attention. Send paramedics to the top floor of the Silver Legacy, in Conrad Gault's residence. He's responsible for the kidnapping."

"Wait, you're who?"

"Replay your recording. Missing people, top floor, Silver Legacy."

Jackie had to get herself and Charlotte out of the building, but she couldn't use the stairs or the elevator. If only she could fly like so many parahumans. Then an idea of the *just so crazy it might work* category came to her, and she sprang into action. She hurried into Gault's bedroom, snagged a robe from the back of a chair and the bedspread. She shrugged the robe over her shoulders and knotted it shut, wishing she'd had time to find clothing a bit more substantial. She rolled up Charlotte inside the blanket, careful to keep her arms at her side.

"I hope you know it's me doing this. If you freak out on the way down . . . I don't have high hopes for surviving any kind of lengthy fall." She paused. "I really hope you're still alive, Charlotte. Or whatever vampires are." She knotted the ends of the bedspread together and slung the entire bundle over one shoulder. Charlotte rode snugly across Jackie's back, leaving her hands free for her crazy idea.

She ran from the apartment, Charlotte bouncing against her back. The fire alarms were still hooting. All elevator doors were still shut and Jackie stopped at the first one, digging her fingers into the crack between the doors. With a grunt of exertion, she forced them open, leaving a dimly lit shaft yawning below her. The cable before her was moving upward. Somewhere below, an elevator was rising, carrying either police or fire personnel, neither of whom she was prepared to face.

Jackie sprang for the cable and slid down. Charlotte bumped against her and the knotted bedspread tightened across her chest, but the knot didn't slip. The stink of industrial lubricants and dust made her cough. She barely had a moment to catch her breath before she saw the elevator rising toward her.

The elevator struck her hard. It felt like she'd been punched through a wall. Shouts of surprise filtered up through the elevator roof. Someone in the car below hit the emergency stop button and the elevator ground to a halt.

In the next shaft over, separated by support crossbeams, another elevator ascended. Jackie leaped between beams and dropped, falling a dozen feet onto the next elevator's roof. Before it drew even with the first, she sprang back across the gap, narrowly missing getting split in half by a beam. Her hands wrapped around the thick, greased elevator cable beneath the first elevator and she slid downward.

She squeezed the cable as tightly as she could but still accelerated. The thick grease didn't let her get enough traction to slow herself. Cross beams and doors blurred past as she dropped. She needed the additional strength and healing of Wolf, but the intellect of the human. There had to be a way to incorporate the two somehow.

She concentrated on the beast, letting it bring aspects of itself forward, creating a form that was neither human nor monster, but somewhere in between. As the transformation took hold, Jackie clamped down upon it still uncompleted. Fur grew over her body, and she sprouted a bushy tail that pushed out from the robe. Her head subtly reshaped itself, snout lengthening and ears becoming more pointy and moving upward. Powerful wolf muscles mixed with her intelligent human ones, striations intertwining in a way Jackie had never achieved before. She found her mind at war with itself, with the animal part clamoring to be released to hunt and slay, while the human part struggled to maintain equilibrium.

The bottom of the shaft couldn't be far below at the pace she was dropping. Stopping herself on the greased cable was out of the question. She was going to have to catch one of the crossbeams blurring past. Before she gave herself a chance to have second thoughts, she pushed herself off the cable, twisting in midair. Her hands glanced painfully off a beam and she continued her fall. Her greasy hands slipped off the second beam, but she did slow herself enough that she caught the next one and held on, arms draped over the steel. The bundle holding Charlotte shifted and she realized the knot was starting to work its way loose.

A counterweight clattered upward as the elevator far above her began its descent. Jackie let go of the beam before the rising weight could take her hands off at the wrists.

She fell again, bouncing painfully off another crossbeam, and came to a sudden, painful stop. The bones in her bare feet and legs cracked with the impact. She fell against the wall and realized suddenly that she was at the bottom of the shaft. There was a door only a few feet above her head. Ignoring the pain in her legs, she leaped for it. Jackie forced open the door and found herself staring into the parking garage.

She'd made it.

Jackie nearly collapsed with sudden relief, but instead staggered into the darker recesses of the garage's lower levels. Charlotte bounced across her shoulders with every stride. Her entire body ached from the abuse.

She got to Charlotte's Corvette and slipped the bedspread off her shoulders. It had nearly torn through at some point in the descent and she'd been fortunate not to lose Charlotte in the shaft. She concentrated on reversing the transformation she'd started, which was more difficult than she'd anticipated. Wolf craved the wide-open outdoors, with room to run, territory to claim, meat to take. Jackie gritted her teeth and pushed Wolf back as hard as she could. *Back down, back into the darkness. You'll have your moment. I'm starting to understand you.*

From her animal brain, she heard only silence, as if Wolf had accepted her control and laid down to rest.

She unwrapped Charlotte from her blanket and leaned her against the rear wheel of the Corvette. She stirred a little, and Jackie felt a stab of joy. She may have been undead, but she still had some life in her. Jackie appropriated her keys and opened the passenger side door, then hurried back to Charlotte and hoisted her in her arms.

"Don't . . . scratch . . . the paint," Charlotte said as Jackie set her in the passenger seat and buckled her seat belt.

"Sorry about the grease stains. I'll pay for the cleaning." Jackie raced back around the car and flung herself into the driver's seat. She was grateful for the darkened, polarized windows and used a dangerous few seconds for some deep breaths. She turned the key and the powerful engine thrummed to life.

Charlotte moaned.

Jackie glanced over at her as she threaded the car through the tight turns of the garage. The vampire's skin had gone an ashen gray color. Her face was scrunched in agony and her fangs were bared. "You look awful."

"Need blood."

"Blood in a bag good enough? Alix has a supply back at the Mine."

"Fresh."

A prowling police cruiser turned into the garage from off the street and chirped its siren. "You! Stop right there. Turn off your motor and roll down your windows," the cruiser's driver ordered over the loudspeaker.

Jackie immediately hammered the accelerator. The engine sang and the wheels screamed in a burnout, filling the immediate area with smoke.

The officer in the patrol car turned on his siren and lights as the Corvette roared up the exit ramp and crashed through the entry gate. The tires squealed in protest as Jackie took a sharp left. She floored the accelerator and the car jumped forward. A quick glance in the rear-view mirror showed her the police cruiser fishtailing out of the building in pursuit.

"If you've got any super-secret spy gadgets on your car, now would be a good time to mention it." Jackie whipped the car into the oncoming traffic lanes to beat a stoplight. Angry horns blared in her wake. The Corvette's fat tires stuck to the pavement as Jackie cut across a gas station tarmac, startling a woman washing the windows of her minivan.

"No . . . tricks." Charlotte's voice was faint.

"Don't you die on me. I didn't go down forty floors of elevator shaft just so you could die and leave me in the middle of this mess."

"Need . . . blood."

Jackie glanced behind. Two cruisers were already in pursuit and as she looked, another squealed around a corner to join the chase. The Corvette could outrun any police car, but nobody could outrun a helicopter or a radio signal. If she was going to lose the police, it was going to require a trick, and she was going to need Charlotte's help.

She took her right hand off the wheel and offered Charlotte her wrist. "*Bon appetit.*"

"Can't feed . . . from werewolf."

Jackie grabbed back onto the wheel with both hands as she steered through traffic. "Look, I can't exactly stop at the local blood bank or something. I'm a little busy trying to save both our lives." She took another sharp left onto Wells and up the on-ramp onto I-80. She dodged around a truck and cut back over to run the exit onto 580 South. Maybe she could lose the cops in the mountains . . . if she could get there. "I can't do this without your help, Charlotte. There's a lot of goddamn traffic and I'm going to need both hands in a couple minutes when the road gets twisty." Jackie cut across two lanes and back, threading the 'Vette through early evening commuters. The one thing in her favor was that the sun had already dropped behind the mountains, and a black car would be tougher to see in the near darkness. She thrust her wrist in front of Charlotte again. "Take it and eat, before I change my mind."

With shaking hands, Charlotte took hold of Jackie's arm and raised it to her face. Her fangs elongated and she closed her mouth on Jackie's wrist.

The sudden, sharp pain made Jackie jump. The Corvette wandered across lanes as she struggled to keep control of the beast raging within her. The fingers of her left hand, clamped around the wheel, sprouted tufts of gray fur and her nails started to thicken into black claws. Her vision altered as her eyes started to transform into Wolf's.

"No, you bitch!" she muttered under her breath. "Stay human."

Tires squealed as commuters braked to avoid the headlong rush of the Corvette with a half dozen Reno Police cars in pursuit, sirens blaring. Jackie struggled to maintain control of the low-slung car with the speedometer pushing toward triple digits as much as she struggled to retain her humanity. One slip on either battlefront would result in a spectacular crash.

She gritted her teeth, willing them to remain human, and drove for her life.

Chapter Twenty-Two

November 2012
Reno, Nevada

Jackie's blood was sweet and spicy, with dark overtones of the beast trapped within her soul combining with the bright vitality of her human side. Her unnatural healing closed the wounds Charlotte opened with her fangs almost as soon as she bit into them. She didn't have enough poison within her fangs to keep dosing the wounds, and at last had to resort to brute gnawing force. Each swallow revitalized her undead flesh. Her cells awakened from their dormancy and her body set about repairing itself.

Charlotte gasped as her body became whole in spite of the damage wrought by the sun and by Blackstone's werewolf-fang gauntlet. That kind of healing wasn't supposed to be possible for vampires. Something about Jackie's werewolf blood was increasing her body's self-healing a thousandfold. It made her giddy.

A sudden motion jarred her hard enough to bang her head against the window beside her. Startled, she looked up, thick-headed with blood-induced torpor.

"I hope you got enough of what you needed." Jackie wrestled the wheel with her left hand. "I can't feel my arm from my shoulder on down."

The lights of the cars on the highway seemed unusually bright to Charlotte, and when she moved her head, they left colorful trails and afterimages in her eyes. She heard the howling of sirens behind her in seventeen-part harmony. The rhythmic swaying of the car soothed her as if she were a baby being rocked.

She took a deep breath and marveled at the sweetness of the air. She hadn't felt so alive in decades. She wanted to laugh, to cry, to scream, to seduce, to celebrate her existence.

Behind them, the chorus of sirens became discordant banging as a police car lost control and was broadsided by another.

"Hey, we're on the highway." She wiggled her fingers before her eyes.

"Christ, are you *stoned*?"

Charlotte burst out in an embarrassed giggle.

* * *

Jackie grasped the wheel with both hands at last. Her arm was still more numb than not, and her hand was full of pins and needles. She'd negotiated traffic reasonably well with one hand, but for the kind of tricky maneuvers she needed to lose the pursuing police, both hands were necessary. If she'd had a third, she'd need that one too.

"Charlotte, I need you to focus." Jackie threaded the Corvette between two gravel-hauler semis. "We may need to leave the car in a hurry, and I can't carry you and still run."

"I'm cool, really." Charlotte's voice sounded airy.

"You may not be in a minute." Jackie stood on the brakes as an inattentive tourist rambled across into her lane. She downshifted and whipped the Corvette around the sedan, nearly getting rear ended by the gravel hauler behind her to the right.

Charlotte's hand lashed out faster than Jackie would have thought possible and clamped around her upper arm with such surprising strength that she winced. "Don't you dare scratch my car, White Fang. I bought it new."

"So you keep telling me. I'll buy you another one. Shit, I'll buy you two. We're going to have a police helicopter on us any minute instead of just a news chopper and then we might not get away at all."

Charlotte shook her head as if trying to clear it. "I feel so weird, Jackie. It's almost like my heart is beating."

"That's fascinating," Jackie said with dry sarcasm. "Hang on and stay sharp. I'm going to need your eyes." She shut off the headlights and cut across four lanes of traffic to charge down an exit ramp, a shadow in the darkness. Tires squealed behind them and metal banged against metal. Jackie ran the Corvette down the ramp shoulder to pass the cars waiting at the bottom for the light to change. The car shuddered once and the passenger side mirror vanished with a loud bang.

"Aww, no . . ." Charlotte whined.

"Sorry." Jackie skipped the 'Vette off a curb and between two cars on the cross street. Then they were in inky black shadow as they headed south on a frontage road near the airport.

The darkness was lit only by the headlights of oncoming traffic or the taillights of others that seemed to stand still as the Corvette tore past them.

"How far does this road go?" asked Charlotte.

"Far enough. Hang on."

A semi going the opposite direction flashed its brights at Jackie—a polite reminder that her own lights were off.

She yanked on the handbrake so as to keep the brake lights off and cranked the steering wheel hard to the left. The Corvette's back end swung around a hundred and eighty degrees into the opposite lane. The police cars braked hard as their drivers tried to spot the black car in the darkness. One cruiser tried to make the same turn but the heavy patrol car couldn't match the nimble 'Vette and it hit a curb broadside hard enough to roll onto its side.

Jackie released the handbrake and used the throttle to powerslide through the full turn. Now they were heading in the opposite direction with very little loss of speed. She hammered the accelerator and whipped around the semi that had flashed her a moment ago. Then she skidded around a sharp left to dive into Quail Business Park. She took her foot off the accelerator and let the car coast without braking.

"That was slick. I don't know if I'd have thought of that."

"We're too close to the airport for the helicopter now," Jackie said. "I figured if I could lose the pursuit, we'd be home free."

Charlotte looked back but saw no headlights or flashing red and blues. "I think you lost them."

"I'm not ready to assume that yet," Jackie said. "Let's get into some real cover and see what happens. They're not going to give up on us just because they lost us temporarily."

"There." Charlotte pointed at some Conex work trailers beside a construction site. "Think you can squeeze her in there without scratching her up too badly?"

"This would be a lot easier if I wasn't driving without lights." Jackie turned the Corvette onto the rough ground of the construction site. Sure enough, something banged hard off the bottom of the car but despite its low ground clearance, the car churned ahead through the soft ground. Then the big, wide tires mired between the trailers and Jackie shut off the engine without even attempting to free the car. "End of the line."

Charlotte looked around. "This is a good spot at least. You can't see the road, and with these trailers here, someone would have to be flying directly overhead to spot us." She smiled, her teeth gleaming in the darkness. "Very professional. So, what happens now?"

"We've got to get out of here and find Blackstone. We have to stop him before he starts his plan all over again."

"And how do you propose we do that?" Charlotte asked.

"Let me use your phone. Mine got blown up."

* * *

Charlotte watched and listened as Jackie dialed a number and got the recorded operator saying "If you'd like to make a call . . ." She punched additional numbers without disconnecting and the recording cut off, replaced by a verbal prompt, "Welcome, White Fang." Thus, having accessed her computer system, Jackie started issuing coded commands.

What would happen to the Midnight Collective in light of Blackstone's betrayal? Surely it would continue—organizations like that were intended to survive long after their founders. It would be tainted by Blackstone's dabbling in the blackest of dark magic, though. No sane vampire should ever seriously consider making a deal with a demonic being. "Not even for the sun," she said aloud. She wouldn't be able to go back to them. Not now. For the first time in decades, she had neither responsibility nor plan, and it was a confusing place to be.

Jackie's selfless heroism had probably saved both of their lives. After fighting Sven and slaying Gault, she'd still found the strength to get them out of the Silver Legacy—and Charlotte had no idea how she'd managed *that* particular feat without getting them caught or killed—and then donated her blood to keep Charlotte from dying. Those were the actions of a hero, not a callous, uncaring beast.

Maybe she did owe Jackie something more than a promise not to kill her.

"Listen . . ." Charlotte stopped, unsure how to proceed. She wasn't in the habit of . . . what was it she was doing, anyway? Forming an alliance? Making a friend of an enemy? Jackie opened the door. Chill air flowed into the car. Goosebumps rose on Charlotte's skin, something she'd taken for granted when she was human. Most of the time she never noticed temperatures. Besides helping her heal her wounds, Jackie's blood seemed to have made her hypersensitive. "Jackie, I want to do something. Let me help you defeat Blackstone." She touched Jackie's arm, feeling the heat burning just beneath her skin. "He betrayed me. He betrayed all vampires. Maybe he didn't kill Nick, but he may as well have. I don't have a lot of friends in what has become my life, but Nick was one."

Jackie nodded. "I'm glad you feel that way. I could use your help. I don't know a goddamn thing about vampires." She laughed suddenly. "Hell, I barely know anything about werewolves."

"My experience is yours. What do you need from me?"

"I presume Blackstone still wants to fulfill his ritual. He still needs an *unnatural* and an *undead* to pull that off. That's us. Unless he wants to start over completely, he's going to try to get us back."

Charlotte shook her head. "That'll never work. We know what he wants, and he knows we know."

"Blackstone knows who I *really* am. He's going to want to make a deal to get you and me back. That means he needs something to trade." Jackie's jaw muscles tightened. "My friends."

"We need to go steal a car. We're not going anywhere in my 'Vette." A hulking black shadow of a vehicle rolled around one of the Conexes and stopped before them, its lights out and operating so quietly that Charlotte hadn't heard it approach. "Where the hell did that come from?" She fumbled with her seat belt, unfamiliar with operating the latch from the left.

"Kentucky originally. More recently my place," said Jackie. "That's our ride. Give me a minute to change into something a little more appropriate." She exited the 'Vette and climbed into the back of the large truck.

Charlotte clucked in dismay at the scratches along the side of her car, foreseeing hours of body work in the Corvette's future. *If the police didn't impound it as evidence*, she thought. It sobered her to realize she might never get to drive it again. She traced her fingers along the curve of the front fender, remembering the evening she'd driven it off the lot and raced it down the Pacific Coast Highway. Perhaps losing it forever was like being cut from the Collective. She was getting the opportunity for a fresh start.

Might as well make the most of it.

She tore away the shreds of clothing that remained and stood naked for a moment, enjoying the feeling of the cold breeze blowing over her healed skin. She felt it saturating every pore. Then she removed her leather body suit from the bag in the trunk. She stepped into it and zipped it up the back, leaving her hands and feet unencumbered. She pulled the full-face mask over her head and strapped a harness across her shoulders. She hung a small quiver of the garlic-infused hawthorn bolts over one shoulder and the crossbow over the other. Her machete in its scabbard went across her chest for easy access.

She looked down at the holstered gun. She still had a clip of silver bullets that wouldn't be any good against Blackstone. If she took it, was she declaring herself still to be Jackie's enemy? No. Blackstone had used a lycanthropic ally once in Sven; he might have another hiding somewhere. She strapped on the holster but put a clip of regular bullets into the weapon instead of silver, her concession to her new werewolf ally.

"You look ready for anything," Jackie said behind her.

Charlotte turned to see Jackie standing proud in her White Fang outfit. The contours of the suit did give her a masculine shape. No wonder she had fooled so many. Charlotte felt her fangs lengthen and she flashed them in a dangerous grin. "I feel ready."

Jackie opened the truck door and engaged her voice modulator, speaking in a baritone growl. "Let's go."

Chapter Twenty-Three

November 2012
Reno, Nevada

Police cars prowled through the area, and Jackie knew it would only be a matter of time before they spotted Charlotte's Corvette. She took the truck onto the highway and headed back toward downtown, keeping it at the speed limit so as not to attract attention. "It's good we got out when we did. I'm sure they'll find and impound your car. Anything they can track back to you?"

"I have no idea," Charlotte said, looking at the White Fang cowl on the seat beside her. "I've been wiped from my organization's computers. I don't have a safety net anymore. For all I know, they could have put me onto the Homeland Security or PRA watch list by now."

"Dominica's pretty sharp about finding and altering records. I'll put her to work on your behalf."

"Why are you doing this?"

Jackie shrugged. "You've got my blood running through your veins right now. Least I can do is make sure it doesn't get spilled."

Charlotte looked around the cab. "It looks like Star Trek in here."

Jackie had grown so accustomed to all her high-tech gear in the cab that she'd forgotten how advanced everything looked. Dominica had loaded the truck with all manner of electronic equipment. Anything she thought would be necessary, useful, or just plain cool had found its way into the truck's cab, bed, or frame. "I guess it is a little crazy," she said at last. "You have to be, to put on a costume and fight crime."

"I think you're damn good at it," said Charlotte.

"Thanks. That means a lot to me."

"Blackstone scares me," Charlotte admitted. "He's an elder vampire. I'm talking nine centuries here. Really powerful."

"Nine hundred years old? No wonder's he's gone batshit nuts. That's a long time."

"Nuts? Yeah, maybe you're right. Raising the dead? Entreating with demons? That's not the mark of a sane mind. He's gone completely rogue. That's the kind of thing that could start a new culling if we don't shut it down. Werewolves hunt humans for food and sport. That's why we kill them—to protect humans so they won't start hunting vampires again."

"A couple of hours ago you were almost dead. If I hadn't been around to feed you, would you have been so noble? Or would you have grabbed some innocent passerby off the street and drained him dry?" Jackie lowered her head, keeping her jawline enshrouded in the shadow of her cowl.

"I might have. I was dying. Humans go to great lengths to avoid death, and their lives are brief flickers compared to the eternal sunset of the vampire. I don't want to die and I'll do what I must to avoid it."

"So, Blackstone scares you because he's a rogue? He's going to bring down the wrath of humanity on your race?"

"Worse. He wants to make a treaty with a demon to remove the ban that keeps us out of sunlight. If that works, he'll be able to do whatever he wants at any time. And what's more, he'll be able to pass that ability on to any vampires he sires because it will be tied to his deal. You'll have a race of day-walking vampires spring up, and that'll spell the end for me and those like me who are still consigned to the darkness. And by doubling the time they can walk the earth, you can bet they'll step up their efforts to make your race only a bad memory. Now do you get why I'm worried? We're both on the deathwatch here."

Jackie sighed and nodded. "I understand." She wheeled the truck through narrow gaps in traffic, making the onboard sonar panic at the near misses. She disabled the system. Using Charlotte's phone, she dialed a number. "I wish I still had mine. I'm lucky I can remember any of these numbers at all." She paused, listening. "Jenn, it's me. I'm on Charlotte's phone. Call when you get this." A second call to Alix was equally fruitless. She felt her pulse pounding in her temples as she tried Dominica.

"Nothing?" Charlotte asked as Jackie handed the phone back to her.

"At least one of them should have picked up. Even if they're in the mine, there's wi-fi down there." Imagining the worst made her press the accelerator a little harder and cut the turns a little sharper.

"We should hurry."

"Way ahead of you." Ahead, Jackie saw dense constellations of brake lights as they approached the exit leading to the winding road up to the VC Highlands. "Hold on." She swung into the breakdown lane. Horns blared and tires shrieked as she slipped down the exit ramp. Cars waited at the bottom for the light to change. Jackie wrenched the wheel over and scraped the truck against the concrete wall to the left, leaving a shower of sparks in its wake.

"Your cute young techie is going to be pissed at the mess you're making of her truck."

The truck hurtled through the intersection, shooting the gap between a northbound bus and southbound pizza driver. "Truck's built for it, unlike your car." Jackie cut straight across the center island of a roundabout. The truck's suspension complained at the abuse but Jackie's face twisted into a feral grin. She weaved around traffic, passing on the left or right as needed.

"Kind of hard to save her life if you kill us getting there," Charlotte said.

"Aren't you dead already?"

"Undead, please."

"Don't argue semantics. I'm the writer here." Jackie yelped as a car turned left in front of her and only through the fortune of the foolish did she avoid pancaking them into it.

When the road narrowed to one lane each direction, Jackie steered the truck onto the rough ground beside the road, speckled with scrub brush, fist-sized rocks, and occasional hidden culverts. Marker posts smacked against the truck's bumper and flopped back and forth in their wake. With a resounding crash, a speed limit sign appeared right before the truck and disappeared beneath it just as quickly.

"That sounded expensive," Charlotte said. "You're going to need to write another book."

"Do you want to do this?"

"Yes, I'd love to."

Jackie didn't have time to snark back at the vampire for she knew a sharp curve was coming up and she took the truck fully off the road. "Fence-buster," she said.

The computer chirped to let her know it had understood her order. Underneath the front bumper, actuators slid two wickedly sharp blades from underneath the truck and rotated them upward until they rested against the heavy-duty front bumper. Jackie hammered down the accelerator. "Hold on," she said. "This worked in all our tests."

"What worked? Oh, shit!" Charlotte braced herself as the truck jolted through a low fence at the edge of someone's property along the hillside.

Sparks sprayed as the blades sheared through the metal. The severed fence banged against the windshield, but not hard enough to crack the military-spec bullet-resistant glass. One of the headlights went out and Jackie activated the extra overhead lights bolted to the truck's roof. Then the truck was through and back on the road.

"You're crazy!" Charlotte shouted.

"Maybe." Jackie passed a car on the right, riding the slope of an embankment. She swung back across both lanes in front of a sedan coming down the opposite direction and bounced up the steady grade of slope littered with more scrub. The truck caromed off a rock the size of a sofa and the steering wheel began to shake. Jackie knew she'd broken something important. The engine took on a labored sound as if it were fighting against its own inevitable lycanthropic transformation from finely tuned machine to inert pile of scrap.

"How long to get back to your headquarters?" Charlotte asked. She had one hand braced against the truck's roof and the other against the dash, pressing herself back into the seat.

"Just a couple more minutes."

The slope took a sudden drop through a small valley with a stand of small trees that looked far too close together.

"You're not going to make it." Charlotte undid her seat belt.

"I can make it," Jackie said through clenched teeth.

The truck hit an unseen rock and suddenly they were airborne. In a blur of motion, Charlotte sliced through Jackie's seat belt and grabbed her by the arm. With one foot, she kicked the passenger door fully off its hinges and sprang into the darkness, pulling Jackie behind her.

They spun through the air to crash into soft dirt among the trees, entwined as they rolled to a stop. Jackie's truck bashed itself into a rock bigger than it was and burst apart.

Despite their close call, Jackie had never felt more alive. "That was close."

"You carried me down from the top of the Legacy. I owed you this much." Charlotte had wound up straddling Jackie when they came to a stop. It was a position that could have led to a kiss, but Jackie's heart longed for a certain blonde-headed assistant. Any attraction she felt toward the vampire was purely driven by the moment. "Also, that's two vehicles you wrecked tonight. Next time, I'm driving."

"That's fair. Aw, shit." Jackie's face fell.

"What is it?"

"My cowl was in there. Dominica's going to hate me."

"Not if we save her life. Wait here for a minute. Catch your breath." She trotted down the hill to the wrecked truck. Jackie heard metal wrench and glass crackle. When Charlotte returned, she had the White Fang cowl clutched in one hand, seemingly not any worse for the wear after the wreck. She handed it back to Jackie, who pulled it over her head. "Now you look right. How far are we from your place?" Charlotte's voice was soft.

"Hundred, maybe a hundred fifty yards up that hill." Jackie sniffed the air, letting the nighttime breeze speak its secrets to her.

Charlotte pulled out her crossbow and smiled from underneath her own cowl. "Race you."

Chapter Twenty-Four

November 2012
Reno, Nevada

The Langdon residence was fully dark. Even the outside security lights were off. "You don't want to go in through your headquarters entrance first?" Charlotte asked as they ran up the hill toward the house.

"No," Jackie said. "If the power's out above, it'll be out in the mine. They're tied to the same backup system."

"You don't know the power's out."

"No, but I don't know it isn't, either. I can't see in pitch black."

"Me neither."

"I thought you could see in the dark."

"Dark means there's still some light. Moonlight. Starlight. Something. Underground is pitch black."

"Then let's make sure the house is clear before checking out down below."

They reached the edge of the property and dropped low behind a deadfall log. A large black van was parked in the circle drive with the words *Washoe County Coroner* printed on the van's side in neat block letters.

She passed Charlotte the binoculars. "Why a coroner's van?"

"Maybe Blackstone needed a few demon zombies," Charlotte said. "We don't know how long it takes him. Maybe he had some ready to go. Or maybe he raided the morgue before coming here. Either way, we're probably going to run across trouble." She handed back the binoculars.

"Yeah, no shortage of dead people in the world. Okay, you take the front and I'll go in the side and we'll search the place."

"Bad idea to split up," Charlotte said.

"You sure about that?"

"Jackie, I've spent fifty years clearing out werewolf dens. I know a little about this kind of operation."

"All right then, I'll bow to your experience."

"And you know the lay of the land better, so you take point."

"Any last tips for taking out that Blackstone bastard if we find him?"

"Stake and decapitate him. Same as you did for Gault." Charlotte raised her machete. "Or you hold him at bay with your teeth and claws and I'll finish him with this."

Jackie shivered. "All right, let's head in. Watch out for zombies. And watch out for my friends. Let's try not to kill anyone who's not already dead."

Charlotte put her crossbow back into its sling and drew her pistol. "Lead on, White Fang."

Keeping to the shadows cast by the waning moon, they approached the house. Jackie headed for the van first, the tungsten claws embedded in her boots making quiet clicks on the asphalt. She crouched behind the van and sniffed. The scent of decaying flesh and formaldehyde permeated the air. The side door was open and she took a moment to verify nobody was waiting inside to jump her.

Charlotte appeared out of the darkness beside her. She touched Jackie's arm and pointed with the machete.

A woman in scrubs stood near the house's open front door. At first, Jackie thought it was Alix, but after a better look, she realized the woman was unfamiliar. She stood unmoving on the cement terrace, staring at the two vigilantes.

"Zombie?" Jackie whispered.

"I don't know," Charlotte said. "Be careful."

They approached the woman. Her head moved as she watched them. Her eyes were wide and staring and Jackie wondered if she might be in shock. Her ID badge was clipped to the breast pocket of her scrubs. Maybe she really was from the coroner's office. The smell of dead flesh and chemical cocktails leached from every surface of the van, making it so Jackie couldn't identify any nearby zombies by scent.

Still, she had to be sure. She switched on her voice modulator. "Ma'am, are you all right?"

The woman's eyes rolled in her head and she swayed in the moonlight. As she turned, Jackie saw the telltale bite mark on the side of her neck. She started to fall and Jackie lunged forward to catch her. The woman opened her mouth and a greenish smoke issued from it. Jackie jerked back in surprise, twisting her head away so whatever it was wouldn't contact her skin and she wouldn't inhale it.

With a whistling sound, Charlotte whipped her machete through the woman's neck.

The severed head bounced into the juniper bushes near front door. The evergreens blackened and shriveled in the darkness as the vapor contacted them. The body collapsed without the expected fountain of blood erupting from the stump of neck. In fact, Jackie realized, there wasn't any blood at all.

"She was drained dry." Charlotte's voice was rife with distaste.

"Why? Just because?"

"Blood is power. The more he consumes, the stronger he becomes."

"So, you're saying he's got a full charge?"

"Yes." Charlotte grimaced, showing her fangs. "We don't do this to people. Not anymore. This is just . . . perverse."

"We'll deal with the moral implications later. How'd you know she was already dead?"

Charlotte hesitated. "I . . . I didn't, for sure. It's what I would have done in Gault's place. He's hurt and being hunted. He needs whatever advantage he can get. And for someone like him, humans are only cattle."

Jackie pointed at her. "Don't do that again. Not unless you're absolutely sure. What if she'd still been alive? You'd be a murderer then."

"I've been worse." Charlotte folded her arms tight against herself.

"All right, let's go, Charlotte."

"Nightfall."

"What?"

She indicated her own mask. "You wear a mask and call yourself White Fang. Call me Nightfall. It was my code name in the Collective. Maybe that doesn't mean anything to them anymore, but it still means something to me."

"Nightfall. I like it."

They entered the house.

* * *

For the first time in a very long time, Charlotte was scared.

It had been years, maybe even decades, since she'd been truly afraid that she might not survive an encounter. She'd been in some real hellholes over the course of her career, but the sheer depravity Blackstone had displayed had made her jump at shadows.

As she followed Jackie into the house, pallid hands closed around her head from behind. Charlotte's nerves clenched and the hot werewolf blood coursed through her veins. She squirmed free of the grip by dropping straight down, her legs moving outward in tandem until she was in the splits beneath her assailant. The stinking, emaciated man had the telltale sores on his face of the habitual methamphetamine user. His right eyeball had burst and spread ruin down his cheek.

Charlotte shot him in the face.

The bullet caught the zombie under his chin and blew most of his head off. Despite the tremendous wound, he still reached down to grab blindly at her. Charlotte froze for a moment. A werewolf would have collapsed and died, and she'd spent so many decades fighting them that she'd expected the zombie to do the same. She dug her climbing talons into his arms to brace herself, and then swept his legs out from under him. He crashed down to the floor and she drove her machete through his throat. With a twist of the knife blade, she sent the remains of his head flying across the room.

Behind her, she heard Jackie snarl and the sounds of fists and feet pummeling flesh. She whirled around to see Jackie battling two zombies, a heavyset black man and a woman who might once have been somebody's beloved grandmother.

Jackie used vicious slashes to keep the two zombies at bay. She dropped to balance on one hand and kick out with both feet in a fluid move that Charlotte would have called *capoeira* if she hadn't performed it completely wrong. Nevertheless, the heavy double-kick impacted the black man's prodigious belly and sent him stumbling backward against the staircase.

Charlotte leaped onto the grandmother's back, wrapped her legs around the woman's waist and her arms around the head and twisted it off with her bare hands. She dropped the grisly lump of reanimated flesh and turned just in time to see Jackie smash a heavy butcher-block coffee table end-first down on the other zombie's head, crushing it into reddish-gray paste.

"Jackie," Charlotte said.

Jackie whirled, splintered coffee-table leg held up like a spear. She didn't look like herself anymore; she looked like a wolf wearing another wolf's head.

Charlotte raised her hands. "Easy, White Fang. It's me. I'm on your side."

The wild glare in Jackie's gaze softened and her face returned to her own as the woman tamed the beast once more. She flung aside the table leg. "I'm having a hard time keeping myself in check."

"It's the stress of all this combat."

"Charlotte . . . Don't let me lose it completely. Promise me if I do . . . you'll stop me."

She found her pistol, checked it, then nodded. "If it comes to that, I will."

* * *

"None of them have any of Gault's potions with them," Jackie said after searching the zombie bodies.

"Maybe Blackstone doesn't have any."

"Maybe, but I think there's something more sinister at work here. I think he still wants to capture us intact and use us in his demonic transaction."

"So why send his undead soldiers after us?"

"Tire us out. Make us use up our resources so they're depleted when we face him." The rest of the house appeared to be abandoned, with no sign of Blackstone. Or Jackie's friends.

"That one outside, she had that smoke inside her," Charlotte said. "Some kind of Gault concoction, maybe? Seemed pretty lethal."

"On the surface, maybe, but she'd have had to kiss me for it to do any damage. Smoke is avoidable."

"I'm grateful you avoided it."

"Me too. Uh oh." Jackie found the bookcase that hid her elevator had been shoved aside and torn from its hinges.

Light burned steady from below in the mine.

"He's down there, waiting for us. Probably with your friends," Charlotte said.

"I know." Jackie turned to look at Charlotte. Her dark eyes gleamed amid the leather of her mask. "You can still walk away from all this. You've done more than enough to help me."

Charlotte shrugged. "In for a penny, in for a pound."

Jackie held out her hand, and Charlotte clasped it. "Let's go."

Chapter Twenty-Five

November 2012
Reno, Nevada

The elevator cage didn't respond to Jackie's call, so she and Charlotte went down the ladder in the elevator shaft. They reached the top of the elevator car and dropped into the cage. The control panel was a smoldering wreck of burnt wiring, adding its sharp tang to Blackstone's vampire stink. Smoke and dust filled the air and Charlotte wondered how much of it was werewolf-killing silver. Jackie could be poisoning herself simply by breathing.

Blackstone sat on a stool by the computer terminals, surrounded by Alix, Dominica, Jenn, and Mark, who were on chairs facing him. Charlotte spotted the telltale wounds on their necks right away. He'd fed on each of them, which she didn't understand because he should have already been stuffed with the drained coroner's blood. Vampires could drink their fill from a single person and if they overfed, they would become torpid and slow. Blackstone showed no signs of that, though, and looked no worse for the wear after their prior battle. The hostages looked listless and barely conscious. Maybe instead of feeding, Blackstone only injected them with the soporific poison in his fangs.

The tunnel to the surface and secret exit for Jackie's truck had been sealed by a great pile of shattered stones. Blackstone must have set off an explosion to make the tunnel collapse.

"Ah, at last, my guests arrive." Blackstone's smile was devoid of humor. "I do hope you weren't terribly inconvenienced by my guards above. Good help is *so* hard to find. I'm afraid I was forced to hire one of them right off the street."

"Give it up, Blackstone. Let them go." Jackie pointed at him.

Blackstone's smile turned ugly. "You're in no position to be making any demands. You've cost me a lot of time and money."

"I'll cost you more than that!" Jackie charged at him, claws spread wide. The animalistic battle-lust tried to take hold and she barely hung onto her human side.

Jackie swiped her claws across Blackstone's chest. The impact knocked the vampire off his stool but the scream of pain came from Mark. Parallel blood lines appeared on his shirt and spread into a large crimson patch. He gasped in agony. Jackie froze, hands hanging at her sides in uncertainty, Mark's blood dripping from her tungsten claws. She shook with the strain of containing the wolf.

Blackstone pulled himself up and held his hands wide as if encouraging Jackie to come at him again.

Charlotte appeared at Jackie's elbow. "Don't touch him, White Fang. He's done something to them. They're psychically connected." Charlotte saw the connection linking Blackstone to the four humans, shimmering like a ghostly burgundy thread. She'd never seen anything like it before.

"Come, beast. Come to me. Punish me. I have been a bad, bad man." Blackstone grinned at Jackie.

"Don't do it, White Fang. You'll hurt your friends." Mark was bleeding badly and Charlotte knew he needed immediate medical attention. She spun around and slapped Alix, hoping the adrenaline from the impact would overcome Blackstone's venom.

Blackstone jerked as if the blow to Alix had affected him, but he recovered his smooth demeanor with a laugh. "Your pathetic attempts at heroics are greatly amusing, Charlotte. I thought I trained you better than this. Kill the wolf and be done with it."

Charlotte took her knife and slit the zip tie binding Alix to the chair. The doctor wobbled and staggered to her medical supplies. The shimmering thread connecting her to Blackstone lengthened, keeping taut.

Jackie clenched her fists. Rage gave her voice a ragged edge. "I'm going to kill you, Blackstone. I swear it on my life."

He deliberately turned his back upon her. "You're going to do nothing, werewolf. Your friends are tied into me now. If you do anything to me, they will suffer the consequences. Cut me, and they will bleed. Kill me, and they will die."

"That's impossible," Jackie hissed, even though she had seen the evidence with her own eyes.

"Is it? I am uninjured, while your pretty young friend is bleeding out his life on the floor. Can you explain it? Of course not." Blackstone's disdain was palpable. "The remarkable thing about demons is that once they know you're looking, you can always find one who will make a deal with you. Always." Blackstone stepped off the platform onto the path that led back to the elevator. "At first, I considered taking you and the vampire woman once more as prisoners, but then I realized it would be far simpler to start over someplace else. There will always be more werewolves and vampires for me to use. And demons, well, they can be extremely patient."

"Then why do this? Why torture these humans?" Charlotte pinched the bloody furrows on Mark's torso together with her fingers, hoping to slow the flow of blood as Alix hurried over with the emergency cart.

"Spite." Blackstone said over his shoulder. "I enjoy being cruel. Nothing more. I'm leaving now."

"The hell you are!" Jackie hurled something past Blackstone that impacted inside the elevator cage. A small explosion boomed through the mine. Rocks and timbers rained down to seal the elevator shaft. "You're not the only one with bombs. You're staying right here, Blackstone."

Blackstone brushed dust off his clothes. "I think not. I'm sure there are other ways out of this mine."

He transformed into a bat. Charlotte grimaced. It felt like they were getting outwitted at every turn.

Jackie glanced back at Charlotte, astonished. "Vampires can really do that?"

"He can. Get after him. Don't let him get away."

"What am I going to do, talk him to death?" Jackie waved helplessly at Mark as Alix worked to stitch shut the wounds inflicted upon him by proxy.

"I've got an idea," Charlotte said. "Trust me. You'll have a chance to take him down. You'll know when."

The bat whipped into one of the old mine passages. Jackie ran after him.

"What are you going to do?" Alix didn't look up from Mark's wounds. She held a tube of medical-grade super glue in her teeth as she stitched, then followed up with a squirt of the glue to seal everything. "Anything Jackie does to him will happen to one of us. Or *all* of us."

"The bond works both ways," Charlotte said. "When I slapped Alix, Blackstone reacted. Anything that happens to you will weaken him. Maybe even sever the bond."

Jenn shook herself, floundering her way back to consciousness. "God, I can't think. That stuff in his fangs is potent. You mean if we hurt ourselves, it'll hurt him?" She made a fist and bounced it off her temple. "I hope you felt that, you asshole. Ow."

"Are you crazy? What are we supposed to do, kill ourselves to stop him? I didn't sign on for this. Goddamn vampires." Dominica's eyes were full of fear.

Charlotte nodded. Her idea had come to fruition between Jenn's self-abuse and Dominica's tirade. "Those freezers. They're large enough for two of you to crouch in. We put you in there with cold water, then use the defibrillator to stop your hearts."

"Wait, you *want* to kill us?" Jenn shook her head as if trying to clear water from her ears.

"No, I see what she's getting at," said Alix. "Shit. I can't think. Why isn't this affecting him?"

"It's bloodborne. The only blood in his body belongs to other people," Charlotte said. "Don't worry. Vampire venom breaks down fairly quickly in humans. What about my idea?"

"Therapeutic hypothermia. We'd be dead but primed for resuscitation." Alix looked down at Mark, who'd passed out either from shock or from the painkillers she'd injected. "God, he's halfway there already, poor thing."

"Would that break the link?" Jenn slapped herself across the face, either to wake herself up or to try to hurt Blackstone some more.

"I think so," Charlotte said. "That would give Jackie the chance to take out Blackstone for good."

"The only problem is reviving us," Alix said. "Unless you're a doctor as well as a vampire."

"I'm not," Charlotte replied. "But I've assisted in reviving someone before. I'll revive you first and you can help with the others."

"This is really risky." Alix sounded doubtful. "Sure, it's possible, and there are lots of cases of it happening, but the circumstances have to be damn near perfect." She looked around. "And we're in a goddamn cave. Even with the hypothermia, we'll only have maybe ten minutes. If I can get right to work, which I doubt since I'll have just been dead, I don't know if we can get the last one of us revived in time."

"You . . . you have to try." Mark's voice was weak and shaky. His hands shook as he felt at the bandage across his chest.

"God, Mark, don't touch that. You'll bleed out." Alix already sounded stronger.

"Stop him. Help Jackie." Mark found a tiny smile. "She has a deadline for her next book."

"That's my line," Jenn said. "All right, I'm in. Please let's do it quick before I reconsider. I really like being alive."

"I can't believe I'm saying this, but okay, I'm in too." Dominica shook her head. "I haven't had anything insane happen to me in at least ten minutes and I'm getting bored."

Charlotte looked at Alix.

"Christ, I think you're *all* crazy, but I want this . . . *thing* . . . gone." The doctor brushed her fingers over the semi-substantial burgundy thread stretching off into the distance where Blackstone-the-bat had flown. "It offends my scientific sensibilities. Let's do it. Charlotte, empty out those two freezers. Jenn, we're going to need a lot of water quickly. Dominica, get the EEG software running on my computer station and four sets of leads. Mark . . ."

"Revive me last," Mark said quietly enough so only Charlotte and Alix could hear. "I'm already hurt, and if I d-die, the end result is the same."

Charlotte nodded.

* * *

Right away, Jackie knew she had a real chase on her hands.

The old mine tunnel ran several hundred feet into the mountain. She and Dominica had reinforced the tunnel so it wouldn't collapse accidentally, but left it otherwise looking as abandoned as ever. A thousand feet in, the tunnel ended in a steep shaft, only fifteen degrees off vertical. That shaft was an emergency exit from headquarters, leading to a narrow path in a steep part of the canyon where the terrain was treacherous.

Blackstone as a bat covered distance in the tunnel faster than Jackie's muscles could drive her. She couldn't see the bat in the dim emergency lighting but smelled the creature ahead of her and knew it hadn't doubled back in the near-darkness. She pelted through the tunnel, knowing with grim certainty she was going to have to let Wolf take over if she had any hope of catching the fleeing vampire.

The last two hundred feet of the tunnel had no emergency lights, and Jackie slowed her headlong rush to avoid braining herself against one of the support timbers. Somewhere up ahead was the steep shaft, and a bat corkscrewing upward. Once the creature got clear of the shaft, Jackie would have no hope of catching him at all. She felt a cool breeze against her sweating face and caught the glimmer of cold starlight as it filtered down the tall shaft. She couldn't see the bat flapping upward, but knew it was in there.

She'd never catch it in time.

Jackie pulled her cowl over her head and let it fall. She unfastened the zippers and snap-tabs holding her Kevlar bodysuit on and stepped out of it. She didn't need her expensive costume parts to be destroyed in the transformation. She took a deep breath, dropped to her knees, and held out her hands wide in a gesture of supplication as she called to her monster within.

Wolf overtook her.

* * *

Stripped to their underwear, the four humans sat shivering in icy baths as Charlotte rushed to prepare the crash cart for revivals. Alix had set up two trays of syringes with cardiac needles. One set was for the potassium solution to stop their hearts, and the other was epinephrine to help restart them.

Alix had two defibrillators with heart monitors, and Charlotte set one up by each freezer. An operating table sat beside each one, along with towels, dry clothes, and a plugged-in electric blanket.

Everything was ready. All that remained was for Charlotte to kill her charges.

"T-two minutes," said Alix, teeth chattering. "T-two minutes d-dead. Then . . ." She struggled to form the words but her violent shivers kept her from doing more than gasping for breaths.

"I understand," said Charlotte. She would start reviving Alix after two full minutes of clinical death. She had eight minutes to bring the doctor back to life. If she failed, she was to move on to Dominica, then to Jenn, and finally to Mark. The chance of her resuscitating anyone who'd been dead for more than twenty minutes was zero. Alix warned her even in the best of circumstances, bringing someone back from the dead only had about a three in four chance.

That meant, statistically, one of them was probably going to die.

Charlotte took up one of the syringes of potassium solution. The longer they waited, the more risk there would be of Blackstone escaping. "Are you ready?" she asked Alix.

Through chattering teeth, Alix managed a "Y-yes."

Charlotte raised the syringe. "See you soon."

She plunged the needle into Alix's chest.

Chapter Twenty-Six

November 2012
Reno, Nevada

Wolf scrambled up through the narrow shaft. Her diamond-hard claws found plenty of purchase in the rough-hewn stone. She smelled her prey ahead, the stink of undead flesh, the false animal guise, the fear. It made her climb even faster. Her tongue lolled out, slapping the side of her face with each bound upward. Saliva flecks dampened her fur in anticipation of the kill.

She saw the bat, a winged shadow against the circle of starlight above. It fluttered upward in a tight spiral, lent speed by its fear. Her legs pounded the stone and she raced to catch it.

The bat passed out of the shaft's mouth and banked hard. Wolf shot from the hole in the mountainside. She snapped at the bat and missed it by inches. Suddenly, the bat became a man and fell to bounce down the slope, cursing and shouting. Ghostly broken threads the color of blood whipped through the air to wrap around the man. Overjoyed and starving, Wolf bounded after him. A bat was only a mouthful, but a man was an entire meal.

The man rolled to his feet and turned, his fingers spread wide into fighting claws. Wolf didn't care; she pounced upon the man, bowling him over. They rolled down the hill, slashing and biting at each other. Claws dug into Wolf's throat as the man tried to force her head away.

Wolf snapped her teeth by the man's face, not quite closing on flesh. Blood leaked from the wounds the man inflicted, matting her fur and making it slick.

The rolling opponents hit an unyielding tree and the man's grip slipped from Wolf's throat. Wolf closed her powerful jaws upon one of the man's flailing hands. Flesh tore and bone crunched and the man screamed. Blood belonging to many other men and women flowed into Wolf's mouth. She shook her head and the hand came away in her teeth. She took her strength from the blood and flung away the stinking dead flesh.

* * *

Charlotte paced back and forth before the freezers as the timer ticked down. At two minutes, she lifted the chilled, dripping body of Alix Duchesne from the freezer and set her on the table. She swiped a towel quickly over Alix to keep the electricity from branching away from its desired path, then placed the defibrillator paddles on Alix's chest and side. She pulled the trigger and Alix's body clenched. Charlotte turned to look at the monitor. Alix's heart was still showing ventricular fibrillation—the state of being *mostly dead*. She did a set of thirty chest compressions and two breaths, forcing Alix's sluggish, chilled blood through her body and oxygen into her lungs.

The timer ticked past three minutes as Charlotte hit Alix with the defibrillator again. "Come on," she hissed. The monitor showed a couple of stray heartbeats before another fibrillation line. She was close. More chest compression, and two more breaths, and then Alix coughed. The monitor showed a regular heartbeat.

Charlotte grabbed the epinephrine syringe and plunged it into Alix's heart.

The doctor emitted a ragged scream and sat up, eyes wide and shaking as the fight-or-flight chemical flooded through her system. Charlotte wrapped the electric blanket around the doctor.

"I'm alive . . ." Alix coughed. "You d-did it."

"Can you move?"

Alix gasped and clutched at her chest. "God . . . it hurts so much. I didn't know it would hurt like this."

"I'm starting on Dominica," Charlotte said. "If you can't work on Jenn, tell me and I'll work on her next." She could tell that Alix was in no condition to revive anyone. If Charlotte managed to save Dominica in a reasonable amount of time, it would still be a good ten minutes before she could get to Jenn, and even longer for Mark.

As she lifted the young woman's body from the ice bath, Charlotte hoped her efforts weren't going to be in vain.

* * *

Something sharp and icy cold jabbed into Wolf's side. She whimpered at the pain and turned her head to snap at the sharp object the man wielded. The man stuck her a second time, then a third before Wolf could do much more than snarl.

Wolf jumped aside to get away from the man's knife, and staggered, for her legs weren't working quite right. Her blood ran down her legs to stain the ground black wherever she stepped. Her head hummed. She shook it and snarled as if she could terrify the pain into submission.

The man got to his feet, cradling his injured wrist against his belly. His gait was slow and uneven as he slipped and slid down the mountainside.

Wolf stumbled and her front legs gave out. Her furry chin split open against a sharp rock. The pain galvanized her, and she found the strength to stagger after the fleeing man.

Four steps. Five. Wolf coiled her strength into her shaking rear legs and jumped at the man. She hit the man high on his back and the two tumbled over, rolling down the hill. A rock banged off the puncture wound in Wolf's side and she yelped from the pain. The man flung her off and hurled a rock at her head. Wolf twisted to avoid the projectile, then launched herself back at the man.

She bore the man back to the ground once more. The man flailed with his good hand and even his savaged stump of wrist, but Wolf fought back with the determination of the trapped wild animal.

Blinded by fury and the lust for the kill, Wolf lunged down and tore out the man's flavorless throat.

The man's struggles ceased.

Exhausted, perhaps dying, Wolf was too worn out to feed on her kill. She remembered one last task she had to complete. She didn't want to do it. It wasn't natural. It wasn't *feeding*. But she'd done it before. With the last of her strength, she bit through his dry spine and tore his head away, flinging it aside in disgust. She laid her head across her blood-dampened forepaws, closed her eyes, and waited for the end.

* * *

Dominica was alive.

Jenn was as well, but only barely. Alix had managed to get herself moving well enough to assist Charlotte with Jenn's resuscitation, but there had been complications. Jenn went into another arrest after the epinephrine shot and it had taken a combination of more CPR and several injections of various chemicals before they'd managed to get her stabilized with a regular heartbeat, although it was far weaker than Alix liked.

Mark had been dead in the ice bath for nearly twenty minutes. Charlotte didn't like his chances. "I'm not even sure I could turn him and revive him by now."

"T-turn him? Into a vampire?"

"Yes."

"We have t-to try to save him, however we c-can." Alix's teeth chattered despite the warm clothes and electric blanket she held around her shoulders. Dominica and Jenn lay unconscious on their respective tables, but the monitors showed they were breathing regularly and their hearts were beating. It was too early to tell if they'd suffered any lasting effects from their brief periods of clinical death.

"His body temperature's down to eighty degrees." Charlotte lifted Mark from the freezer. The young man's icy skin was colder than any vampire's. Most vampires would have written him off as a loss. There were always other humans, but to this group of women, he . . . *mattered*. Charlotte hadn't been human for a century, but maybe it was time for her to learn how to be one again. This group could teach her.

Alix coughed. "He's not dead until he's *warm* and dead. Start chest compressions and respiration. I'll run the defib and injections." She limped over to the crash cart and gathered a handful of syringes. She lifted an empty one and looked at Charlotte. "How does it work when you make a vampire? Like, what's the mechanism?"

"He has to drink blood that has been inside my body." Charlotte laid Mark upon the table.

"Okay, but then what happens? It goes into his stomach and gets absorbed through the lining into his own bloodstream, right? What if we just inject it directly into him? Will that turn him into a vampire?"

"I don't know." Charlotte began chest compressions.

"Shit, I hope we don't have to do that. Breathe," Alix said.

Charlotte bent down and blew two breaths into Mark's lungs.

Alix checked the monitor. "Compressions."

Charlotte performed another round of CPR.

Alix positioned the defibrillator paddles on Mark's torso. "Clear." She hit the trigger and Mark twitched.

"Nothing." Charlotte checked the monitors.

"Charging," Alix said. "Take that syringe and fill it with your blood. Last resort, like I said."

"I need to tell you something. Something important. My blood isn't . . . vampires don't have our own blood. We have to get it from feeding."

"Clear." Alix hit Mark with the paddles again. "And?"

"No response yet. The blood in me right now . . . it's Jackie's."

Alix froze. Charlotte could tell she'd shocked the doctor with the admission.

"I don't know what her blood will do to Mark filtered through me. It might make him into a vampire. It might make him into something else. Or maybe it'll just kill him. I don't know."

Alix shook herself. "This is all new territory for me. Start compressions again. We're running out of time."

Charlotte bent to the task of compressing Mark's heart. She breathed twice for Mark, then stood back for Alix.

"Clear!" Alix gasped. The strain of her own recent resuscitation showed on her pale face as she triggered the defibrillator again. "Come on, goddammit, Mark!" She set down the paddles, grabbed a syringe full of epinephrine, and punched it into Mark's chest.

Charlotte turned to the monitor. "Still nothing."

Alix handed her an empty syringe. "Blood. Fill it. Now. Clear!" The defibrillator hummed and then made an unfamiliar hum and pop. A curlicue of smoke rose from the machine. Alix swept it onto the floor. "Shit!"

Charlotte jammed the syringe into her wrist and wiggled it around until blood found its way in through the tip. Alix tried to do chest compressions herself, but her strength was fading and Charlotte knew the woman wouldn't manage fifteen before she fainted, much less the thirty required.

"H-here," said a weak voice. Charlotte turned to see Jenn push the other cart with the spare defibrillator over to her. Tears streamed unchecked down the blonde woman's face and the effort of moving the cart seemed to take everything she had. She sank to her knees and bowed her head. "P-please."

Alix stepped back, winded. "I can't . . . anymore. I can't . . . breathe . . ."

Charlotte handed the doctor the syringe full of her blood. She bent to breathe twice for Mark and then did another series of compressions to let the doctor catch her breath. Then she straightened up and said, "Do it."

Alix raised the syringe, her face stretched into horror at what she was about to do, and plunged it into Mark's chest.

Chapter Twenty-Seven

November 2012
Reno, Nevada

Consciousness came to Jackie slowly. She saw bright lights against a dark, rocky backdrop and knew she was back in the mine headquarters. She found herself lying on a cot with an IV in her left arm. Her belly ached where Blackstone had stabbed her.

"Welcome back to the land of the living," Charlotte said. She'd changed into civilian clothes—jeans and a t-shirt. "You're one lucky bitch, you know that?"

Jackie pushed herself up onto her elbows and licked her dry lips. "What happened? Is everyone okay?"

"Dominica told me where your emergency shaft exited on the hill. From there I found where you and Blackstone wound up. You were pretty messed up. More dead than alive. You didn't even fight me when I wrapped you up and carried you back down here." She shook her head. "Saving werewolves. I don't even know what I am anymore."

"Blackstone?"

"He's not undead anymore. He's just dead. You got him, Jackie. After a full day in the sun, he's probably ashes on the breeze."

"I've been out that long?"

"You're lucky it wasn't longer. You'd lost so much blood when I found you that I wasn't sure you could even be saved. You weren't healing. Fortunately, Alix had enough of your own blood stored down here to give you a full transfusion after patching those holes back up." Charlotte paused. "She's really amazing, you know. She saved your life after reviving Jenn *and* Mark *and* being dead for two minutes herself."

"Dead? What happened?"

"I killed your friends to break the psychic bond Blackstone forged with them, and then with Alix's help we brought them all back. They're all alive. I still don't believe it." Charlotte cast her eyes down for a moment as if she were embarrassed or hiding a secret.

Jackie didn't miss the flicker of shame. Her healing powers had kicked in and she felt more alert by the second. "What is it you're not telling me?"

"It's Mark. We had to . . . infect him, with my blood, to bring him back."

"So, he's a vampire now?"

"We don't know." Charlotte sat on a chair beside Jackie's cot. "He hasn't awakened yet. But that's not what's concerning me. Jackie, I was full of your blood. Werewolf blood. It had a weird effect on me, and I still don't know what kind of lasting side effects there might be. Your blood, filtered through my undead system, is now flowing inside Mark's veins. It might make him a vampire. Or a werewolf. Or something unknown." Her face clouded. "Or it might kill him anyway. We just don't know. To my knowledge, this has never happened before in vampire history. Alix said she knows someone at the Institute of Parahuman Medicine in Paris and sent them an email detailing everything. She didn't name names but besides that . . ."

Jackie shivered. "So the secret is out." Was this the end of her career or something worse?

"Well, she said there's confidentiality rules, and if anybody knows about the existence of vampires and werewolves already, it's the people in Paris. I guess the director is the daughter of the founder of Just Cause or something like that." Charlotte shrugged. "I never paid much attention to the whole superhero side of things."

"Maybe it's time to start." Jackie swung her feet onto the cold stone floor. She wished she had some slippers, or Wolf's tolerance for chilly toes. "I'd better see Mark. And the others."

Charlotte smiled. "The others are sleeping. Even Alix. I figured nobody's going anywhere until we get that elevator shaft clear and dig all the rubble away from your exit, so they may as well rest here."

"Not that they'd do much better in the house. It's pretty well trashed as I recall. So's my truck. And your car. It's been a costly couple of days. I'd better get this next novel finished and delivered so they don't void my contract."

Jackie padded to the cot where Mark lay, an IV in his arm and EKG sensors stuck on his forehead and chest. His skin looked almost radiant. Jackie brushed a stray lock of hair away from his forehead. Mark didn't respond to the touch at all.

Jackie looked back up at Charlotte. "You think he'll be okay?"

"I have no idea. I don't even know if I'm going to be okay." She dropped onto the floor to rest her back against a cabinet.

"What are you going to do?"

Charlotte shrugged. "I've been cut loose from the Collective. Excommunicated. I don't know if that was solely Blackstone's doing or if it runs deeper in the organization than just him. The entire thing could be rotting from the inside out. If they labeled me a rogue, I may as well be walking around with a target on my neck. Until I can get that cleared up—*if* I can—I don't have anywhere else to go. I should reach out to them, let them know about Blackstone, but I'm tired. I've been running nonstop for thirty years. I need a little downtime before I lose . . ."

"Lose what?"

A surprising, genuine smile came across her face. "My humanity. Or rather, what's left of it. I've been thinking *vampire* for so long that I forgot where I came from. You've managed to take being a werewolf and turn it into something positive, something good for humans. Maybe I can try to find that in me too."

Jackie looked around her headquarters. It felt more like home than it ever had before. Her friends—her *pack* —were alive, safe, and even thriving. She'd done her duty to protect them, to fight for them, in spite of finding out that the world was a much larger, darker place than she'd ever dreamed. Zombies. Werebears. Vampires. Even *demons*. She wrote urban fantasy and still had difficulty believing it. Maybe she should go introduce herself to Just Cause. Tell them the truth. Maybe they'd even believe her; in a world where people could fly, shoot lightning, and walk through walls, were vampires and werewolves so unbelievable?

No, she couldn't do that. She'd worked too hard to preserve her own secret, and she owed it to any of her brothers and sisters out in the world, who'd been hunted just because of their monthly struggles against their own beasts. It would be better if she worked outside the big superhero organizations. As a vigilante, she wouldn't have her hands bound by red tape and bureaucracy. She could be effective. Maybe she could even find a way to help other werewolves.

But she couldn't do it alone. She held out her hand to Charlotte. "Join me?"

Charlotte looked down at the hand. Jackie could tell Charlotte was thinking hard about the idea of a permanent alliance with a werewolf. Then she shrugged and clasped the offered hand. "Why not?"

"White Fang and Nightfall. We do make a hell of a team."

"How come you get top billing?"

"Well . . . I started the whole vigilante thing, right?"

"We're going to have to talk about that . . ."

ABOUT THE AUTHOR

Ian Thomas Healy dabbles in many different genres. He's a multiple participant and winner of National Novel Writing Month. He created the popular ongoing superhero series, the *Just Cause Universe*, and is also the creator of the *Writing Better Action Through Cinematic Techniques* workshop, which helps writers to improve their action scenes.

When not writing, which is rare, he enjoys watching hockey, reading comic books (and serious books, too), and living in the great state of Colorado, which he shares with his wife, children, house-pets, and approximately five million other people.

Visit *www.ianthealy.com* for more information.